Sherlock Holmes

and the

Return of the Whitechapel Vampire

by Dean P. Turnbloom

Paperback ISBN 9781780928180
ePub ISBN   978-1-78092-819-7
PDF ISBN   978-1-78092-820-3

Published in the UK by MX Publishing
335 Princess Park Manor, Royal Drive,
London, N11 3GX
www.mxpublishing.com
Cover design by www.staunch.com

Grateful acknowledgment to Conan Doyle Estate Ltd. for the use of
the Sherlock Holmes characters created by Sir Arthur Conan Doyle.

For Esther

Acknowledgements

Writing the Whitechapel Vampire trilogy was truly a labor of love for me. My first exposure to Sherlock Holmes was watching Basil Rathbone and Nigel Bruce on Saturday afternoons with my mother when I was a young boy. I found the characters fascinating from the start and began to read the original stories. Somewhere along the line I wondered why it was that Doyle never penned a story about Holmes investigating the most notorious crime of his era, the Ripper murders. When I was a bit older I became enthralled with the vampire legends and especially the film adaptions from the Hammer studios in London starring Christopher Lee and Peter Cushing. This combination of influences lay dormant for many years and finally bubbled up to become the genesis of Sherlock Holmes and the Whitechapel Vampire and the two succeeding novels that complete the trilogy. Thus I begin, in this last edition of the trilogy, to acknowledge those I owe my thanks, beginning with my mother, for introducing me to Sherlock Holmes. I also thank Basil Rathbone, Nigel Bruce, Christopher Lee, and Peter Cushing for giving me hours of entertainment and forming unknown the nuggets that became this trilogy. I also want to thank my wife, Nanette, who's always been my biggest fan, and Theresa and Adrienne, my beta-readers. I owe a special thanks to Bob Gibson of Staunch Design for creating three of the most amazing book covers ever. Lastly, thanks to Steve Emecz and everyone associated with MX Publishing.

Chapter 1
"...Barlucci is on the loose again..."

The adventure to follow originated, as have most others, from the unexpected call of a visitor. I remember it was in the late afternoon on a sunny July day. I'd just returned from a long walk in the park. The previous two weeks had been cloudy and unusually cool for the middle of July and this was the first day conducive to a leisurely stroll and I took advantage of it.

My leg, still sensitive to changes in weather thanks to the wound I'd received in Afghanistan so many years ago, portended change still to come. That the change would be more than mere climate had yet to be revealed.

As I arrived home I placed my walking stick, a gift from Sherlock Holmes when he retired from London to Sussex, in the umbrella rack just inside the door. That's when I noticed a letter waiting for me in the basket beneath the mail slot. I picked up the plain yellow envelope and was very much surprised to see it was from Holmes. It had been some months since I'd last corresponded with him, when I received a thank you note for a signed copy of the book titled, "Body Snatchers—A Sherlock Holmes Adventure", it being a retelling of the curious circumstances surrounding the disappearance of the remains of Miss Abigail Drake. I put a kettle on and sat at my kitchen table to read the letter while I waited for the water to boil.

A letter from Holmes was certainly a sign of the times. I recall when we shared our rooms at Baker Street, and indeed after when the game was afoot, he rarely resorted to the post, and then only when there was some purpose in so doing, much preferring the immediacy of a telegram. This signaled to me the object of the letter must be quite mundane and I found myself somewhat wistful for that exhilarating era of excitement at 221B—wistful and nostalgic. I owed much to Holmes and the adventures we shared. It was in an early episode that I met my Mary, the first Mrs. Watson, but even before that, it was our association and those adventures that pulled me out of the deep melancholy in which I found myself after my tour of duty with the 66th Berkshire Regiment.

As I sat there at my kitchen table, I remembered how meeting Holmes had really been the beginning of a new life for me, one that I could never have imagined while I lay recovering in the base hospital at Peshawar from the wounds I'd received at the hands of an Afghan with a Jezzail rifle. My association with Holmes acted as the scalpel that excised the cancer of depression from which I suffered. During those heady years at Baker Street and indeed for many years thereafter, my friend involved me in such a strange and varied series of cases that I scarcely had time to build my practice, let alone allow myself to fall victim to any depression of spirit. In point of fact I would say that the lowest ebbs of my spirit appear as bookends at either side of our long association.

The first bookend was, as I've alluded, the period of physical recovery just prior to our meeting and the second was after the passing of my third wife. Both times it was Holmes who saved me from my despondent disposition, the first time unwittingly but the second most purposefully. A finer friend no man could know.

Using a butter knife I opened the envelope and removed the letter. In it, Holmes wrote about the weather, its effect on his bees, and how he was planning soon to visit London. All of this idle chit-chat seemed to me to be most uncharacteristic and as I read I began to speculate where this might be leading. And then, in the last paragraph, was the second shoe for which I'd unconsciously been waiting to fall. He wrote of an article in the Sussex Agricultural Express in which had been reported a number of bodies washing ashore on the eastern coast of Newfoundland. The item further mentioned there'd been no reported ship wrecks or debris that might account for the bodies. Holmes wrote that he'd not given the piece more than a passing glance until near the end it noted that one of the bodies appeared to be completely drained of blood.

I thought to myself, so that's it, he's still haunted by the baron, and felt a pang of guilt. Had I realized all those months ago the effect that dredging up the Barlucci murders, or as the press knew them, the Ripper murders, would have on Holmes, I'm quite certain I would have left my notes wrapped in twine, along with the leather journal of Inspector Walter Andrews, unopened at the bottom of my old steamer trunk, foregoing recording the account of our adventures in America. Had I known the dangers that lie ahead, I'm quite certain I would never have written a word about Abigail Drake and our adventure with the Body Snatchers.

But it was at Holmes' own prodding that I wrote the story that had its beginnings with Barlucci. Besides, how was I to know that retelling this adventure would stir in him such an obsession? After all, it had been twenty-five years since we'd last heard anything of Barlucci and his name had come up only sparingly in the time that intervened. I could hardly be expected to know how the escape of Barlucci bore on Holmes' mind.

It wasn't that Holmes had never been bested before of course. There was the matter of the Paradol Chamber, the Candlewood Papers in which John Clay had a hand, the matter of the Coptic Patriarchs controversy, and of course there was Irene Adler. But none of these had quite the impact on Holmes that the Barlucci affair had had.

4

Something about the baron was eating away at Holmes, and yet I couldn't quite diagnose the cause of the cancer.

Perhaps it was the cold-bloodedness of Barlucci. But he'd met cold-blooded men before, Moriarty for one. But then again, he'd beaten Moriarty in the end. Could it be that was it? Could it be that having such a fiend as Barlucci elude him not once, but twice was finally taking its toll on his psyche, his ego? Even though the baron's second escape ended beneath a mountain of ice and snow?

It was a certainty that we'd never faced a more grizzly murderer, though from what Holmes had told me about his stay as Barlucci's 'guest', the scoundrel thought he was doing both society as a whole and his victims in particular a service by ending their dire existence and ridding the East End of such creatures. In addition, there was the baron's assertion that he could be no more blamed for taking victims than a wolf can be denounced for hunting sheep, the pronouncement being made with no more emotion than if those women in Whitechapel had indeed been sheep.

It was just at that moment when the kettle began to whistle. I got up to fetch it for my tea and when I turned around again, in the seat I'd so recently vacated sat Sherlock Holmes.

"I'll take mine with just a drop of milk, if you don't mind, Watson?" he said as though I'd known he was there the entire time.

So stunned was I that it took a moment before I could ask, "Where the devil did you come from?"

He smiled as he answered, "Why, Sussex, of course." His quips are always accompanied by that smug little smile.

"No, I mean what are you doing here?"

"You read my letter. And I assume you still read *The Times*. Come, come, Watson, surely after all those years at my elbow you must have absorbed some of my deductive method, if only by osmosis."

I sat down in the chair opposite my guest and poured two

brimming cups of hot tea, offering Holmes the milk. I began going over in my mind what I'd read in the papers in the last few days. "Of course there's been much in the tabloids concerning that unfortunate incident at the Epsom Derby…" My voice trailed off as I saw he was looking down at his tea, shaking his head. I reined in a different direction, "Well, then, perhaps the treaty signing…" Again it was obvious the protocol I was following was in error, evidenced by the crinkling of his eyes. "I see," said I, growing a bit tired of this variation of dumb crambo. There were always tales of impending war carried by the papers or some change in government, but I didn't think these would interest my friend to any great degree. "What about the Pettifer murder, then?"

"What about it? It's quite obvious the nephew is the murderer. Even the official police couldn't miss that." Eyeing me with what appeared to be good humor Holmes tapped the rim of his teacup with his slender forefinger. "I can see retirement or even your self-proclaimed semi-retirement has only proven to dull what once I'd thought to be at least a middling degree of talent for detecting and deduction." He reached behind his back and pulled out a section of yesterday's edition of *The Times* he had rolled up in his pocket and which had become flattened during the train ride from Sussex to London. "Here. Read this," he commanded of me as he unfolded it and pointed halfway down the page—page sixteen I might add. These days I seldom read much beyond page three.

The Times reported the grounding of a ship on an island in the East River, near Manhattan Island, in New York. That in and of itself wouldn't have excited Holmes' imagination, but as I read on, I found that this particular ship wreck had quite an air of mystery surrounding it. There was only one person on board when it ran aground, and he was found dead at the wheel apparently by his own hand, a mortal wound to his throat.

After reading the article, no more than four small paragraphs,

I looked up incredulous. "That article has gotten you to leave your bees and to show up here unannounced?"

"Frightfully sorry if I've disturbed you, Watson, but after your latest literary masterpiece and our long and ardent discussions about the object of that work I thought you'd be at least somewhat interested in an investigation that would tie up all the loose ends to that tale."

"I don't know what you mean, Holmes. I think we've tied them up quite nicely."

"Yes, all of the loose ends save one, I'm afraid. And I believe that loose end is," he said tapping the newspaper, "loose once more."

I looked at him with uncomprehending eyes.

"Barlucci," he said simply.

"Barlucci? How can you..." I took a long slow inhalation before continuing, "the bodies," I breathed as the realization of what he was saying struck home with me.

"There's my Watson of old," he said with a smile on his face reaching inside his jacket, only to have it emerge seconds later clutching his black clay pipe. "Have you any old shag around? I'm afraid I didn't pack the slipper." He held up the empty pipe.

It was then I'd noticed the valise he'd left standing just inside my front door. "There's some Arcadia in the blackamoor on the mantle," I said, pointing out the tobacco jar. "So, you believe the bodies are from this...what did the papers call it?"

"A ghost ship," he said, curling up his left eyebrow. He crossed the room to the fireplace and with a slight grimace dipped his pipe into the jar. He preferred tobacco of a much darker blend.

"Yes, a ghost ship. Then you believe the bodies you wrote of washing up along Newfoundland—"

Holmes interrupted, "And the coast of Canada, and Maine in the U.S. I did some checking. I wired several of the papers that reported the bodies washing ashore and asked whether any of them had been identified and if there were any unusual circumstances discovered. Most of the bodies, I was told, were too badly decayed to get any sort of identification. But the Bangor Sentinel told me the body that washed up recently there had papers still on him and I was able to ascertain the corpse was found with two large gashes in his throat and without a drop of blood in his body as far as they could tell."

"'Gad, Holmes, you don't think…"

He tamped the tobacco into his clay pipe and said, "But there's more. I wired the New York Police Department and received a response from an old friend of ours."

"Mylo? Yes, he would be the one. He's a commissioner now, you know."

"Quite, though how he managed it is beyond me. Be that as it may, he tells me they found certain artifacts onboard the derelict vessel, artifacts that I think will interest you."

"What sort of artifacts?"

He paused to light his pipe. After extinguishing his match with an exhalation of smoke he continued, "The papers failed to say what kind of ship it was that was wrecked, they were a bit too interested in making as much as they could from the fact that the only person found onboard was dead."

"What kind of ship is she then?" I asked.

"The *Redeemer* is a salvage ship. On her last voyage, she was commanded by Captain Thor Cutter, an experienced mariner."

"Was it his body to which the Bangor newspaper referred?"

"No, that body belonged to an able seaman by the name of Billy Bright. He was known to have shipped on the *Redeemer* with Captain Cutter. It was the captain who died at the helm."

"Dear God. And what of the artifacts?"

"Ah yes, the artifacts. There were quite a few, but the most interesting ones were those that bore the name of the ship they'd been engaged in salvaging—the *Animus Lacuna*."

"No. The ship that belonged to that miscreant, Barlucci?"

8

"The very same. As improbable as it may seem, I believe Barlucci is on the loose again."

"But Holmes, it's been over twenty years since…since…"

"Since he's disappeared? Yes, for twenty-some odd years he's been dormant or lost or perhaps prisoner, but now he has returned. I'm certain of it. This is his obscene handiwork. Surely you haven't forgotten that once you eliminate the impossible whatever remains, however improbable, must be the truth."

"Yes, but Holmes…"

"And don't forget," he said with a broad smile on his face, "Barlucci believes himself to be a vampire, and to a vampire the sands of time stand forever still."

I'd been long aware of how the events of two decades ago had affected Holmes. How he'd felt cheated somehow when it was discovered Barlucci had apparently been buried in ice and snow and thereby had permanently escaped justice, not unlike those scoundrels involved in the murder of John Openshaw. It was clear that Holmes took it as a personal defeat and blamed himself for allowing Barlucci to slip from between his fingers in London.

As the years passed though, from all outward appearances that injury had healed. But I suppose I must bear the brunt of having opened that wound by causing him to relive certain details during his review of my most recent work. I noticed then how he became quite agitated. I thought it only natural at the time and was certain it would soon pass. But now, with him sitting in my kitchen telling me Barlucci was at large once again, I could not help but think he might be reading a bit more into these events than were warranted just in the hope of having a chance to put right at last what he'd come to think of as his greatest failure. I was also concerned that his retirement might have dulled that keen insight of which he'd been so proud and I had always been in such awe.

With all the tenderness and subtlety I could muster I said, "Are you sure the facts add up to that, or are you allowing your desire to close the circuit on this particular case to cloud your judgment?"

Holmes gave me a wry smile, "I see," he said followed by a prickly silence. "So, you think my retirement has blunted my senses. Is that it?"

As he'd done so often in our association, he now appeared once again to read my very thoughts. "I didn't say that exactly. I mean, it's certainly understandable that you would want to tie up loose ends." I could see the storm clouds gathering behind those steel gray eyes.

"And it is your considered professional opinion that my desire to 'tie up loose ends', as you put it, has driven me to see connections that do not exist?" He spoke with the calmness of a school master remediating a recalcitrant student. "Surely you know me better than that, Watson."

"Well, you are in retirement and it has been some time since you've actively pursued a case, and—"

"You forget, do you not, the 'Raven's Call' and what of the 'Lion's Mane'?"

"Yes, but even though you were technically in retirement in the first instance, that case as you well know was completed before you'd been so six months. As for the Lion's Mane, I believe, as familiar as I am with aquatic life and as a medical man, I could have solved that case myself."

"So, you desire a demonstration to prove my powers of observation and deduction have not suffered by lack of exercise?" With a long sigh he said, "Am I reduced to performing parlor tricks?"

The tired look on his face made me instantly repentant of my evident accusation and yet I was astonished that what I thought was a prudent argument for caution he had apparently taken as an affront.

After what seemed an interminably long and awkward silence, he spoke in a voice brimming with a tranquil turbulence, "I assure you, my dear Watson, I'm very happily ensconced in the life of the country squire, tending my bees and writing my entomological monographs. I would not choose to interrupt my idyllic existence were I not convinced that a peril unlike any other and one far beyond the feeble abilities of the official police has once again appeared out of the darkness. But, if it will serve to convince you, then very well."

He sat upright in his chair and gazed out of the window toward the roses along the path to the hothouse. "The first thing I noticed when I arrived at your rooms was that you've changed gardeners. I suspect your former gardener has retired and his son has assumed the role, though the son is left-handed. Further, I'd like to congratulate you on a successful series of lectures you've recently given at the King's Library in the British Museum. Finally, I'm happy to see you're feeling well enough to entertain again and I see the woman with whom you've been keeping company has had a profound impact on your sensibilities."

I must admit I was surprised by the combination of facts he'd presented and my mind went to work immediately to decipher how he might have made such accurate deductions. "Well, I suppose you might have seen an article concerning my lectures, though how you might have deduced their success is more likely a kind indulgence rather than any elucidation of fact."

"Not at all, I noticed the stack of congratulatory telegrams and a program by the secretary in the anteroom."

"I see, then perhaps we should chalk up that deduction to base snooping," I said in as dismissive a manner as I could muster. "As far as my gardener, it took no great amount of intelligence to guess he might be retired. The last time you were here you noted to me the uneven pruning of my roses and suggested to me it might be time for him to leave my service. It was probably a mere guess that his son has taken his place."

"You wound me, Watson. You know I never guess and you are forgetting my assertion as to his left-handedness."

"Posh. Theater. I don't have a recollection of his being either right or left-handed."

"And you needn't have to, it's in the angle of his pruning, which is much improved over his father's, although clearly the elder has instructed the younger on the fine art of horticulture."

"I shall make a special point of checking on his next visit. As for my sensibilities, what makes you think they've changed?"

Holmes smiled broadly and said, "My old friend that is the easiest deduction of all." He leaned forward and patted my arm. "In all our years together I don't remember one poem you either recited or to which you made reference, yet I now see Shelley on your bookshelf, along with Yeats, and Dickinson beside your reading chair. And carefully tucked between its pages I can see a delicately tatted bookmark. What am I to think?"

I laughed in spite of myself, "Very well, then, I can see you're still on the top of your game. And yet, I cannot believe Barlucci would disappear for over twenty years only to reappear in the one place in which he'd most likely come to notice."

"Au contraire, if we take the position he was somehow unavoidably detained on his voyage to New York, I believe Barlucci would, upon his earliest opportunity, complete his journey."

I could tell from the sparkle in his eye he meant to travel to New York and seek the elusive Baron Barlucci and he meant to have me by his side when he found him. "I suppose you've already booked passage."

"Indeed. We depart Monday morning on the Olympic and arrive in New York on the following Sunday."

"You take much for granted, Sherlock Holmes," I said in my gravest tone.

"Come, Watson, how often have I noted your constancy in what is an ever-changing world. I know you will come with me if for no other reason than to ensure I haven't become the doddering old fool you fear." He smiled as he said this and I felt a touch of shame at how close he was to the truth.

Chapter 2
Crickets, dreams, and vampires...

I was soon to discover the pleasures of a summer crossing in contrast to the winter one I'd experienced years before. In the winter the wind on deck was bitterly cold; in summer the breeze was gentle and refreshing. In winter the seas were in a state of constant turbulence, pitching the ship to and fro; in summer the gentle rolls of the ship were quite relaxing. In winter the threat of icebergs were ever present; in summer the only iceberg we saw came in the salad.

The *RMS Olympic,* sister ship to the ill-fated *Titanic,* was a vessel of extraordinary luxury and the largest ocean liner of its kind in the world. Holmes and I spent the long days walking on deck, playing chess with other passengers and each other, enjoying the exquisite cuisine, and reading. I'd brought along Dickinson and Yeats, while Holmes spent much of his time engrossed in something he said he'd attained before we left London.

As our destination grew ever closer I could tell my friend was keen on getting started with the investigation. Along with the mysterious book he'd been reading, Holmes brought along every newspaper article he could find that carried any description of the shipwreck or the bodies that he was convinced had been left in its wake. In the last forty-eight hours of our trip he spent so much time reading and re-reading them that no doubt he'd committed them to memory by the time we'd arrived.

I, on the other hand, became increasingly apprehensive as we got steadily closer to our objective. The cause of my trepidation was that Holmes had asked Commissioner Strumm to meet us upon our arrival and I knew very well Holmes' opinion of Strumm. To put it mildly, I knew he never truly appreciated Commissioner Strumm's professional prowess. In fact, he was quite candid with me that he was more than mildly surprised when he'd discovered Strumm had been promoted to the Board of Commissioners. In fact, his exact words on the topic were, *'a man's faults do not cease to be simply because they are ignored'.*

But when I was last in America a mere two years previously I got to know the Strumms and came to especially appreciate Mylo Strumm's rise through the New York Police Department. Certainly Mylo had his faults, but he also had a fine family and career. One doesn't acquire such wealth without merit.

I was researching the *Body Snatchers* chronicle, and I remember how Commissioner Strumm, along with his wife Emily, was exceedingly gracious. They opened both their home and their lives to my curious questioning. Without their kind support I could never have written the story of which this trip, according to Holmes, is a continuation, a last chapter if you will. I spent a good deal of time with them as they made Mylo's study available to me and my work and I came to feel very close to the entire family. I wasn't looking forward to their reuniting with Holmes.

For this reason I was feeling exceedingly uneasy and was reticent to engage Holmes in any but the most mundane conversation at dinner on the night before we arrived in New York,. But before we'd finished our meal, I gained an uncomfortable insight into my friend's psyche, one that in hindsight proved quite prescient. We'd just finished our soup when Holmes said rather matter-of-factly, "Watson, I had a most unusual and disturbing dream last night. I wonder if you'd venture an opinion on its meaning."

I thought perhaps this was some trick or jest of his but decided I should probably play along, "I would be happy to offer my impression, but as you know the interpretation of dreams is not my specialty."

"Merely as an intellectual exercise, then?"

"Very well, as an intellectual exercise," I answered, intrigued that he appeared anxious to share an unguarded look into his very soul. "Please, tell me what you dreamed."

I should have known what was coming. "I was in a heated pursuit of Barlucci, physically chasing after him. I followed him down a hole in the surface of the street. It was deathly black inside and for a moment I stood waiting for my eyes to adjust to the darkness. After a bit all was shadow, but I could clearly see the outline of everything within. I followed a long tunnel, which at the end opened into a large cavernous chamber. There, in the middle, was a shining black box—a coffin."

"It was shining, even though there was no light?"

"Yes…yes, it was most peculiar now that you ask, but it was shining. It's difficult to describe but it seemed to glow, to emanate a sparkling black aura." Holmes' eyes took on the glassy look of one seeing what I could not and he gestured while he spoke, "I approached the coffin, but at having long last attained my goal, I hesitated. This was the hiding place of Barlucci. After making sure there was no other exit to the room, I went back to the coffin and placed my hands on the edge of the lid. Slowly, I lifted it. As it opened, I could see the outline of a body—it was Barlucci. But as I stood there, my eyes transfixed upon my quarry, it dissolved into a gray fog, and then—nothing."

"Dear God."

"Yes, it was quite a shock to me as well. As I began to close the lid, a pair of eyes stared at me from the other side. They glowed red like burning embers. I closed the lid and that's when I awoke." His eyes cleared and he once again looked himself, "What do you think it means?"

"I think it means you've been thinking too much about Baron Barlucci, and possibly reading too much from that tome you brought with you."

"Ha. Just the sort of answer I expected. You never disappoint, Watson."

This recounting of his dream opened the door for me to ask about a topic we had never actually spoken about in depth before. It was a subject that although we'd certainly talked around several times after our previous adventure in New York and again during Holmes' review of my latest book, we had never addressed it in detail. It had always been, like the piece of spinach stuck in the vicar's teeth, a thing obvious to us both but never remarked upon—the topic of vampirism.

I began the conversation shortly after the second course had arrived. "I say, Holmes, do you truly believe in this whole vampire business? I mean, the entire matter of Miss Abigail Drake seems almost a fairy tale with the passage of time, don't you think?"

"That is an interesting question, Watson. It's a bit like asking if I believed in magnetism without the benefit of being able to examine the magnet. I might believe in the effects caused by the so-called magnet that I would be unable to explain by other means," he said between bites of the chicken fricassee. As he supped he appeared to be thinking of something and then he said, "What if I were to tell you that I can, without error, tell the temperature of a summer's night in Sussex with no other instrument than my own ears?"

"I'd say you'd gone round the bend."

"Nevertheless, my ability to do so is a scientific certainty."

"Impossible."

"You say that only because you cannot see a connection between the two, but what might seem an impossibility at first, when properly examined, explained, and tested, sometimes becomes a scientific fact."

"But to tell the temperature with one's ears stretches the bounds of credulity a bit too far."

"That's precisely what Amos Dolbear thought."

"Dolbear, you say? Who is Amos Dolbear?"

He put down his fork and refilled his cup with coffee as he said, "That, my dear Watson, is a story I believe you will find both interesting and instructive. I was vacationing some years back, it was the summer before that matter at Shoscombe Old Place. You had been too busy with your practice to accompany me and I made the acquaintance of a remarkable man, an American inventor by the name of Amos Dolbear. He was visiting relatives in England and we happened to be staying at the same hotel. One evening we were sitting on the veranda having a libation when he commented that it was a rather warm evening. I sat in silence for a minute and then said, 'I'll wager you I can gage the temperature more accurately than you.'"

"Whatever did you do that for? You aren't a gambling man, Holmes."

"No, and this was no gamble. At any rate, he accepted my wager and we both recorded our guesses and then asked the bellboy to bring us a thermometer. When we checked the temperature on the thermometer, I was within a degree of the actual temperature while he was off by several."

"Pure luck."

"Luck is on the side of the diligent. On the contrary, I could do it every time, so long as there were crickets about."

"Crickets? Poppycock. What have crickets to do with it?"

Holmes chuckled as he offered me a cigar, "I'm sure you realize that whenever my mind is unstimulated by a case I seek stimulation in other forms."

"Yes, I am quite aware," I said, as I extended a match to his cigar, thinking of his former habitual use of cocaine and less often morphine.

"Well, since I'd long ago forgone the needle at this point, thanks to you in no small measure, I entertained other stimulations, one being the study of nature, particularly the insect world."

"Bugs? Whatever engendered in you an interest in bugs?"

"Bugs, as you name them, are abundant in an almost infinite variety. Their study is most instructive as many are of a most social nature. Take the noble bee, for instance. But I digress. In any event, having observed in passing that crickets appeared to chirp at greater intervals when the air was cooler, I hypothesized there might be a direct correlation between the temperature of the air and the rate at which this simple creature chirped. If that was so, I theorized, it might be possible to devise a way to calculate temperature from the number of chirps heard per a set unit of time. I worked out a simple formula that uses a count of the number of chirps in a minute, multiplied by my constant, which is dependent on the cricket species I discovered, to come up with the air temperature in degrees centigrade."

"You must have been exceedingly bored at the time, chum, but it does sound fascinating. And it worked?"

"Unfortunately for Mr. Dolbear, it worked well enough to win five pounds from him."

"I say, Holmes, you didn't keep it, did you? I mean, it seems almost as though you were cheating him."

"Well, I did tell him how I was able to calculate the temperature so precisely and we shared a good laugh and proceeded to meet nightly to repeat the experiment. I offered to return his five pounds, but he would hear none of it."

"Seems he was a good sport, then."

"And a good listener. He took my simple little calculation, adapted it to degrees Fahrenheit, and wrote a small manual on the subject, '*The Cricket as a Thermometer*'. I understand he earned back his investment of five pounds with quite a healthy interest and today his formula is known as Dolbear's Law. "

"No."

"Indeed. And if I'd told him beforehand that I could predict temperature based upon nothing other than my senses, he would not have believed me, any more than you did. But once I'd shown him the effect, he could hardly but believe the cause. Do you see? Amos Dolbear would have thought using a cricket as a thermometer was a fairy tale until he saw the effect."

"That's certainly a long but very circumspect answer. Undoubtedly we saw the effects of Abigail Drake."

"Yes, but I think we both agree that Miss Drake was mad. The possibility of her madness manifesting itself with unusual physical strength is not without its antecedent, you know."

"Yes, she was quite strong for a drowned woman. How do you explain her death and resurrection?"

"Elementary. It should be quite obvious, especially to a man of medicine such as yourself, that Miss Drake was not dead, but was most probably in some sort of comatose state that simulated death. This sort of thing isn't without precedence."

"That's true enough. I understand that the fear of vivisepulture was so common at one time that escape provisions devised for coffins were commonplace. I believe the topic was even the subject of some of Poe's works."

"Indeed. There have been numerous cases of people who've contracted disease and have been pronounced dead only later to be discovered alive and well. There are also some well documented cases of persons being buried alive."

"But Miss Emily Drake obviously believed her sister to be a vampire."

"Ah, but what sort of vampire. From what Miss Emily told us, her sister subsisted on blood, although she'd never herself witnessed it. The only other symptom she spoke of was Abigail's supposed hypersensitivity to light. That might easily be feigned."

"Yes, but you're forgetting Abigail Drake's victims were all drained of their blood."

"True. But you saw the amount of medical and scientific equipment present in the ruins of Abigail Drake's home. Who's to say she didn't drain the blood of her victims by more conventional means, a symptom of her madness?"

"So then, you are saying there is no such thing as vampirism after all?"

"What I am saying precisely is that vampirism is, to the best of my current knowledge, merely a legend. I have no data indicating vampires exist, other than the stories of two people whom I believe are, or were in the case of Miss Drake, quite mad. I therefore deduce that to believe in vampires without additional data would be tantamount to madness. As I have commented on many past occasions, it's not possible to—"

"—not possible to make bricks without mud. Yes, yes, I know. I remember."

"Good. It's gratifying to know you've been listening."

I let his sarcasm pass without comment. "Then why did you assist that doctor, what was his name?"

"Dr. Rudalac?"

"Yes, why did you assist Dr. Rudulac in removing Miss Drake's head from her corpse?"

"I thought it the best course. Both Dr. Rudalac and Emily Strumm, née Drake, appeared convinced Abigail Drake was a vampire. I could offer no proof, beyond simple logic, to the contrary, hence if removing the dead woman's head gave them comfort what was it to me?"

"And yet you are now traveling to America in pursuit of Barlucci, a man who went down in a shipwreck over twenty years ago and hasn't been heard of since. All because of a supposed ghost ship."

"Ah, but Barlucci's ship didn't go down and we have two instances of the wreckage of that ship being found. The first was by Mandible Pierce and his fellow crewmembers. We know from that account Barlucci was left buried under a mountain of snow. The second instance is this ghost ship, the *Redeemer,* which has apparently brought back a number of items from the *Animus Lacuna.* I submit that either by accident or by design, one of the things they brought back was Barlucci himself."

"If he can survive in the frozen north for two decades he is an extraordinary man indeed."

"Yes, I believe Barlucci is extraordinary, and extraordinarily evil. And it will most certainly take an equally extraordinary effort to defeat him."

Chapter 3
Animosities and old friends…

The *Olympic* moored alongside the Chelsea piers on the west side of Manhattan early on the morning of July twenty-seventh. The last time Holmes and I came to New York we were to have been met by Inspector Walter Andrews, but before we arrived the unfortunate inspector had met Abigail Drake and, consequently, his death.

This time however we were met by former Detective Sergeant and now Commissioner Mylo Strumm. Having seen him less than two years ago, I had no trouble spotting him on the pier as we arrived. He was a tad bit heavier than when we'd first met and had thinner, graying hair, but other than that he looked much the same and it was easy to see that married life had agreed with him, although the strain of his occupation was beginning to show in his face even more than I remembered. His eyes were a bit bloodshot, no doubt from excessive paperwork, his face was somewhat pallid and a sheen of sweat showed on his brow even though the temperature was quite moderate. Were he my patient I would prescribe fresh air and exercise.

"Commissioner," I waved and called out to him as we walked down the gangway to the pier. The crowd of people jostled us, slowing our progress as we made our way to the vehicle beside which Commissioner Strumm was standing.

"Mr. Holmes, Dr. Watson," Strumm said, hand extended, as

we approached.

"I understand you are one of the commissioners of police, now," Holmes said shaking his hand. "Congratulations."

"Thank you, thank you, but actually there is no longer a board of commissioners. There is only a single Commissioner of Police. One of the reforms instituted by Teddy when he was governor."

"I'm sorry, did you say Teddy?"

"Why yes, Teddy...Teddy Roosevelt," Strumm said, emphasizing the first syllable of the last name. "Former President Theodore Roosevelt," he continued, apparently feeling further explanation was required, "he was President of the Board of Commissioners here before going on to become Governor, and then President."

Holmes said, "Ah, yes, I see. I'm afraid I don't follow American politics." But I knew he was merely being dismissive. There's not a major country in the world of which Holmes wasn't aware of its politics.

"If I were you, Mr. Holmes, I'd start," Strumm said with a wink, "your former colony will someday be an even greater power than Great Britain."

"I think that day may be a bit too far in the future to see just yet," said I, and we all laughed cordially as we climbed inside the conveyance at Strumm's disposal.

"I'm glad you came this month rather than last," Strumm said as we began motoring toward Police Headquarters. "You are two of the first outside the department to ride in one of our newest police wagons. It's a Packard four-seater," he said with obvious pride.

"I'm afraid I'm a bit old fashioned," said Holmes with an obvious coldness. "I prefer a hansom."

"I agree," I said, then pinching my nose, "unless the horse has recently had too rich a mixture of oats and molasses." My jest had the desired effect of lifting the mood a bit.

"I'm afraid we can't stand in the way of progress," said Strumm.

Holmes took this opportunity to steer the conversation in a direction more to his liking, "Speaking of progress, Commissioner, how is the investigation of the shipwreck coming?"

Strumm became suddenly serious. "Mr. Holmes, despite my wife's and my joy at seeing you and Dr. Watson again, I must admit when I got your wire concerning your theory that this Barlucci fellow may have arrived at last in New York, I have to say at first I thought you were yanking my chain."

"Beg pardon?" I said.

Strumm saw the quizzical look on my face and explained, "Pulling my leg, making a joke."

"Oh, I'm afraid it's no joke."

"I should say not," said Holmes shifting in his seat to look Strumm in the eye. "Don't you find it terribly coincidental that the ship that has apparently discovered the whereabouts of the *Animus Lacuna* would come to rest, or I should say come to wreck, in New York harbor void of life and with a trail of bloodless victims in its wake?"

"I'm aware you don't believe in coincidence, Mr. Holmes, but that's exactly what this is. Coincidence, nothing more. It's been twenty-five years. The fact that the *Redeemer* has dredged up some artifacts from Barlucci's barque does not mean Barlucci has come back to life. I'd hoped we might wait a bit before opening this can of worms, but by God, Holmes, Barlucci's dead and that's that. Most of the bloodless victims, as you call them, have been too long in the drink and too far gone from being eaten by sea life to tell one way or another whether they're bloodless. And for the life of me I can't figure what difference it makes anyway."

"What about the man at the helm, Captain Cutter?"

"What about him?"

"Is he still in the morgue? I'd like to examine the body as soon as possible."

Strumm appeared a bit uncomfortable at the question. "I'm afraid that's impossible. We buried him a few days ago."

"I'm disappointed to hear that. When we spoke on the phone I asked you to hold off."

"Yes, but we had some, er, problems with the refrigeration units and, well, in this heat, I'm sure you can understand."

Holmes nodded his ascension, but appeared annoyed.

"My God, man, the ship ran aground over ten days ago. I'm having trouble enough with the mayor over keeping the ship tied up where it is so long so you can have a look before the crime scene is released. He'd have had my head if I hadn't buried the captain before now."

With reluctant resignation in his voice, Holmes said, "What's done is done, I suppose. What was the official cause of death?"

"Loss of blood. He'd apparently managed to slit his own throat. The knife was still lodged in him when we found him."

"And the blood?"

"There was plenty of blood, Mr. Holmes, if that is what you're getting at."

"I see," said Holmes as he settled back in his seat, his forehead creased and his chin resting on his chest.

When we arrived at the headquarters of the New York City Police Department it was late morning and Commissioner Strumm invited us up to his office for coffee.

"How is your charming wife, Commissioner, and your daughter, Lucie?" I said, hoping to get Holmes and Strumm into less volatile areas of discussion.

To Holmes, "Her name is actually Lucinda but we call her Lucie. We named her after my wife's late aunt, you remember?" He poured three cups of coffee and handed one to Holmes and one to me.

26

"Thank you," Holmes said taking his cup. "I do indeed, a most charming and caring woman as I recall. It must have been quite a blow to Mrs. Strumm when she died. They appeared to be very close."

"Yes, Emily was terribly upset when she died. She'd raised Emily and her sister after their parents were killed. Ah, but you were asking about Lucie, Doctor. Both she and Emily are fine, thanks. In fact, they're better than fine."

"Oh? How so?"

"Lucie's become engaged since you were last here, to young Phillip."

"Phillip Tremaine?" Turning to Holmes, I said, "When last I was here I had the pleasure of meeting Phillip. He was in his last year of medical school. I remember that, except for his fair hair and complexion, he's the spitting image of his father." I turned back to Strumm and said, "Has he passed his boards, then?"

"Passed with honors. Phillip is now a full-fledged doctor, Dr. Alan Phillip Tremaine. He's taken a position at St. Vincent's. That's the same hospital where his father was on staff and his grandfather was President."

"Yes, I remember," Holmes said. "What a pity about his father, struck down in his prime by the malignancy that is Barlucci."

"You mean Abigail Drake, don't you Mr. Holmes?"

"Abigail Drake, my dear Commissioner, was merely a monster of Barlucci's making. I don't know how he came to own her mind so completely in so short a span of time, but own her he did. And in so owning, turned her to his own wicked ways."

"Yes, well," said I, once again trying to steer away from the rocks, "and a pity about his mother also. Time has certainly taken its toll these past twenty years."

"A pity, yes. I remember we were shocked when we heard of Julia Tremaine's passing. We were under the impression she was doing well when we departed." As Holmes said this, I noticed Strumm shifting in his chair and moving his gaze out the window. This, of course, was not lost on Holmes who said, "What is it, Commissioner, what's the matter?"

"I'm afraid that's a bit of a sore topic right just now."

"I don't understand."

Strumm sat down his coffee, cleared his throat, rose from his chair, and began pacing across his office. "No," he said at last, "I don't suppose you do. How could you?" He looked from Holmes to me and then back to Holmes before saying, "Julia Tremaine isn't dead."

"Not dead? What does this mean?" I said, somewhat agitated. But Holmes only sat there impassively, bent forward, his elbows resting on his knees, fingers steepled before his eyes in the pose I'd seen so often, signaling rapt attention.

"Just that. Julia didn't die after giving birth to Phillip as was reported."

"What? Then why the pretense, why the charade?"

"We did it to protect Phillip."

"Protect him? From what?"

Strumm took a deep breath. He sat on the edge of his desk and spoke in a quiet tone, "After Alan Tremaine's funeral Julia became more and more depressed. Her family, of course, thought she was just going through a tough patch with all she'd been through so they had her brother Charles move in to stay with her a while."

"I was under the impression he was with the Army, in Egypt," said Holmes.

"That's true. At the time Alan died Charles was still in Egypt. I'm surprised you took such an interest, Mr. Holmes."

"I believe in being thorough, Commissioner."

"I see," understanding Holmes' unspoken meaning. "Anyway, Charles had been wounded, which was why he hadn't written in some time. The wound resulted in the loss of his right leg."

"A pity," said I.

"Certainly, but because of it, he was mustered out of the Army with a pension and shipped home. At first, with Charles living with Julia, it appeared she was improving. But soon she got worse, much worse. Poor Charles. Julia would awaken in the night screaming for her dead husband, claiming he'd been buried alive."

"Dreadful."

"It gets even more disturbing," Strumm said. "Charles would find her walking around through the streets at night, sobbing and gibbering about hearing a voice calling to her, Alan's voice. It soon became plain she'd gone completely out of her mind. She sat vigil at his crypt, insisting he be dug up and brought to her and on more than one occasion they found her kneeling at his tomb babbling as if speaking to him."

"Good heavens."

"The Cabots had no choice. They had to put her away."

"That's absolutely horrifying. But why pretend she was dead? And why tell us the truth now, after so much time has passed?"

"As I said, the Cabots wanted to protect their young grandson from the shame of having been born in an asylum and of having a mother who's a permanent resident. So, they concocted the story of her death due to complications of childbirth. Charles maintained this version of events even after his parents passed on. I think he must have felt it would have been a disservice to their memory to do otherwise, but what's happened recently has made it necessary for young Phillip to know the truth."

"What's happened?" I asked.

Before Strumm could respond Holmes said, "Julia Tremaine has escaped from the asylum. Isn't that so, Commissioner?"

"Yes, but how did you know?"

"We read about a prison break before we left England. The rest was simple deduction."

"You're awfully well informed, Mr. Holmes."

"It is my business to stay so, Commissioner. I should like to speak to the guard that was on duty at the asylum after we inspect the ship in the morning. Would you be so kind as to arrange it?"

"Of course, if you wish, but what's your interest there?" said Strumm, apparently sensitive to the feeling Holmes might be overstepping.

Holmes smiled, "Commissioner, you've just had a ship run aground, a ship with no one on board except a dead man at the wheel, his throat lacerated in a most ghastly manner. A singular event, wouldn't you say?"

"Yes," said Strumm, cautious expectation in his voice.

"Add to that a simultaneous breakout from a prison workhouse and an asylum, on the same night, on the same island, at practically the same time."

"Are you seriously suggesting these events are related?"

"Are you seriously suggesting they are not? Surely even you can see the coincidence of these three events."

"That's just it. They're coincidences. How could the prison and asylum breaks have anything to do with the ship wreck?"

"How indeed, Commissioner. The answer to that question, I'll wager, is the key to the mystery. I'm sure Dr. Watson can tell you that more often than not—"

Anticipating Holmes' recitation of an axiom I'd heard more times than I care to remember I interrupted, "More often than not, you will find in coincidence the residue of design."

"Thank you," Holmes said.

"And the residue of exactly whose design do you believe is to be found in this instance?" Although Strumm asked the question, it was evident from his tense posture that he already knew the answer.

"Isn't it obvious, Commissioner? Barlucci's."

"Once again I remind you, Mr. Holmes, Barlucci is dead."

"Unfortunately, Commissioner, the only people who would be

able to attest to that are, themselves, dead."

"Yes, that may be true but we do have the Captain's log. It gives us a pretty good idea of what was going on aboard the *Redeemer* on the voyage to New York."

Holmes looked surprised. "You didn't mention it in your wire."

"No, it was only discovered a few days ago in the Captain's cabin. It was in a hidden compartment in his armoire."

"May I see it?"

"I thought you would be interested. You may inspect it here, but until we've concluded the investigation, it must remain in police custody. I have, however, had it transcribed. You may have a copy to read at your leisure."

"Very kind of you, Commissioner, although I would like to examine the original if you don't mind."

"Of course, I expected you'd ask." Strumm moved to the safe sitting in the corner of his office and a few moments later presented Holmes with the log book of the *S. S. Redeemer*, Commercial Salvage Ship, New York Harbor. "Here you go, sir."

"Thank you," said Holmes who had already removed his glass from his jacket pocket. As Strumm and I sat having a second cup of coffee and conversing about the events of our lives since we'd last seen one another, Holmes examined the book in the minutest detail. A few of the more telling entries I've recreated here:

6 July 19—

Despite my attempt to keep secret the article trapped in the block of ice brought aboard, rumors abound. As it melts down, I'm concerned the truth of the rumors will be proved. I've had to put it under lock and guard as the crew is grumbling about the ship being haunted.

7 July 19—

The crew is becoming increasingly tense. A fight broke out this morning in the galley when a deck hand threatened the cook over the preparation of his food. *The First Mate had him locked in the compartment with the ice block. When he came out, he was frightened senseless, murmuring about ghosts and goblins. He was so agitated he broke away and after running to the forecastle of the ship, jumped overboard. After hitting the water, he surfaced laughing hysterically, shouting of being free before submerging once again, lost to the sea.*

11 July 19—

There appears to be some kind of mass hysteria affecting the crew. We've been sailing in a blind fog for three days now. Two crewmen disappeared two nights ago without a trace, presumably overboard. Today Simmons, the radio operator, destroyed the radio equipment before taking a pistol and blowing his brains out on the forecastle in clear view of the entire crew. I had the First Mate post a guard on the armory. He, the Gunner, and myself have all taken to wearing side arms. The mood of the crew is getting uglier by the day.

13 July 19—

The last two days have been murderous. The First Mate and six crewmen attempted to take over the ship, demanding we jettison the ice block over the side. A handful of loyal followers assisted me in putting down the mutiny. Four crewmen were lost over the side, some of them wounded. The fog was so heavy that no rescue was possible.

14 July 19—

Three more suicides in the last two days have convinced me I cannot keep that thing in the ice onboard any longer. We dropped it off the fantail this morning. Perhaps that will be the end of this madness.

After at least forty-five minutes Holmes closed the book, holding it across his chest as he said to Strumm, "Thank you, Commissioner, that was most informative."

Strumm looked at him querulously, "Then you agree that Barlucci is dead?"

"On the contrary. I'm more convinced than ever he is indeed alive, well and on the loose in your fine city."

"How can you say that? Even if you were to believe it was Barlucci in that block of ice and that somehow he could be alive, the captain had it dumped over the side. Surely that ends it."

"Does it? The block of ice is almost certainly a red herring. It's just the sort of thing Barlucci would devise. He could have secretly gained access to the ship and stowed away, working to confuse and deceive the captain and crew. A man of Barlucci's intellect would easily be able to use the superstitions of these simple-minded seamen to do his work for him, pitting one against the other, fostering suspicion amongst the crew until finally they turned on one another."

"That's a nice story, Holmes. But we have the log."

"Ah yes, the log. That in itself is somewhat suspect in my eyes."

"Why? Because it disproves your theory that Barlucci is alive?"

"It doesn't disprove Barlucci is alive at all, Commissioner, but it is curious…" He offered the book to Strumm, "Perhaps you can tell me why there is a page missing."

Strumm started forward, "What are you talking about?" He strode over to where Holmes was sitting and snatched the log out of his hands. "There are no missing pages."

"You are mistaken, Commissioner. Look more closely," Holmes said calmly, offering his glass. "Look between the entries for July 13th and July 14th."

Strumm held the log under the desk lamp, examining it with the glass. Finally, he looked at Holmes, "All right, there's a page missing. That doesn't…" his voice trailed off, clearly disturbed by the discovery.

"Doesn't prove anything? Perhaps not, but I believe it's against maritime law to extract pages from a ship's log, which is a legal document, is it not?"

"True enough, but we don't know when that page was removed. It could have been removed months ago, for perfectly innocent reasons. Regardless," Strumm said in a less confident tone than just a few minutes before, "it certainly does not prove Barlucci had anything to do with what went on aboard the *Redeemer*."

"The fact is, Commissioner, while it doesn't prove Barlucci's involvement, it does imply there was something going on that someone did not want to come to light. When you add that fact to there being no one left alive on board that ship, we cannot be absolutely certain what occurred. These are but threads, threads that I believe will eventually lead directly to Barlucci."

Strumm looked from Holmes to me and I tried, without allowing Holmes to see, to indicate with a subtle movement of the eyebrow furthermost from Holmes that I, like Strumm, had my doubts about the logic of Holmes' arguments. I then broke the awkward silence saying, "I think we should be getting along to our hotel. It's been a rather long voyage and I could use a hot bath before dinner."

"Dinner," said Strumm. "That reminds me, Emily will have my hide nailed to the barn door if I don't insist on the two of you joining us for dinner tomorrow night."

"We have no wish to put you out, Commissioner," said Holmes. "I'm sure the fare at the Gilsey will suit us quite nicely."

"Nonsense, Mr. Holmes. Emily is looking forward to seeing you again. She's spoken often of your kindness in the days after her sister was killed. She would be very upset if you refused. Besides, you've never met Lucie. You must come."

"We accept," I said in the pause that followed, before Holmes could refuse. "A good home-cooked meal will be a pleasure after a week at sea, eh Holmes."

"Please tell Mrs. Strumm that Dr. Watson and I have accepted your kind invitation, Commissioner. It will be a pleasure to see her again."

"Splendid. Shall we say about seven?"

"Seven it is," said I.

"That will give us plenty of time to visit the *Redeemer* and the asylum beforehand," Holmes said.

We took the underground, or subway as New Yorkers say, from City Hall to 29th Street and from there walked the short distance to our hotel. Holmes thought it would be fitting to stay once again at the Gilsey. I, of course, had stayed there myself while gathering material for 'The Body Snatchers', but I hadn't thought to mention to Holmes much about the state of my accommodations. I was certain he would be pleasantly surprised.

"So yet another coincidence inserts itself, Watson."

"You mean the bit of news concerning Julia Tremaine? A tragedy to be sure, but I don't readily see a connection to the rest."

"Nor do I, yet, but it's an interesting tidbit nonetheless, don't you think? There are several threads already in this case. We have but to gather them together and discover their collective meaning." A wry smile crossed his lips, "It appears our Commissioner has again taken to drink, did you notice? What's bred in the bone comes out in the flesh, I'm afraid."

"No, what do you mean?"

"On the side table, near the bookshelf, there was a carafe of water and a near empty glass."

"What of it? There's certainly no mystery in wanting water near in this weather," I said wiping my brow with my handkerchief.

"The glass didn't contain water, at least not merely water. I had occasion to swipe my finger in it as I passed. Alcohol, bourbon I would say, was the former contents of that glass."

"Doesn't mean it was Mylo's…could have been poured for a guest."

"You give the commissioner too much latitude. His entire

physical being displays his return to his former ways. The paunch he carries, his rheumy eyes, profuse sweating, pallid complexion except for shine of the nose, all point to a man who all too often climbs into the bottle."

"Pah, that paunch is more likely his wife Emily's good cooking; whereas his complexion could be the result of too much time spent indoors, going over paperwork, the bane of a position such as his. And who could help but sweat in this climate. As for his eyes and his nose, he might have a bit of summer allergy, or perhaps they're irritated from the noxious fumes of his automobile."

"Did you happen to notice he twice fumbled the combination to his safe?"

"No, I didn't but that might be easily explained by a number of things other than excessive intake of alcohol."

"Watson, you are indeed a faithful friend, always ready to find the best in mankind. I shall endeavor to keep an open mind about Strumm, if only for your sake."

"I'm glad to hear it," I said. With that passed, my mind wandered to young Phillip Tremaine. "I can't help wondering what the effect of discovering his mother alive and escaped from an asylum will have on young Phillip. Wait till you meet him, Holmes—so young and bright and eager—I hope he manages the news well."

"Yes, it would be a hard thing on many levels to find out all of this now. To learn not only of his mother's circumstances, that would be difficult enough, but to also learn of the conspiracy of silence that kept it from him."

"Conspiracy of silence, you make it sound almost sinister. I'm sure they had the best of intentions."

"Ah, but you know what the proverb says about good intentions."

"Yes, of course, though I dare say it was a kindness to the boy all the same."

"How so? Bestowing this kindness as you call it may indeed have altered the very course of this young man's life."

"All the better, I say."

"Perhaps, perhaps…but what if, had he known about his mother, instead of being solely a medical doctor he'd studied the mind and how it works. Perhaps he could discover some principle or treatment that would restore his mother to her sanity, thereby giving both their lives meaning. You know of the work of Freud and Jung. Perhaps young Tremaine would be carrying on in their tradition or even blazing new trails in the understanding of the human mind."

"I can certainly see your point, though I'd not considered it before." Happily, at this point we arrived at our hotel. "Ah, here we are, Holmes. I think you'll find the Gilsey much as you remember it." We ascended the steps and walked into the lobby.

"If I'm not mistaken," Holmes said, "the carpet has been replaced as well as the wallpaper. And they've had lifts and telephone stations added."

"Yes, well, you must allow for the ravages of time on some things and the modernization of others, old boy, but look there, at the desk."

"Dr. Watson," a middle-aged man in a blue suit and an oval pin bearing the title 'Manager' called to them.

"As I live and breathe, Abel Jenkins. You're manager here? How excellent," Holmes said turning to me. "Watson, you might have told me Mr. Jenkins was still at the Gilsey."

"I did try to hint at it. I would think someone as adept at deduction would have caught on to that."

"Pish-posh," he said and turned his attention back to Abel. "Tell me, Mr. Jenkins, how's the family? How's your cousin, Ernie?"

Abel's face visibly fell as he answered, "Ah, Mr. Holmes, it's quite a sad thing. I'm afraid our family has suffered a great loss." His sad eyes looked at us reproachfully, "Influenza."

"Dear me," said I, "we're sorry to hear that."

"Indeed," Holmes said, "How old was Ernie?"

"Ernie? Oh…did you think…" his face brightened, "I didn't mean Ernie; I meant Opha, my pig."

Holmes said, "Aha, the pig. Your pig has died of influenza?"

"Yes, oh, she was quite old, for a pig, but she was such a joy, really."

"I see, then Ernie is well, I assume?" Holmes said.

"Certainly, and doing real good, too. He's been working as a telegrapher these past fifteen years. And," he said with an important pause, "he's gone and gotten himself married."

I said, "I didn't know that, Abel, why didn't you tell me."

"Oh dear, Dr. Watson, it's fairly new news. Ernie's only been married since January. Met his wife right there in the telegraph office."

"How fortuitous."

"Nah, she works at the police department, she's a secretary, Mr. Holmes. She ain't no fruitoress.

Chapter 4
Salvage ships and lost souls…

The following morning we took a landau from Strumm's office to the Ward's Island ferry. It seems the new patrol wagon had developed some sort of mechanical problem and was unavailable, a decided disadvantage when compared to a horse-drawn carriage as Holmes was quick to point out.

Since the bridge from Manhattan was destroyed in a storm in 1821, the only way on or off Ward's Island was by means of the ferry, making it an ideal location for both the prison and the asylum. Unfortunately, on the night of the prison break, the additional boats making use of the ferry landing to bring on mariners to examine the wrecked *Redeemer* provided, as authorities later theorized, the means for a number of prisoners and asylum escapees to make good their escapes.

The day was warm and a bit humid, but out on the island there was a favorable breeze coming from seaward improving the overall comfort, though it also brought with it the odor of the fisheries just up the river.

The ship, a rather ugly cutter of about seventy-five feet in length with twin steam-driven winches at the stern, had been pulled off the rocks where it had landed and undergone the repairs necessary to bring it alongside a dock until it could be towed to a yard for more extensive repairs. We began our investigation on the bridge where the last victim was found.

Holmes walked around the wheel, bending down to look at the worn paint with his glass. "Where are the chains?" said he.

Seemingly surprised, Strumm said, "What chains?"

"The chains used to secure the captain to the wheel."

"I didn't say anything about any chains, Mr. Holmes."

"There was no need, Commissioner. Observe," Holmes pointed to the wooden interior of the ship's wheel. "These marks here and here," indicating first one side of the wheel and then the opposite. "They're new and unique. The wheel has other various older scuffs and scrapes, but the manner of these gouges and cuts appears the same on either side. This points to an unusual circumstance of recent origin that would leave identical cuts in the wood on opposing interior points of the wheel. Also, since the captain was the last known occupant of the ship and it was while he was steering it the ship ran aground, he either ran aground on purpose, or could no longer steer a course to avoid it. That he was found dead at the wheel suggests the latter. This leads us to the conclusion his death occurred prior to the grounding of the ship and indeed was the cause of it. It's a dedicated captain indeed who would remain at the wheel with the wounds you have described, Commissioner. Hence the deduction that the dead captain was chained to the wheel."

"That's remarkable," was all Strumm could manage to say.

"Please," I chided, "don't encourage him." Inwardly I was quite proud to know that beekeeping had not dulled the man's insights. I'd quite forgotten that during the Abigail Drake business years before Strumm had only limited occasion to observe Holmes in action and at that time the enmity between them flowed in both directions in equal measure.

"You guessed that in the scant seconds we've been on the bridge? Is there anything else you can guess?"

"Oh dear," I said. I saw a familiar twinkle in Holmes' eye.

"I never guess, Commissioner. To do so is a shocking habit, one I find to be destructive to the orderly use of logic. No. I never guess; I observe, I surmise, I interpret, I deduce. But I never guess."

"I beg your pardon, Mr. Holmes, what else can you, uhm, deduce?"

"From the position of the manacles that bound the captain, I would say he is five feet six inches to five feet eight inches in height, has blonde hair, and is or was most probably left-handed."

"I warned you," said I.

"Astounding."

"Not at all. The height and handedness can be deduced fairly easily by a combination of the manacle placement on the wheel and the difference in the amount of chaffing in the two areas."

"And his hair?"

Holmes pulled a strand of hair from the hub of the wheel. "I expect your man was found slumped with his head against the hub."

"Yes. Brilliant, Mr. Holmes. The stories written by Dr. Watson, here, appear not to be exaggerated."

Holmes smiled and visibly seemed to thaw a bit at this. That was something else beekeeping hadn't dulled, his appetite for praise. "But I must say, Commissioner, you are completely wrong in your assumption that he committed suicide."

"What makes you say that?"

"Do you mean aside from the fact that the wound you described began on the left side of his throat. Since he is left-handed, this would be a very awkward movement. Besides, what would be his reason and why would he be manacled to the wheel?"

"The ship's crew was suffering from some kind of mass hysteria. No doubt it affected the captain as well."

"Nonsense. All of this was a construct of Barlucci to throw the official police off the scent."

"Barlucci again? Holmes, I'm afraid you'll have to come up with some hard evidence, something more substantial than a missing log book page, before I can believe one man could have taken on an entire ship of able bodied seamen."

"Then for the present, Commissioner, we must agree to disagree." He looked out across the island toward the asylum. "Was the prison break before or after the ship ran aground, Commissioner?"

"After. We believe the prisoners used the confusion around the ship wreck as a diversion. They killed a guard and took his uniform and then, to add to the chaos, they overpowered one of the asylum custodians and unlocked the southernmost wing allowing the inmates there to escape as well."

"And how many prisoners and inmates are still at large?"

"We were able to round up the majority of both the same night. But there are two inmates from the asylum and four prisoners who've eluded capture thus far."

"And Mrs. Tremaine is one of these?"

"Yes, I'm afraid she is. That is why it was necessary to tell young Phillip the truth about his mother. We were afraid she might try and contact him."

"And has she?"

"No, Phillip would have told us if she had. He took it pretty hard, I'm afraid."

"No doubt," said I.

"Where were the artifacts from the *Animus Lacuna* found, Commissioner?"

"There were some items discovered in the Captain's cabin, mostly coinage, a ship's compass, and the like. The rest were in a storage room just aft of the crew's quarters."

"May I see the storeroom?"

"Of course, right this way," He led Holmes and me to a small but rather cluttered room just aft of the wheel house. "We haven't removed anything quite yet. We're having our properties custodian come this afternoon and catalog the items. I didn't want the scene disturbed until after you'd had a chance to take a look."

Holmes gave a sidewise smile, "Except for the body of the captain."

"Yes, well, as I said, that was of necessity."

"Yes. And the two guards who were found murdered?"

"I have already explained that, Mr. Holmes. They were victims of the prison break, found nowhere near the ship and their necks were broken. If they were victims, as you would have us believe, why was their manner of death not similar to the others?"

"Another mystery, Commissioner. Perhaps Barlucci didn't wish to tip his hand." Holmes went quickly round the room, inspecting all the items one by one, part of a life preserver, brass plating, ship's bell, assorted china, and clothing. He paid particular attention to the clothing, but said nothing. At last he spoke, "Thank you, Commissioner, you've been most helpful, but I don't believe we can learn anything more here. Let's get on to the Asylum Director's office. You've made arrangements for us to interrogate the warder on duty?"

"Yes, Doctor Small should be waiting for us when we arrive."

As we were departing the ship and Strumm was arranging our transport to the hospital, Holmes pulled me aside. "The clothing in the store room," he said cryptically.

"What about it?"

"It is of Italian manufacture," he said with a hint of a smile. "It's been said the apparel oft proclaims the man." Before I could say anything the carriage pulled up and we got in beside Strumm.

The New York Asylum for the criminally insane was built on the Kirkbride plan with tiered wards radiating in opposite directions from a central building. The further the wards were from the main building, the more severe were the cases. The central office structure was built in a grand gothic style and the office of the Asylum Director was resplendent with the finest Persian tapestries and carpets. Centered on three palladium windows was a large desk of rich mahogany. There stood along the walls on either side of the windows two large book cases in which were housed a number of awards and certificates of achievement earned by Dr. Small and the hospital.

As we entered the Director's office we saw two men. One was seated behind the desk, Dr. Small, and the other was standing before it, the warder. It was when Dr. Small walked from behind his desk to greet us that I realized I'd been mistaken in believing he'd been seated and it became most obvious his name well-suited him. He could not have been more than four feet six inches in height. His beard was full but graying as was his hair, what little of it that was left circumscribed around his bald and shiny head. He wore thick black-framed glasses that made even his face appear small. "Commissioner Strumm, we've been expecting you," he said, extending his hand. "This is Jonas Hone. He's been a warder here for twelve years," indicating a man in his forties, a beard stubble on his scowling face. It was evident he was not happy at being called to the Director's office.

Holmes stepped forward, "Thank you, Doctor Small. My name is Sherlock Holmes and I will be questioning Mr. Hone. Dr. Watson, my associate will take notes, if you've no objection."

The Director looked at Strumm who nodded his assent. "No, no objection, Mr. Holmes."

"Splendid. Now then, Mr. Hone," Holmes turned toward the warder, "do I understand that you were knocked unconscious and your keys were taken from you?"

"That's right, knocked cold as a pike and left locked in my room," Hone said, slumping his shoulders, his hat held loosely in his hand. Jonas Hone stood nearly six feet tall and was approximately two hundred pounds. He wore his thinning hair short and had no facial hair other than stubble.

"But you were found later in the wards, and without your pants."

"They tooks my pants as a joke when they tooks my keys. I keeps a spare key in my room." All the while he spoke, his eyes darted from one of us to the other, never lighting in one place for more than a second or two.

"And yet you failed to secure a second pair of pants? Very curious, Mr. Hone."

"There was quite a bit of confusion at the time, sir," he said, his voice rising in insolence.

"And your keys were later found in the lock of one of the wards?"

"Yah…"

"May I see your keys?" He held out his hand as Hone fished them from his belt and handed them over.

"This key here," Holmes said holding out one of the brass keys. "It is to your quarters, is it not?"

Hone looked at the key and then at Holmes, "Yah…how'd you—"

"And this one, here…" he held out another key, "…what does it open?"

Hone glanced at the key and suddenly appeared to be uncomfortable. "One of the wards, I reckon."

"Indeed. Isn't it true it was this key that was found in the lock to the ward?" Holmes stood glaring at Hone who was silent. "You work the women's wards, do you not?"

"I do…what of it?" he said, squirming in his chair.

"And some of those wards are small, are they not?"

"Some is…the more violent cases are kept t' themselves so's they don't hurt no one."

"Is that the only reason to separate them out?"

"What do you mean?" Hone asked.

Holmes ignoring the question asked, "Are you married, Mr. Hone?"

"I am, sir, fourteen year come this November."

"Happily?"

"What's that got to do with...?"

"I suggest you have your wife see a doctor, Mr. Hone."

"Whaaa...?"

The Director stepped forward, "What's going on, Mr. Holmes? I don't understand. This is quite irregular."

"Doctor Small, can you tell me which ward this key opens?"

"Certainly. Each key has a number that corresponds to the lock and door it opens. Why is this key of particular interest, Mr. Holmes?"

"I believe it will show Mr. Hone was lying about his whereabouts when the patients under his charge were released."

"That's a serious accusation, Mr. Holmes. I hope you have good cause for making it." Director Small wrote the key's number on a slip of paper and then opened the door to the outer office. "Miss Walstone, look in the files and tell me which ward this key opens."

"Yes, Doctor," she said taking the slip of paper from Small. After reading it, she turned and hurried off to a bank of filing cabinets, returning only a minute later. "It's Ward 5 South, Room 124. Lorelei Baker is the only resident."

"I see. Thank you, Miss Walstone," he said and closed the door.

"Explain yourself, Hone," Small said with a grim look.

"I...I...she...she was causing a lotta ruckus and so I...well...I had to calm her down some."

"Do you often find it necessary to, er, 'calm her down some' Mr. Hone?" Holmes asked smiling, with a conspiratorial intonation.

The warder, a smirk on his face, said, "I may have, on one or two occasions…" and as he looked at the director his smirk disappeared and he grew silent.

Holmes asked, "What is the diagnosis of Miss Baker, Dr. Small?"

"Traumatic shock. She was the only survivor of a fire that killed her husband and three children. She hasn't spoken a word since she's been here." Small turned to address Hone, "You know the rules regarding Miss Baker. At no time are male warders to enter the isolation wards without a female warder in attendance." Small's face turned bright red in contrast to the gray in his hair and beard. He took the keys from Holmes, examining the one to 5S-124. Looking up at Hone he said in a voice much calmer than the expression in his eyes, "Pack your things. I want you out of this facility today. You're discharged immediately." Small pressed a button on his desk and two armed security guards entered. "Escort Mr. Hone back to his quarters and when he's collected his personal effects, make certain he leaves the premises." Without another word but scowling at Holmes, Hone walked out of the office with a guard on either side.

"Mr. Holmes, I owe you my thanks, but how did you know?"

"The chancre sores on his mouth were the first clue. The man is in the early stages of syphilis, which tells me he is not a man of monogamous habits. That, along with his keys, made me suspect he may not be telling the truth of his whereabouts."

"What did his keys have to do with it?"

"I noted that the key you are holding has far less verdigris than any other except the one to the warder's quarters. This indicates that its use is only second to that of Mr. Hone's own room. Institution workers are creatures of habit. I submit Mr. Hone was on this night, where he is accustomed to spend a good deal of his time when he is on duty, in the room of the unfortunate Miss Baker. I'd wager the bump he claims to have received was either faked or self-induced. No doubt his attention was occupied and he didn't notice his keys being lifted. By the way, I'd have Miss Baker checked for syphilis as well as for signs of pregnancy."

"That's astounding, Mr. Holmes, and we shall without delay. This all comes as a monstrous shock."

"I shouldn't doubt it, Director Small," said Holmes with a sharpness to his tone. "As a director, you should always expect that which you inspect."

"I beg your pardon, sir?"

"Shall I make it plainer? Very well," as he said this I cringed being familiar with Holmes' intolerance for the mediocre performance of bureaucrats, "if you spent more time inspecting your hospital wards and less time polishing the awards on your bookshelves, you would know better what's going on right under your nose within the walls of your own asylum."

"You astonish me, sir," said the Director turning on his heel, the veins in his neck becoming distended. "I believe you forget yourself."

At this point I interjected, "You'll have to forgive my colleague, Dr. Small, but Holmes has made a habit of astonishing me for many years. However, just now I fear we must be going." In order to prevent Holmes from making an awkward situation worse by expounding on the rather obvious observation that the Director was ignoring his duties, I took hold of one arm and indicated to Strumm he should take the other and together we left the Director's office, with Holmes between us and Dr. Small still in a huff.

Once we'd taken our leave of the asylum, Commissioner Strumm reminded Holmes and me of the dinner invitation for that evening, "Don't forget, now. If I know Emily, dinner will be served promptly at seven. I can't wait to tell Emily how you blasted old Dr. Small. It'll make an amusing story for dinner conversation."

As Holmes looked a bit bemused at the fuss, I said, "Yes, I'm sure it will. Please tell Emily we are very much looking forward to seeing her again and Holmes is most anxious to meet your equally lovely daughter, Lucie."

"Yes, please do, but I still don't understand why you rushed me out of Director Small's office before I'd finished advising him on how better to administer his hospital." And with Strumm still chortling, we departed by way of a passing hansom to our hotel.

Chapter 5
The other Dr. Tremaine...

We arrived at the Strumm home promptly at half-past six o'clock. The Strumms live in a lovely house in upper Manhattan, unpretentious yet elegant in its own way. It is larger than the homes on either side with trellised rose bushes leading to the rear of the house on one side and a wraparound porch containing swings and wooden furniture enough to entertain a dozen guests on the other. Our second knock was answered by Emily Strumm. "Come in, gentlemen. I'm sorry to leave you standing out here for so long. Ilsa, our housekeeper, was stricken last week with consumption and I'm afraid she is still confined to her bed."

"Dear me," said I. "Consumption, you say?"

"Yes, and of an unusual variety according to Phillip. He's had one of his colleagues from the hospital examine her, a specialist. He's quite perplexed. Says he's never seen anything quite like it," Emily said, dabbing her eyes with her handkerchief. "Poor little thing. She's not been long in our employ, having only arrived from Sweden two months ago. But still, we've grown quite fond of her."

"Is there anything I can do to help?" I said.

"No. Thank you Doctor, but you're our guest. We wouldn't dream of imposing on you. Besides, Phillip and his associate both agree it will just have to run its course."

Holmes said, "I'm sure she'll pull through. The Swedes are a sturdy stock."

"I hope you're right, Mr. Holmes," Emily said. "Yes, well please come in, let me take your hats and your cane, Doctor." As she spoke, Emily felt nervously about her throat.

"Are you all right, dear?" I asked, handing her my hat and cane.

"What?" she said and then realized what she was doing. "Oh, my necklace."

I looked at her curiously, "Your necklace? My dear, you aren't wearing a necklace."

"Yes, I know…I've misplaced it." She smiled as she took our things, "It belonged to Abigail. She was wearing it when she…" her eyes began to tear.

"Yes, I remember," said Holmes. "Dr. Rudulac recovered it."

"Yes, the dear man. He gave it to me…it's all I have to remember her by." As she said this a dark shadow passed over her eyes. "I can't for the life of me think of where it might have gone. I faithfully place it on my dresser each night and retrieve it upon awakening, and then one morning it was gone."

"How odd. Is it valuable?" said Holmes.

"Not terribly, I'm sure. Abigail wasn't what you would call extravagant, a bit of gold with a carved bloodstone setting."

Seeing the troubled look on Emily's face, I attempted to reassure her, "I wouldn't be too concerned. It'll turn up, and when you least expect it I'll wager."

"Oh, I'm sure you're quite right, Doctor. It was just a queer piece of jewelry anyway, and of such an unusual design."

"Do you know anything about it, anything of its origins?" Holmes asked.

"I'm afraid not. Only that my sister wore it always, and so it's become very precious to me as well."

51

"Of course," I said and patted her delicate hand.

"Well, I believe we should find my husband in the drawing room. This way, gentlemen."

As we entered the empty drawing room Emily said, "Mr. Holmes, I never got to thank you for the trouble you went to and your kindness after my sister..." her voice trailed away as the episode of some years before was again recalled to mind.

"I assure you, Mrs. Strumm, it was my pleasure and no trouble at all."

"Please call me Emily. I think of you and Dr. Watson as family, our British cousins, if you will."

"Very well, then, Emily. I'm sure we are both most honored."

"Indeed," said I.

Warming to the occasion and to the charm of our hostess Holmes said, "I must say, Emily, you haven't changed a hair in the twenty-five years since I've seen you. If I didn't know better, I would swear you had ridden Mr. Wells' time gadget from that time to this."

"Mr. Holmes, you are too kind. I'm afraid I'm not the young girl you met at that unfortunate time."

"I say, there's a bit of a surprise. Holmes referring to popular literature."

"Yes, well, just as you have found a belated interest in poetry, Watson, I find in my retirement a good deal of time to spend on things that might never have occurred to me when I was actively consulting."

"That's most encouraging, but I must say I disagree with you when it comes to Mrs. Strumm," I said, turning with a little bow, "You're much prettier with maturity if one were to ask me," said I.

"And Doctor, you are as flattering as ever." She broke into an exuberant smile, "Oh, it's so good to see you both again. What is it that brings you to New York? Another book, Doctor?"

Holmes said, "No, I'm afraid not, Mrs. Strumm," but before he could conclude his thought he was interrupted by Mylo who'd just entered the room.

"Ah, gentlemen, if you're quite finished turning my wife's head, can I interest you in a cigar?" Strumm asked retrieving a walnut humidor from the bookshelf.

"I can always tell when my husband wishes to be left alone with his guests. He offers them one of his God-awful smelling cigars." She paused as we laughed. "Gentlemen, I believe this is my cue to leave. But Mylo," she said, starting to put her hand on her husband's arm and then drawing it back, "don't be too long, dinner is almost ready."

Something unspoken, but evidently understood, passed between them.

"I promise, Emily dear." He smiled sadly with the genuine admiration and affection of a man thoroughly in love with his wife. Once she'd closed the door behind her, his smile faded and he turned to face Holmes and myself. "I'm sorry, gentlemen, but I haven't said anything to Emily about your theory regarding Barlucci."

I took a cigar from the humidor and said, "I understand completely. We shouldn't have been so thoughtless," I cast an accusing eye at Holmes. "Bringing up Barlucci might certainly stir up strong emotion in her. You saw how visibly upset she was at losing her keepsake."

"Come now, gentleman," said Holmes, "I think you underestimate the inner strength of Mrs. Strumm." He took a cigar and passing it beneath his nostrils inhaled deeply. "Besides, at some point she will most certainly have to be told. Hispañola?"

"Only if you are correct, sir, but until we are certain of our facts, I would prefer it if you did not speak of him in front of Emily." Lighting Holmes' cigar he said, "Yes, I get them from a tobacconist in lower Manhattan."

"As you wish," Holmes said adding, "for the present." Puffing several times, "It has a very pleasing aroma." His gaze turned stern,

"Tell me, have you considered the possibility that he may seek your wife out?"

"Seek her out? You mean assuming you are correct and he is in New York, which I find quite improbable. Why would he seek out Emily?"

"Barlucci has been out of touch for some twenty years. It's probable that he is unaware of Abigail Drake's death. He most certainly would be looking for her and if he cannot find her, he would naturally seek out her sister."

"If he does, I assure you, you'll be the first to know," Strumm said with a somewhat sarcastic smile.

"I hope so," said Holmes, looking quite serious.

Just then the door to the study opened once more. A beautiful young woman was standing there, and for just a moment I was breathless with the sight of her. I'd met Lucinda Strumm on my previous visit but that had been over two years ago. She had matured a good deal in that time and I was astonished at just how much she looked like her mother, and her aunt, at her age. She smiled shyly and said, "Papa, Mother says you and your guests should extinguish your cigars before dinner is ruined."

"Tell your mother we'll only be a moment, but first, come in, I want you to say hello to Dr. Watson and meet Mr. Sherlock Holmes." He extended his hand to her and waved her inside. "Mr. Holmes, this is my daughter, Lucinda, but we call her Lucie."

"Of course." Holmes gave a shallow bow and extended his hand, "Miss Lucinda, it's a pleasure. I'm sure I don't need to tell you, but you are the very image of your mother."

Lucie curtsied and shook Holmes' hand, "Thank you, Mr. Holmes, but Mother always tells me I look just like my Aunt Abigail. Please, call me Lucie."

"A distinction, I dare say, only visible to a sibling," said I. "It's good to see you again, Lucie, and congratulations."

Her cheeks reddened and the smile on her face widened as she gave me a friendly hug. "It's good to see you too, Doctor. Then Papa's told you I'm engaged?"

"Yes, and I must say you couldn't have picked a finer young man if my opinion is of any consequence."

"I agree wholeheartedly," said Strumm. "A fine young man."

"Who is a fine young man?" said Mrs. Strumm standing in the doorway with her hands on her hips.

"Phillip, Mama."

"Yes, well fine young man or no, dinner is getting cold. Gentlemen?" she said sternly, turning to lead us all through the door and toward the dining room.

As we began to follow Mrs. Strumm, Lucie turned and said, "Mr. Holmes, I wonder if I might speak to you for just a moment," placing her hand upon his arm to detain him. "Papa, you don't mind, do you? I'll only be a moment, I promise."

"Of course, dear, but don't keep your mother waiting, and don't impose too heavily on our guest."

"Not at all," Holmes said. "How could such a lovely young lady be an imposition?" And with that, Strumm and I went on ahead into the dining room. Miss Lucie and Holmes entered only a brief time after, she with a very satisfied look on her face.

Mrs. Strumm needn't have worried, dinner was excellent and we all ate our fill. I, myself, had three helpings of Mrs. Strumm's peas and carrots. It was while we were enjoying an excellent peach cobbler with our coffee that there came a knock on the door.

Lucie nearly jumped in her seat at the sound. "That's Phillip. We're going to the Aeolian tonight. Alex got us tickets for a private box. I'm hoping the music will cheer up Phillip, he's been so glum since getting the news of his mother. May I be excused?"

"Certainly, dear," said Mrs. Strumm. "But bring Phillip in to meet our guests before you two leave."

Pushing herself away from the table, she said, "Of course, Mama," and disappeared out the door. Moments later she returned pulling a seemingly reluctant young man behind her. "Mr. Holmes, this is Phillip. Phillip, Mr. Holmes. You already know Dr. Watson."

"It's good to see you again, Doctor," he said to me and then extending his hand to Holmes, "I've heard and read a great deal about you, sir. I'm glad to meet you at last."

Holmes stood and shook the young lad's hand, "I'm afraid my colleague has a penchant for romanticizing events that aren't nearly so melodramatic as they appear in print." He looked piercingly at the boy for a moment so much so that it seemed to make young Phillip a trifle uncomfortable.

"Is there anything wrong, sir?"

"I'm sorry to stare," said Holmes, "it's just that you are every bit your father, except your hair, of course, the fairness of which comes from your mother, does it not?"

He looked at Holmes for a moment, then down at the hat he carried in his hand. "I'm afraid I've never seen my mother, sir," he said.

"I can see the remark has troubled you, I apologize."

Mrs. Strumm said in an effort to turn the conversation to more pleasurable topics, "I understand you are going to the theater tonight, who's playing?"

Lucie took Phillip's hand and said, "The Philharmonic is presenting works by various composers, Verdi, Paganini, Vivaldi to name a few. They're featuring a young violinist, Max Pilzer. He's said to be quite good."

"Yes," Phillip said. "Lucie is making me take her."

"Well, young man, I certainly wouldn't want you to feel coerced into taking my daughter out," Strumm said with a stern look on his face.

"Oh no, sir, I didn't mean…"

"Oh, Papa, stop. Don't listen to him, Phillip, he's only teasing you," Lucie said laughing at Phillip's embarrassment and both Strumm and his wife joined in.

"Phillip, really. You know how Mylo and I feel about you. We couldn't be happier."

"Thank you, Mrs. Strumm, Mr. Strumm." Looking at Lucie he said, "We had better get going, Lucie, we don't want to be late." He helped her on with her wrap and then said, "It was good to meet you, Mr. Holmes, and I hope I will be seeing you and Dr. Watson again soon."

"I'm sure you can count on it," said Holmes, with a wry smile.

It was while we were on our way back to the Gilsey that Holmes confided in me his conversation with Miss Lucie and his impressions of the evening. "Miss Lucie and I had a very interesting conversation, once you take into account young Dr. Tremaine's demeanor."

"Oh, and what was that about?" I said.

"She asked me if I might look into the matter of the disappearance of Julia Tremaine. She said young Phillip is most distraught, first with only just learning of his mother's tortured existence in an asylum and then of her escape and her whereabouts not yet being discovered. Lucie says he is very worried about her safety."

I looked at the expression on Holmes' face and could see behind the steady gaze that he was working on some mystery in that great mind of his. "And you have reason to doubt this?"

"Very perceptive of you. Did you see his face when I mentioned his hair favoring his mother's, when he volunteered he'd never actually seen her?"

"I didn't notice anything unusual."

"Hm…the cobbler, no doubt, distracted your attention at the critical moment. I thought his answer was unusual and somewhat evasive. He wouldn't have to have actually seen her to know of the similarity in their hair color. Surely he has a photograph of her. I recall there were several in the Tremaine home of both his father and his mother. And yet he felt compelled to deny having met her."

"Or perhaps he just said it without an ulterior motive? Not every peach contains a pit, old boy."

"Ahh, had it been only the statement, I might think you right, or at least might give the lad the benefit of the doubt."

"What else was there, then?"

"He looked away as he said it, as if unable to look me in the eyes while making the denial. That, my dear Watson, is what I call a 'flag'."

"A 'flag'? What do you mean, what's a 'flag'?"

"A signal, in the sense of a semaphore flag, in this case it's an indicator of a falsehood, an unconscious revelation. When an habitually honest person purposefully tells a falsehood, they quite naturally feel an amount of guilt in the telling of it. If that feeling of guilt is strong enough, they react physically, by looking away, or by placing a hand near the mouth as if to cover it and not let the falsehood escape. They thus signal their true feeling. One only needs to know how to read these flags in order to interpret them."

"Then you believe young Tremaine was lying, that he has met his mother?"

"Yes, and recently. I'm certain of it. I've made quite a little study of these unconscious movements, I've even—"

I interrupted, "—written a monogram on the subject no doubt. What do you propose to do?"

"Miss Lucie asked me to investigate Julia Tremaine's disappearance."

"It's curious that Phillip didn't confide in Julia."

"Most curious," Holmes agreed, "Perhaps he is too ashamed. If Julia Tremaine has sought out her son, she most probably wants to involve him in some scheme involving the place in which she was known to be obsessed."

"Do you mean you think she intends to have her son help her to rob his father's grave, to remove the remains from the vault in which they lie? Phillip would not agree to that. Surely he must have turned her away."

"Undoubtedly, which of course would only serve to increase his shame."

"What do you intend to do?"

I intend to do just as Miss Lucie requested. Tomorrow, you and I will visit the Marble Cemetery."

Chapter 6
Murder in the Marble Cemetery…

"I'm terribly sorry Doctor, Mr. Holmes, we'll have you inside shortly." Lionel Manfried, Superintendent of the Marble Cemetery, appeared frazzled as he fumbled with three rings of brass keys from under his jacket, finally producing the one that would gain our entry. "We're interviewing for a new caretaker. I'm afraid the last one walked off the job one day and hasn't been back since."

"I see, walked off you say?" said Holmes. "How long ago did he disappear?"

"It's been nearly a week now. At first we thought perhaps he'd gotten drunk and just not showed, but after the third day, we sent someone round to his house to see about him. No one was there and his neighbors said they hadn't seen him or his brother for days. It's all very unusual. He's been with us for nine years now." He unlocked the gate as he spoke and swinging it open said, "Here you go, sirs. Which resident were you intent on visiting today?" He pulled a piece of folded paper from his hip pocket, running his finger down a list of the names of his 'residents' and the tomb numbers in which they reside.

"We'd like to see the final resting place of Dr. Alan Tremaine, if you would be so kind," Holmes said with a saccharine tone.

"Let's see, Tremaine…Tremaine…ah, here it is, vault forty-three, southwest, near the south wall. This way, gentlemen," he said as he walked briskly across the stretch of green lawn. The Marble Cemetery was unlike any funerary I'd ever visited. Enclosed by four walls it had more the appearance of a peaceful park than a cemetery. There were no signs of headstones marking graves, just a wide expanse of grass broken only by the numerous squares of marble covering the entryways into the subterranean tombs. Scattered throughout the grounds and along the walls where plaques contained the names of the guests, were benches that gave it its park-like atmosphere. "Was Dr. Tremaine a family member?"

"No, as a matter of fact we'd only met the man on one occasion, although we knew of him," I said.

As we neared the place of interment, our guide indicated with the toe of his boot which marble cover sealed the tomb of Alan Tremaine. "Here you have it. Dr. Tremaine's remains are just below here and in the tomb closest to the south wall."

"Thank you," Holmes said and then he asked, "It's my understanding that each of these covers allows entry unto two tombs, one on either side, is that true?"

"That's correct. We have a total of 156 tombs with 78 marble covers. Each tomb has its own brass door, which is locked. I have a key and the family can, if they so desire, have a duplicate made. Each tomb can accommodate up to six adult members."

"Have there been any recent interments in either of the two tombs beneath this particular cover?"

Manfried consulted his list, "No…no, the most recent in the area was three months ago, two tombs over, a Mr. Griswold in tomb thirty-nine was laid to rest beside his wife who died a few years prior."

Holmes examined the stone lid, "Hmm…" He ran his fingers along the edge of the lid. "This stone has been recently removed."

"Impossible. We have a caretaker here every night and the gate remains locked outside of visiting hours, during which the grounds are patrolled."

"Except for the past week," I reminded him.

"Well, yes, that's true, but the gate has remained locked the whole time."

"Nevertheless, observe." Holmes knelt down on one knee beside the tomb cover. "I am able to run my finger the depth of the lid all round on this tomb, but earth has filled in the gaps of the tomb lids on either side."

"Dear me. Yes, I see you're right. That is a little odd."

"Watson, bear a hand," Holmes said as he tried in vain to lift the lid.

"The stones are much too heavy," Manfried said. "We have a lift-wagon to remove them. Wait here and I'll get it." And with that he hurried away to a small brick building in the corner of the cemetery. He returned minutes later pulling a yellow steel wagon. It rolled easily across the grass on raised wheels and had a small ladder affixed to it. He brought it to rest directly over the tomb's lid. From beneath he fastened a steel 'lifter' in the shape of an 'L', the lower leg of which fit into a hole drilled into the cover at each corner of the stone. To the lifter a chain was attached through a welded 'eye'. The chain led into a gear box on the wagon. Once the lifters were in place, Manfried turned a crank and, through the action of a very efficient system of pulleys, slowly lifted the marble lid from its place until it was sufficiently high enough for the wagon to be pulled away leaving the open tomb beneath.

"Ingenious," I said.

"Watson, get the ladder. Let's have a look." He turned to Manfried, "You have the key, I believe you said," he held out his hand.

"Uh...I...I...this is very unusual."

"Very well, then, Watson and I will wait up here while you go down and take a look."

Manfried swallowed hard and slowly handed the keys over to Holmes. Evidently as Cemetery Supervisor he limited his supervision to matters above ground.

"Come, Watson," Holmes said as he clambered down the wooden ladder into the dark abyss. I followed.

On either side of the ladder was a brass door with two seraphim wings in bas-relief between which was suspended a scroll with 'R.I.P' written in script upon it. Holmes took the key given to him by Mr. Manfried, who was nervously attending the top of the ladder, and turned it in the lock. Taking the hinged brass handle, he swung the door open. Instantly our senses were assaulted with the noxious fumes that could only be coming from the putrefied remains of man or beast. We both instinctively reached for our handkerchiefs and held them to our faces as we entered the pitch-black tomb.

Fortunately, Holmes had the foresight to bring with him a pocket-lantern that he withdrew from his jacket and lighted. In its cold stare, we saw a horrid sight. On the slab of marble meant to hold the coffin of the deceased Dr. Alan Tremaine was the body of a man with two garish gashes in his pale throat. On the floor of the tomb in front of the shelf lay the empty casket, its lid torn from its hinges. On the other side of the tomb lay the body of yet another man, with the same fatal furrows cut into his throat. Holmes withdrew the glass from his inner jacket pocket and began a thorough examination of everything within the tomb.

"Wh-what's going on down there?" I heard Manfried call out. "And what is that stench?"

Welcomely, I stepped away from the scene of carnage and into the small passage between the two tombs, where the air was only slightly less ghastly. "You'd better call for the police," I said. "I fear we may have found your former caretaker."

Manfried ran off to call for the police. By the time he'd returned, Holmes had completed his work and we were climbing back up the ladder. Holmes said to Manfried, "I believe the mystery surrounding the disappearance of your caretaker has been solved but leads us to the mystery of what caused him to enter this crypt and who murdered him and, if I'm not mistaken, his brother therein."

"His brother?"

"Twins, from the look of them. Identical. Here are your keys," he said handing the ring to Manfried. He turned to me, "Come, Watson, we must give Commissioner Strumm a call."

We hailed a cab and proceeded to Commissioner Strumm's office on Park Row. "What do you make of it, Holmes?"

"I'm not sure, but it looks very grim. If Julia Tremaine is at the center of the desecration of this tomb, and the missing remains of Dr. Tremaine attest she must be, then I fear she has somehow become linked to Barlucci, possibly as a victim."

"Then those men were—"

"Murdered by Barlucci, yes."

"The same modus operandi as in London, then?"

"Essentially, but there are differences."

"How so?"

"For one thing, he didn't bother to slash the throats with a knife. Instead, he's left their punctured throats with symmetrical gashes, not unlike the victims of Miss Drake, indicating he acted hurriedly and without regard for their eventual discovery."

"But how would Barlucci and Julia Tremaine come to be together and working in league with one another?"

"I suspect it was Barlucci who instigated the asylum break. Don't forget, the asylum break took place shortly after the ship ran aground."

"I see, but what on earth would Barlucci want with Julia, and how would he even have known she was in the asylum?"

"That remains to be seen. But look at the facts. The tomb of Dr. Tremaine has been opened and his body exhumed, the very thing

Julia Tremaine insisted on before being committed to the asylum. Remaining in the tomb are the bodies of two men whose wounds are nearly identical to the ones we saw on Inspector Andrews and the couple from the park twenty-five years ago."

"But Barlucci had nothing to do with those murders. It was Miss Drake who—"

Holmes interrupted me with a sharpness of tone that shocked me. In a tenor I can only describe as a wrathful bitterness he said, "Damn it all, Watson, can't you see what's in front of your nose? Don't you understand? Whether he was on the scene or not, it matters little, the evil in Miss Drake was directed by his hand. But now, now he has returned to visit evil upon the world himself. My first mistake was to ever believe Barlucci could disappear from the face of the earth in a ship wreck like those scoundrels from our 'Orange Pips' adventure. No, I should have known from the beginning it was a trick, a ruse. Barlucci must have read and been familiar with that story of yours and through his pretentious arrogance thought he would stage just such a disappearance to discourage our pursuing him." While I'd heard Holmes speak forcefully many times, he'd never before directed that force toward me and all the while he spoke his face was set in as fierce a look as I have ever seen.

For him to ascribe to Barlucci such a personal enmity was only to demonstrate his own obsession with the man. This was not the first time Holmes alluded to Barlucci with such a peculiar acrimony and each time it was with a noticeable detachment from the presence of mind for which I'd long admired him. I later noted this particular outburst in my journal and determined to keep a weather eye for other signs of dementia in the future. It was acutely disturbing to think he might be on the verge of a breakdown. I was so stung by his tone I recoiled somewhat in my seat.

His face, minutes before sharp and hard, softened visibly and he reached out his hand and patted my arm. "You must forgive me,

Watson. Of all the men in the world, your good comity is the most important to me. My only defense is my ardent belief that this man Barlucci is of such cunning and evil intent that he must be stopped at all cost. I feel at least partly responsible that he is still at large and it eats at me, day and night it eats at me."

His hand was still on my arm and I patted it as I said, "I knew when you were reviewing my manuscript that the case was not closed in your mind. I didn't know, however, that I'd opened the wound so cruelly and so completely. I pledge you this, old friend, if Barlucci is truly at large again, as you say, I shall stand with you shoulder to shoulder until he is hanging from the gibbet."

"You are as constant a man as I have ever known, and I thank you heartily for it."

Thankfully, at this awkwardly tender moment we arrived at the headquarters of the Commissioner.

Chapter 7
A familiar modus operandi…

As we were on our way up to see him, Strumm met us on the steps of his offices. "Holmes, Watson, good. You may want to see this," he said as hurried down the steps toward his awaiting vehicle.

"What is it, Commissioner?"

"There's been a murder. One of the prison escapees, fellow by the name of 'Bone-crusher' Braden. Would you like to come with?" Holmes and I followed the Commissioner to his Packard, much to Holmes' chagrin. "Get in, we can talk on the way."

The automobile lurched forward as we gained our seats. "I say, that's a chilling moniker, 'Bone-crusher,'" said I with a shiver.

"And well earned. He started out as a wrestler, then became an enforcer for one of the Irish gangs in midtown. Somewhere along the way he discovered he enjoyed snapping necks. He's one of several really bad ones that escaped during the prison break. We've rounded up two of them already, but we believe he's probably the one who killed the guards."

"That's right, you did say the guards had their necks broken."

Holmes said, "Where was he found, Commissioner?"

"Inside a comfort station at Grand Central. The custodian noticed his shoes up under one of the stalls when he began his workday and they were still there at the end of it."

"Very observant of him," Holmes said.

"They were a mismatched pair, he said, hard to miss. When he tried to rouse him, Braden made no response, so he took his broom and hooked one of the big man's feet. When he did so, Braden fell to the floor. He could see his throat had been slashed. We believe he may have had a falling out with one of the other escapees."

"Slashed, you say? Interesting. By the way, Commissioner, Watson and I made a murderous discovery of our own. We were just on our way to tell you about it."

Commissioner Strumm turned around to look at Holmes and me in the back seat. "You've discovered a murder?"

"Two in fact. We were looking into the disappearance of Mrs. Tremaine, per your daughter's request."

"Lucie asked you to find Phillip's mother? I told her we were doing everything possible to find her," Strumm said, reddening about the ears, obviously disturbed by this news.

"Yes, well, be that as it may, we made the discovery in the tomb of Phillip's father, Dr. Alan Tremaine. There were two dead bodies, the caretaker and his twin brother. Alan Tremaine's body was nowhere to be found."

"Oh my God, that's awful. Poor Phillip. First he learns his mother's not dead, that she's been in an institution since his birth and he's only finding out because she recently escaped. Now his father's tomb's been desecrated and the body stolen. What's next, for God's sake?"

While we rode along we discussed the tragic circumstances of young Phillip's birth until we arrived at the Grand Central Terminal. I must say I was quite impressed with the terminal building as we entered it. Not only was it colossal in size, it had a grand design that included a large and I may again describe it as a grand marble staircase on the west side of terminal. The ceiling had a depiction of the heavens across it replete with constellations that I must say appeared to me to be life-size. Holmes had the audacity to exclaim the entire ceiling display was portrayed in reverse, but I believe he was only being petulant.

A uniformed policeman met us as we arrived and ushered us to the comfort station where three other uniformed policemen stood guard outside. Holmes and I followed Strumm past the guards, through an anteroom and into the comfort station. It was quite a massive room with shining white marble floors and walls pillared in the four corners with alabaster columns. It had a row of thirty water closets with mahogany doors standing side by side and situated directly across from thirty mirrored wash basins. All of the doors were propped open and at the distant end two detectives were standing outside the stall where the body of 'Bone-crusher' Braden lay sprawled half in and half out.

"Has anyone touched the body?" said Strumm as we hurried down to where the detectives stood.

"No, sir, not since the custodian called us. We got word no one was to touch a thing until you arrived."

"Good. Stand aside," he said. "Mr. Holmes, would you like to examine the scene first?"

The two detectives looked stunned. The taller of the two said, "Pardon me, Commissioner, but who is this? I don't usually like—" He stopped as Strumm fixed him with a cold stare. "Uh...but of course, since you...uh, would you like Gardener and me to wait outside?"

"That won't be necessary, just make sure to stay out of Mr. Holmes' way." The two young detectives took exaggerated steps backward. Ignoring them, Holmes removed his glass from his jacket pocket and proceeded to examine the body of 'Boner-crusher' in minute detail. From head to toe he examined every inch of the man, stopping here to check his scalp, opening his mouth, bending down to sniff for any odors that might be present, now looking at the fingers, taking his pen knife and scraping beneath the nails, examining the scrapings with his lens, then discarding them. Finally, he carefully went over the man's pant legs and shoes, scraping some soil from the heel, examining it and then at last wiping his pen knife clean on his handkerchief. Concluding, he stood between Strumm and me, polishing his glass with his necktie.

"This man's throat has been cut cleanly through the mastoid and through the jugular."

One of the detectives who'd been looking on as Holmes conducted his examination said under his breath in a mocking tone to his partner, "Came all the way from England to tell us this stiff's throat's been cut. Tell us somethin' we don't know, Limey."

Strumm bristled at the insult, "Keep a civil tongue in your head, Miller, or you'll be pounding a beat in Harlem."

"That's all right, Commissioner. I'm sure the detective here is just anxious to get back to his gaming."

Miller stammered while his partner snickered. "What's that supposed to mean? I've been on duty for the past six hours."

Holmes said, "I was unaware the New York Police Department had a billiard room."

Sputtering, Miller said, "Billiards…whataya mean billiards? You're crazy."

"Am I? I first noticed the talcum near the pockets of your trousers when we entered. As we drew nearer, I could see the green chalk on your fingertips."

Strumm shot a glance at Miller's hands, which he quickly put into his pockets and walked around behind his partner.

Holmes gloated just a bit as Strumm asked, "What else can you tell us, Mr. Holmes? I'm sure detectives Miller and Gardener here could benefit from hearing your views."

"I can tell you these slash wounds were made posthumously, that the cause of death was from two punctures in the same area. I've seen this modus operandi before. I can also tell you the murder was committed elsewhere and the victim was placed here to be found."

"I'm sorry, Commissioner, but this Li—er, this gentleman's off kilter now."

Holmes said, "Perhaps then you can explain why there is almost a total absence of blood on the floor."

"We was just thinkin' about that when you got here, weren't we Gardener?"

"Yeah, that's right. We figure the murderer must have held Braden's head in the commode while he cut his throat. Probably knocked him out first."

"Oh?" said Holmes. "And did you find evidence of his being hit on the head?"

"Well, no, but how is the murderer s'posed to've carried this stiff through the middle of Grand Central without no one seein' him? What, did he sprinkle pixie dust and float Braden in here? Why hell, he must weigh close to three hundred pounds."

"How do you explain that, Holmes?" asked Strumm.

"Observe," said Holmes as he stooped over the body. "His heels here are scuffed and dirty, as are his trousers. This suggests to me he was dragged at least part of the way. Now observe the dust. Do you notice anything significant about it?" He held out a sample in the palm of his hand for Strumm to examine.

"Not particularly. It looks fairly non-descript to me."

"Not at all, Commissioner," Holmes said as he rubbed a bit of the dust between his thumb and index finger. "See how fine it is, and the color, how it's a dull gray. Have you ever observed the edges of an electrical air circulator?"

"A fan?" said Strumm.

"Yes, a fan. This is the type of dust that you'll find accumulated on the edge of the blades on a circulator fan."

"What the…you tellin' us this Joe was dragged over a fan?

You're looney," the disgusted detective said.

"I was merely making an observation from which we might make further deductions. For example," he said as he stood looking around the room. "Halloa." He walked to the far end of the room where, at about chest height was a square grating about two feet by two feet. He pulled his glass from his pocket again. "This grating has recently been removed and replaced. The paint along here has been disturbed," he said indicating the edge of the grating. "It was grasped from the interior and pushed out until these fasteners were forced out of their holdings. They were clumsily replaced, except for..." and he looked around on the floor. "Aha," he said as he bent down to pick up the missing grate fastener.

"Remarkable," said Strumm.

"Baaaah..." said the detective. "That don't prove nothin'. So what, it's been moved. Anybody could've done that. Maintenance man most likely."

"If you remove the grate, Commissioner, I believe you'll find evidence of this man's heels having been dragged and scuffed along the ventilation shaft."

"What a crock," said the detective.

"There's one way to find out, Gardener. Take down the grate, detective," said Strumm. And as we waited the two detectives removed the grate from its place. Peering inside with a pocket lantern lent him by Holmes, Strumm whistled and then said, "I'll be a sonofa..." Inside were long irregular lines in the disturbed dust as though a body had been dragged along the shaft, the heels making scuffing marks as they went.

Strumm, obviously impressed with this bit of deduction, said, "From here the murderer just had to watch and when the room was empty, he could remove the body and leave it there to be found later. After that, he could walk out unnoticed. Ingenious, Mr. Holmes."

Looking at the two detectives who stood there with their mouths agape he said, "Miller, you and Gardener could learn a thing or two from this 'Limey'."

I noticed Holmes could barely contain his smile as we left the comfort station.

Chapter 8
Watson's mystery...

It was late in the morning when we returned to the Gilsey where Abel Jenkins appeared locked in a serious conversation with his cousin, Ernie. Holmes was deep in thought and proceeded up to our rooms, but I was intrigued and walked over to the desk. "What serious world problem are the two of you are working on?" I asked.

Ernie stood silent, his head hanging low giving an overall appearance of abject dejection, but Abel, patting Ernie on the arm, said, "Actually, Doc, we was hoping to speak to Mr. Holmes. Ernie's got a little problem he wants to see if Mr. Holmes mightn't be able to help him with."

"Oh? And what is the problem that has your cousin in such a state?"

"It's about his wife, Matilda...a domestic matter," he said with a knowing nod.

"She's runnin' around on me, Doc," Ernie said, unable any longer to contain himself. "I know she is, and if I catch the rum-running son of a snake she's a-running with, I'll...I'll..."

"Take it easy, Ernie, you got no proof."

"Proof you say? What about her goin' out the last two nights in a row? And, what about her borrowing four dollar and not having nothing to account for it?"

"She paid that back the very next day." Abel explained as Ernie only scowled, "Matilda borrowed four dollar from me last week and asked me not to mention it to Ernie."

"And naturally you told her what with blood being thicker than water and all…"

"Well, I never was no good at lying anyhoo. So, you see, Doc, we could really use the help of Mr. Holmes to set this straight, to see if Matilda truly is runnin' 'round or this is just Ernie's imagination."

"Ain't my imagination, Abe, I done told you that," said Ernie stalking off to the dining room.

"Yes, well," I said, "I'm afraid Mr. Holmes is a bit busy right now; he's already carrying on two investigations. I'm afraid he'd be hard pressed to find time to help you, no matter how much he'd like to do so."

"But Ernie's on his last nerve, Doc. I don't know what he'll do if he don't get this settled."

"Well," said I, "As I said, Mr. Holmes is occupied at the present, but perhaps I might be of assistance."

"You, Doc? Forgive my asking, but what can you do to help?"

"I don't wish to blow my own horn, but I have stood alongside Mr. Holmes during innumerable investigations and must say that I've studied his methods. I think I'm quite capable of investigating this matter and arriving at a satisfactory conclusion."

"Pardon me for saying so, Doc, but I think we'd be more comfortable with Mr. Holmes."

"I really think that's out of the question just now, Ernie. Perhaps you'd be convinced I'm equal to the challenge if I gave you a small demonstration of my abilities."

"Well, okay, Doc," he said with little enthusiasm. "How you gonna do that?"

"Well, let me see…" I said as I began to ponder how I might suitably impress Ernie and his cousin. Then it struck me. "Do you have in your possession an article belonging to one of your guests?"

"What? What do you mean? In the safe? I suppose, but what do you want with..." his voice trailed off.

"Anything at all will do, a watch, jewelry, whatever is convenient."

"Well, since it's you, Doc, I guess it'd be all right so long as you don't go nowheres." He turned around slowly and kneeled in front of the hotel safe and began to spin the dial, being extra careful to keep his body between me and the dial face. I could hear the tumblers click and then Abel said, "Here's something, but what are you fixin' to do with it? I could lose my job if I was caught parceling out a guest's goods given me for safekeeping."

"Don't worry, I only wish to examine it. From that, I shall describe your guest to you. That should give you confidence I am equal to the task of investigating Ernie's problem." I felt it should be a fairly elementary feat to deduce a sufficient amount of information about the owner of whatever article Abel provided. I'd seen Holmes perform similar tasks many times before and I was quite confident that I could follow his example with more than satisfactory results. In so doing, I felt both Abel and Ernie would be convinced that I was up to the task of investigating their little domestic affair. After all, it was merely a matter of observation and deduction.

"So, what have you got for me?"

"Here you go, Doc," Abel said and he handed me a rather crudely crafted silver brooch with an amethyst setting.

I took the thing between my thumb and forefinger and leaned over the desk to take better advantage of the light. At first I was stumped. Then I became inspired. "Aha," said I. "Look here, where the pin is affixed. It's been recently repaired. That tells us it's a piece of great sentimental value, probably a keepsake, for the cost of repair was undoubtedly nearly as much as its intrinsic worth. The elderly woman to whom it belongs, for we can be sure from the piece and style she is elderly, has apparently been recently upon hard times for the repair is one of an amateur and not a master jeweler." I could see that Mr. Abel Jenkins was in awe thus far, his mouth agape and his eyes transfixed upon the brooch. I continued, "I would say the woman who owns this is obviously in her late sixties to early seventies, most probably of southern European extract judging from the Italian silk in which the bauble was wrapped." I was most certainly on the mark now.

"Pardon, Doctor," said Abel at this point.

"Yes, Abel, what is it?"

"Well, sir, I'm afraid the owner is coming down the stairs just now."

I turned my attention toward the wide staircase leading to the first floor mezzanine overlooking the lobby. There at the top of the stairs, just beside the bank of lifts, was a silver-haired dowager in evening attire, complete with a fox stole. I turned and smiled toward Abel, but his attention was elsewhere. "Ah, Mr. Potter, how are you this evening?" Abel said, as he took both the brooch and its silk wrapping from my hands and placed them beneath the counter. "I trust you are finding your stay with us pleasant."

Potter was nearing forty, bald with bushy brown eyebrows and nearly as wide as he was tall. He had an unpleasant look on his face as he approached the desk. "Jenkins, was that the brooch I gave you for safekeeping that you were showing this gentleman?" As he said this he gave me a most discourteous look.

"Yes, sir. He was admiring the handiwork."

"Bah…he was doing no such thing. What is the meaning of this?"

"I'm dreadfully sorry, sir, this is a misunderstanding and it's entirely my own fault," I said, hoping to extract poor Abel from a delicate situation with his guest. "I'd merely remarked to Mr. Jenkins here that it was a quaint talent of mine to be able to judge a person by examining an article they own. I'm afraid I asked if I might examine the article to demonstrate my prowess."

"Oh, I see, a trickster, eh? Get this boob to put his hand into the safe and you walk away with a pretty piece of jewelry, replacing it with a fraud."

"See here, sir. I'm nothing of the kind. How dare you?"

"Well, and what was your judgment about the owner of this piece of jewelry?"

I cleared my throat most audibly and said, "Well, I'd concluded the owner was undoubtedly a dowager who for some reason had recently been down on her luck, that she was most likely around seventy years of age and most probably was from or had spent a good deal of time in southern Europe, perhaps France or Italy."

"Remarkable," said the man.

"Well," I said chuckling in a pleased manner, "it's really not all that difficult, you see—" but my explanation was cut short.

"No, what I meant was it is remarkable that you could be so very much wrong. This is a piece of jewelry my daughter made for my wife, with her own hands. And we are from Indiana, not the south of France. So you see, you were wrong on all accounts." He laughed and then said, "Therefore in fact you are remarkable, you see, a remarkable fraud."

"Please sir, I hope you won't..."

"Won't what? I've half a mind to complain to the owners of this hotel and if we weren't checking out today, I would." And with this he seized the brooch and stormed across the lobby to meet his wife and young daughter as they came out of the lift.

"I'm terribly sorry, Abel, I don't know how I could have..."

But Abel Jenkins was smiling nearly ear to ear, "Aw, that's all right, Doc. You may not be right today, but who says that little girl won't grow into being one of them dowagers one day and move right on over to France."

#

When I returned to our hotel room, Holmes was already on his way out the door. "Where are you headed in such a hurry," I said.

"I'm on my way to the office of the Chief Engineer for the Interborough Rapid Transit Company, or the IRT as it's called."

"What do you expect to find there?"

"Barlucci's nest, unless I miss my guess," he said with a smile on his lips.

"Barlucci's nest? Why would you expect to find Barlucci in a nest?"

"A nest, Watson, is the diurnal resting place of a vampire. It's just the sort of place in which Barlucci would choose to hide." And with that he was out the door.

This left me quite disturbed. I was unsure if Holmes' obsession with Barlucci had mutated into an actual belief in vampires. Surely not. Perhaps it was only that Holmes believed Barlucci might, in clinging to his own illusions, manifest the habits of a vampire by adapting the habitat of one. Of the two possibilities, I wanted with all my heart to believe the latter. But the look in Holmes' eye as he departed gave me little cause for relief in that direction. I desperately wanted to speak with someone in an effort to sort this out.

With the rest of the morning and afternoon to myself I decided to have a bit of lunch and then visit with Commissioner Strumm. Surely if I could talk this matter out with him, I could decide what to do.

I found the commissioner in his office, reading over some reports on the twin brothers whose corpses Holmes and I had found in Dr. Tremaine's tomb. His door was open, so I availed myself, "Pardon, Commissioner, I find myself on my own this afternoon and I thought I'd come by to see if you'd made any head way on the 'ghost ship'. I hope you don't mind." I said nothing about Holmes at first, not wishing to be too open with my misgivings.

"Not at all, Doctor, but I'm surprised you aren't out chasing ghosts or some other such nonsense with your friend Holmes." said Strumm.

"Please, Mylo, Holmes is one of the most brilliant men I've ever known and my dearest friend."

"Perhaps twenty years ago he was brilliant, Doctor, but from where I sit, he's just this side of being locked up for a loon. Barlucci indeed. Thank God he hasn't convinced you of that nonsense." He looked up at me from his desk and his features softened, "Forgive me, I didn't mean to bark at you like that. Come, sit down." It must have been evident to him that I had something on my mind. He reached into the bottom drawer of his desk and pulled out a half-empty bottle of bourbon and two glasses. "Care for a little drink?"

"I thought you'd sworn off drinking."

"Ha, you sound like Emily," he said with a wry smile, his eyebrow cocked. "A drop now and again can't hurt. This job'll drive you into the ground...you've no idea. A little drink helps take the edge off," he said pouring himself a short glass. "What do you say?"

"I suppose I could use a dram with a bit of water, if you please."

"Sure, Doc, here you go. By the way, Emily wanted me to tell you and Mr. Holmes you're invited to come to dinner again this evening if you can make it. We're having over a guest we'd like you to meet."

"Oh, and who might that be."

"He's a friend of Lucie's and Phillip's. We've only recently made his acquaintance ourselves, but we were both very impressed with him." He handed me a glass with bourbon and water, downed his own in one gulp, and refilled it just a bit fuller this time. "Now, what is it you came to see me about?"

"Well, I can't promise Holmes will be there, but I'd be delighted," I said, taking the drink. "Now, for the reason I'm here. As

I told you in my wire, I am becoming a bit concerned about Holmes."

"Yes, I was a little surprised when I received your wire, but once your letter arrived a few days later it was all too clear."

"I didn't know what else to do. When he arrived on my doorstep telling me that Barlucci was alive and back to his murderous ways, I thought at first he was jesting, but I soon realized he was quite serious."

"But I don't understand why you would just leave your life in London and follow him on this mad adventure."

"You forget our long partnership. Holmes and I have a bond, our friendship has been forged in the fires of deathly danger. It's more than a partnership, it's a friendship, a kinship. Holmes is like family to me. Something inexplicable if you've never experienced it."

I could see a pained look cross Strumm's noble features like a shadow and new immediately he was remembering Michael Murray, the partner who'd died at the hands of Abigail Drake. "I understand completely, Doctor," he said as he downed his second drink and refilled his glass.

"Yes, well, I could hardly let him travel to America on his own in his frame of mind, so I wired you."

"But what will happen when the crime is solved and there is no Barlucci?"

"Don't underestimate Holmes, Inspector. As you witnessed in the comfort station, even if Holmes is not what he used to be he is still a remarkable mind capable of astounding observation and deduction."

"Yes, even I have to admit that. But aren't you concerned?"

"Of course I'm concerned. My hope is that once the solution to this mystery is revealed, he will realize Barlucci is long dead and will at last be at peace."

"And so, in the meantime you tolerate his lunacy?"

"Yes, but I'm afraid his dementia has taken a disturbing turn."

"Oh? In what way?"

"Well, I'm sure you remember the talk at the time about Miss Abigail Drake being a vampire? Your own wife made that accusation."

"Yes, but she explained that was just a medical condition that took the name from the old legends, but the facts were far less mysterious and twisted."

"Mmm, yes, well I'm afraid Holmes has been studying up on those old legends and I believe they may be having an effect on him."

"In what way?" He put his glass down on the desk.

"I fear he may be starting to believe them, or at least the possibility of them."

"Nonsense. Holmes may be deluded about Barlucci, but I really can't believe he could give any credence to such ridiculous tales. I was only joking before when I—"

"I sincerely hope you are correct. That's what I thought when first he told me what he'd been reading, but his actions lately, and a few slips have led me to the unmistakable conclusion that if he doesn't believe this drivel, he's certainly gotten far too wrapped up in it. What really has me frightened to my wits end is that if he persists in this he may truly become unsettled in that genius mind of his. I've long held that genius is a first cousin to madness."

"Dr. Watson, this is incredible. I mean…I mean, I may have said he's delusional, even demented, but I didn't really think that…" Strumm looked at me with unbelieving eyes. "Surely you can't be serious."

"I'm afraid I am. Just this morning he told me that he was going to look for Barlucci's 'nest'."

"His nest? What does it mean?"

"I fear it means he may truly believe Barlucci is a vampire."

Chapter 9
The inimitable Mr. Hume…

While Holmes roamed the uncompleted tunnels of the Interborough Railway in search of the phantom Barlucci, I dined once again with the Strumms. Arriving promptly at six-thirty in the evening I was greeted by Lucie Strumm who led me into the parlor where she and Phillip were entertaining another guest.

"Dr. Watson," said Lucie, "I'm so glad you're here, I want you to meet someone." She took me by the arm and practically dragged me over to a tall young man with long, dark hair that flowed around his shoulders and met and blended with a luxuriant beard. Behind a pair of tinted glasses his piercing steel blue eyes looked somehow older than he otherwise appeared, although with all of that hair, it was difficult to tell precisely his age. If I were to guess, I'd say he was somewhat older than Lucie and Phillip, though how much was a mystery to me. His manner of dress was stylish and the clothes themselves appeared to be well tailored. "Doctor, this is Alexander Hume. He's a musician. Alex, this is Dr. John Watson, an old friend of my parents."

"I have heard of Dr. Watson. In fact, I've read a good many of the stories he's written about his colleague, Mr. Sherlock Holmes. This is a great privilege, Doctor." He extended his hand.

"How do you do, Mr. Hume. You flatter me," I said and as I

shook his hand I was taken by its pale delicacy as well as by the strength of his cool grip. "I can certainly see you are a musician, Mr. Hume. Your hands have an artistic look to them. By the way, I should admit that I've also heard of you, sir."

Hume's eyes narrowed as he looked at me more intently. "Oh, is that so, Doctor? And from whom have you heard of me? I'm afraid I'm not very well known out of certain circles."

"Why from Miss Lucie here, that is if you are the same Alex who got her the tickets to the concert she and Phillip attended last night."

He seemed to visibly relax at this. "You are very perceptive, Doctor," Hume said, apparently as impressed with my memory as with my ability to make accurate judgments from simple observation.

I chuckled, a bit amused, "Well, I suppose I should thank Mr. Holmes. I've been in association with him on so many adventures I expect I've picked up some of his arcane habits of deduction, by osmosis most likely," echoing Holmes' own words.

Hume was an odd character to find in the home of the Strumms. He was quite as tall as Holmes and carried himself with an almost aristocratic bearing, which I'm sure was affected for our benefit. His clothing was of good quality, but appeared to be a bit the worse for wear. I imagined he wore the tinted spectacles because his eyes were made sensitive through long hours of reading music in a poorly lit bohemian apartment, perhaps even composing on a dilapidated piano. "Do you play the piano?" I asked.

"Yes, among other instruments."

"We hope to coax him into playing for us tonight, Doctor."

"Splendid. I only regret Holmes isn't here. He'll be deeply wounded he missed it." Then, being a bit inspired by the company I said, "Perhaps the two of you might play a duet sometime."

"Oh? Your Mr. Holmes is a musician, then?" asked Hume.

"Yes, he plays the violin. Though I'm sure he's not up to your standards."

Hume smiled for the first time, white teeth showing behind his mustache. "Nonsense. I would consider it an honor to play with him."

"I'm sure he would enjoy that. Tell me, how did you become acquainted with Miss Lucie?"

"It's the most exciting story, Doctor," Lucie said. "Tell him, Alex."

"It was really nothing special, Lucie, I just happened to be at a place and time that was fortunate, for myself as well as for you and Phillip as it turned out."

"Nothing? Don't be so modest, Alex," said Phillip. "Dr. Watson, Alex saved our lives, Lucie's and mine. It was the most amazing act of heroism I've ever seen."

Hume said, "I assure you, it was nothing of the kind. I was very lucky."

"He was wonderful, Doctor. Phillip and I were on our way home from the theater. It was a warm evening and we decided to walk when we were accosted by two men with a gun. They wanted to rob us. We didn't know what to do. But then Alex came out of nowhere and pummeled them."

"I say, that does sound exciting. You weren't hurt, were you?"

"No, thanks to Alex," Phillip said.

Hume, evidently embarrassed by the attention said, "And thanks to that, I've found two new friends in New York."

"I say, your accent isn't quite American, is it? That is, I mean to say, it sounds American, but with a certain coloring I've not heard before. From one of the western states, perhaps?"

Mr. Hume looked at me over the rims of his glasses, "You have quite an ear, Doctor. I've travelled around quite extensively, both here in America and in Europe. I suppose I may have acquired some coloring, as you put it, in my travels."

"Ah, well, that explains it."

At that moment Emily Strumm entered and with her appearance there seemed to me to be a change in Hume's countenance, a softening of his features or at least of what features I could discern through his beard. "Oh, good, our guests have all arrived. Lucie, did you introduce Dr. Watson to Alex?"

"Yes, she did, Emily. I was just asking Mr. Hume about his European travels."

"Good, dinner should be ready shortly. It's a pity Mr. Holmes wasn't available this evening." Turning to place herself between me and the other guests, she said to me in a low voice out of Lucie's hearing, "Doctor, may I see you for a moment, in the study?"

"Yes, of course, dear." We stepped into the study, leaving Lucie, Phillip, and Mr. Hume for a moment. "What's wrong, Emily?"

"Doctor..."

"Come now, please call me John."

"Very well, then, John, this is very difficult for me. I mean, I don't know quite how to begin."

"Holmes always recommends starting at the beginning."

"Very well then, you are aware that when Mylo and I met, he had a drinking problem?"

A bit embarrassed by the direction of the conversation, I stammered a bit before admitting, "Yes, I was aware of it."

"Well, I'm afraid he's started drinking again. Or perhaps he's never really quit, I don't know," she said and turned toward the window, away from me so I couldn't see her tears.

"Well, I'm sure there's nothing to worry about, Emily. He has a very stressful job."

"Yes, very stressful. I know. And I've tried to ignore it, hoping it would go away. But in the last few years, he's gotten much worse. He comes home late from work, smelling of liquor." Although her back was turned I could see the reflection of her tear-filled eyes in the window. "I'm afraid I may have to leave him."

"Emily, no...I mean, perhaps he can change."

Tears were now flowing down her cheeks as she turned back to face me. "I've begged him to change. For so long, while Lucie was growing up, I just didn't know what to do. But I've made up my mind. After Lucie and Phillip marry, I'm going to give Mylo a choice, his bottle or his wife."

"I'm so sorry to hear this, Emily. You and Mylo are both very dear to me."

"That is why I wanted you to know. And I also wanted to ask you, have you seen him drinking? He tells me that he only stops on his way home, to take the tension of the day off before he comes home to be with his family, as if he's doing it for our benefit. But today, when he telephoned that he'd invited you for dinner tonight, he sounded… Have you seen him drink at work, Doctor?"

I was torn. I couldn't lie to Emily. I remember how Strumm had tried to explain his drinking to me that very afternoon, giving me a not too dissimilar explanation. He hadn't asked me not to say anything and with Emily asking me directly I really had no choice, "Yes, Emily, just this afternoon he offered me a drink in his office."

"Did he have one? Was he going to have it even if you declined?"

"I'm afraid so. I'm so sorry, Emily."

"No. It's all right. I thought as much. Thank you for not lying to me." She dried her tears and composed herself. "Well, no matter. Let's go back to the parlor and get the others. Dinner is waiting." I followed Emily back into the parlor where she announced, "I'm afraid I have to apologize for my husband's tardiness. He's been working very hard, but I can't leave you waiting your dinner any longer. Come, let's all go into the dining room."

"But Emily," said I. "I'm sure we shan't perish from hunger if you wish to wait a bit longer." Lucie and Phillip agreed, as did Hume who couldn't seem to pry his eyes from Emily.

"No, if we wait any longer it won't be fit to eat. Mylo will be along—" but before she could finish her sentence, in walked Strumm, looking tired and serious. "Well," said Emily in a scolding tone but with a smile that belied her manner, "I was beginning to think you'd forgotten we have guests for dinner."

"My apologies all round. Is dinner ready?"

"I like that," she said a little coldly. "Of course it's ready."

"Then let's eat. I'm starved. This way, gentlemen," he said and we all went into the dining room.

The conversation was light as we consumed our soup. Young Phillip was quiet but not quite morose as Lucie tried to interest him in conversation. Mr. Hume, on the other hand, was an engaging conversationalist versant in a variety of topics. It was evident the Strumms had welcomed him into their home almost as if he were family. He had, quite understandably considering the circumstances of his making their acquaintance, made a most favorable impression on both Mylo and his wife. When the conversation turned inevitably to his rescue of Phillip and Lucie, to his credit he tried to downplay it.

Emily said, "Alex, please tell us again how you saved our Lucie and Phillip from those ruffians."

"Thank you, but it actually wasn't all that remarkable," he said in a very self-effacing way.

"Don't be so modest, Alex. You were brilliant," said Phillip suddenly roused from his quietude. "The way you beat them off was truly impressive."

"Thank you, but it really wasn't at all exceptional. When I was much younger I was trained in the French art of cane fighting."

"Cane fighting?" said I. "Is that anything like singlestick?"

"Very much so, although while singlestick is a sport, cane fighting is more along the lines of self-defense. I'd never actually used it before."

"Well, we're certainly glad you used it that night," said Emily. "No telling what harm might have come to these two."

"Yes, I'm afraid they don't teach much self-defense in medical school these days," said Phillip and we all laughed.

"So what was it that kept you at work tonight, dear?" Emily asked her husband in voice barely above a whisper and yet it still contained considerable force behind it.

Strumm's eyes darted to me and then to young Phillip. "Oh, nothing much, just some routine business. Besides, you know I don't like bringing my work home with me."

"Yes, I'm sorry. Mylo is very good about that, Doctor," she said addressing me. "Some wives have to put up with their husbands' dour moods when things don't go well at work, but I have to say Mylo has never let his work interfere here at home," she said, emphasizing the word 'work'. "It makes for a very pleasant domicile."

"Life is too short, darling," said Strumm with an odd look in his eyes.

"You're quite right dear," she said, removing her hand from the table as his crossed to take it. Somewhat embarrassed, he drew his hand back and forced a smile. I happened to glance at Mr. Hume during this little exchange and while it might be my imagination, I could swear he had an amused look behind those tinted glasses. Lucie and Phillip apparently didn't notice, so busy they were talking among themselves.

After dinner as the women cleared the table, the men gathered in the parlor for a cigar and a brandy. While Phillip was attempting to get Hume to play something at the piano, I had a chance to have a quiet word with Strumm. "What did keep you, Commissioner? I saw your furtive glance toward the boy when you were asked."

"You're nearly as observant as your colleague Mr. Holmes. It's that business at the tomb. I received a note from Holmes saying he's convinced there is some connection between that and the murder at Grand Central."

"Yes, he's quite convinced of it. That's why he's not here tonight, said he wanted to check on some threads he'd picked up, to see if he could make a connection, something concrete I believe he said."

Suddenly, the air was vibrating with the haunting opening notes of what I later learned was Beethoven's Piano Sonata Number 8 in C minor. The passion with which Hume played was quite remarkable. By the time he stopped, the entire company had gathered round the piano in rapt attention.

"Bravo, sir, you play splendidly," said I when he'd concluded.

"Yes, I quite agree," said Emily, who with her daughter had entered the parlor and both Strumm and Lucie murmured their admiration while Phillip applauded.

"Thank you, that's very kind," Hume said, rising to address Emily, "but I'm afraid it dragged a bit toward the end."

"Don't be silly, it was lovely," said Emily.

"I'm very gratified that you find it so, Mrs. Strumm." He said this looking so intently at Emily that she flushed a bit and her lashes fluttered as she looked down at her hands. Hume must have realized he made her uncomfortable and said, "I couldn't help notice the picture on the piano, is it of you and your sister?"

"Yes, that is the two of us, just before she left New York for London. We were just children then, really."

"And where is she now?"

Strumm came up behind Emily and slid his arms around her waist, "Mr. Hume, Mrs. Strumm's sister died some years ago."

"I'm very sorry to hear that, please forgive me."

"It's all right," Mrs. Strumm said as she patted her husband's hands, curling her fingers around them. "It was long ago. That picture is almost the only thing I have now to remember her by. That and a necklace that she wore faithfully when last I saw her."

"And where is the necklace? I see you aren't wearing it."

"I'm afraid it's missing," she said, touching the place around her neck where it usually hung.

"You must have loved her very much."

"More than anything. We had always been very close," she said, wiping away a tear.

"I'm sorry, I didn't mean to…"

"It's all right. As I said, it was a long time ago. Time heals all wounds, you know," she said with a smile.

"Some wounds take a considerable amount of time to heal, but I wouldn't worry, I'm certain you will find the necklace. Do you know where it comes from? Does it…does it have any special…significance?"

"Well, if it does, we have not been able to discover what it is," said Strumm.

"How did your sister die, Mrs. Strumm?"

Emily grew quiet. I felt it was imperative to speak, "I'm afraid the circumstances were quite tragic, and unusual."

"I'm sorry. Mrs. Strumm, Mr. Strumm, I didn't mean to pry. I feel foolish. Of course it's not something you'd wish to speak about, especially with a stranger."

Strumm began to speak, but Emily stopped him saying, "That's perfectly all right, Mr. Hume. You had no way of knowing." As she said this, she moved out of Mylo's arms and put her hands over Hume's. "And as far as being a stranger, I certainly hope you don't remain so. You're welcome in our home any time. After all, it seems we owe the health and safety of our Lucie and Phillip to you." I noticed Strumm appeared a touch uncomfortable with the attention his wife was paying Hume. But what could he say? After all Hume had saved their daughter's life.

Hume looked deeply into Emily's eyes, perhaps a bit too long, and then clicked his heels together in a very European manner and gave a slight bow, "At your service, Mrs. Strumm."

When it came time to leave the Strumm's, Hume asked if we might share a cab. I was more than happy to do so as I found him a most worthy companion, knowledgeable on a variety of topics, including poetry. He and I began talking about Yeats but before we'd gone two blocks from the Strumms' home, the theme of our conversation turned to history, the history of Mrs. Emily Strumm and, more to the point, her sister Abigail Drake. He asked, "You seem to know the Strumms quite well. Do you know what became of Mrs. Strumm's twin sister?"

"Well, yes, I do know what occurred. Abigail Drake was a very disturbed young woman."

Hume's eyes widened, "Disturbed? In what way?"

"She suffered from delusions, delusions that led her to believe..." I stopped, realizing he was leaning toward me, his penetrating gray-blue eyes fixed on mine, seemingly drawing the words from me. "I say you seem awfully interested in what must to you be ancient history," I said with a chuckle.

Hume sat back in his seat, "I'm terribly sorry, but it does seem to me to be quite the mystery—a missing piece of jewelry of unknown origins, a sister who died in a tragic fashion. Since it's a topic that doesn't appear to lend itself to a quick dismissal, such as an accident or a fall, it carries its own mystery."

"Well, when you put it like that, I suppose it does seem quite mysterious." I took a long look at this young man seated across from me. "Very well, then. If you are to be a friend of the family, I suppose it best if I tell you. That way it won't be something you need bring up with the family itself."

"Yes, I don't wish to cause any pain to them, I assure you."

During the next thirty minutes it took to drive to my hotel I gave young Mr. Hume the entire story of Miss Abigail Drake, from our first encounter with her in London to the night of her tragic death.

When the cab pulled up to the Gilsey and I got out, I looked up at him and said, "If you'd like a more detailed history, you'd do well to pick up a volume of my account of it titled *The Body Snatchers—A Sherlock Holmes Adventure.*

"Yes, I shall do that, Doctor. And thank you, you've been most informative...most informative indeed." With that he settled back into the cab and for the second time that evening I noted a most pleased look on his face.

Chapter 10
Dr. Small's secret...

The following morning, as Holmes and I entered the hotel lobby on the way in to breakfast, Abel Jenkins flagged us down with the furious waving of his hand. Approaching the desk Holmes said, "Yes, Abel, what can we do for you?"

"I've got a message from Commissioner Strumm."

"Thank goodness, for a second I thought you'd come down with St. Vitus' affliction," I said with a smile.

"He said it was very important you get it as soon as you come down for breakfast," he said, handing Holmes the message.

Holmes opened the note and began reading it while we continued toward the dining room. Strumm had apparently come by very early and left the note in Abel's capable hands.

"What is it, Holmes?"

"Hm?" he murmured, absorbed in what he was reading, and then looking up he said, "It appears there's been another murder, at the asylum this time. Strumm would like us to come by and have a look at our earliest convenience."

"Dear me, another murder, do you mean...?"

"Yes, he says the circumstances are very much like the one at the Grand Central Terminal. What's more, we know the victim—it's Jonas Hone."

"Hone? What was he doing at the asylum? He was discharged."

No sooner had I uttered the question than I felt my stomach rumble and thought hungrily I would certainly be missing my breakfast this morning. But Holmes' reply quieted my discomfort, "Yes, it's very curious. I shall have to ponder it over my sausage and poached eggs. Come, Watson, I'm famished." Surprised, but extremely grateful, I followed him into the hotel restaurant.

Holmes barely spoke during breakfast nor did I. I had no wish to disturb his ruminations. Instead, I used the time to commiserate alternately between what this new murder might tell us and how odd was Holmes' reaction to the news of it. I had expected him to rush off immediately to the scene of this new crime. But instead he turned rather introspective and seemed not in a hurry at all. I and my stomach were most thankful, but at the same time just a trifle disturbed.

Following our meal, we caught a taxi out to the Ward's Island Ferry. As requested by Strumm in his note, we called ahead to let the commissioner know we were on our way and we were met at the ferry landing by both Commissioner Strumm and Director Small, along with Detectives Gardener and Miller. The short ride to the asylum was an extremely chilly one for such a warm August morning. "Who discovered the murder?" said Holmes.

After a moment of stony silence, Commissioner Strumm offered, "The director, here, found him. He was on an inspection tour of the north wing."

"Splendid, Dr. Small. It's most gratifying to find you've followed my advice."

The director signaled his distaste for Holmes' comment by turning his head and staring out the window of the cab. Holmes turned to me and quietly observed, "I often wonder why it is that those in most need of good advice are the most reluctant to take it?"

Strumm continued, "It seems there'd been some petty thefts as well as an odd migration of vermin that prompted the investigation."

"A migration of vermin, you say? What on earth does that mean?" I said.

Small, his chin up as well as his back, turned toward me, "The older parts of the north wing are in some disrepair," he volunteered grudgingly. "We've become accustomed to the cellars being populated by rats. Of course it's not something we relish, but it's become more or less accepted as the exterminators have thus far failed to rid the building of them."

"But what about the migration the commissioner spoke of?" said Holmes.

"Yes, I was coming to that." He cast a cold eye in Holmes' direction, "As I was saying, we've become somewhat accustomed to a certain level of infestation and so long as they remained in the disused cellars of the north wing, we weren't too concerned. But recently, we've noticed signs that the rat population was on the move and now inhabiting the cellars of the newly renovated sections of the wing, where we store a good deal of our spare linens, beds, and equipment. So, I, along with my head custodian, was inspecting the cellars of the older section to determine why the rats had decided to leave. In the second cellar we entered, there was a foul odor of decaying human remains. That is where we found him."

"I understand you know the victim, Dr. Small?" said Holmes, although he was well aware of the victim's name and of course was equally aware that Small knew him. He was obviously enjoying the priggish director's discomfort.

"Yes. It was Hone."

"Not Jonas Hone. I was under the impression he was discharged at our last meeting. What was he doing here at the asylum?"

"I don't believe that is any of your business, Mr. Holmes."

"Ah, that's where you are wrong, Dr. Small. I have been asked here to consult on the matter of Mr. Hone's death. What he was doing on the grounds could have a decisive bearing on why he was murdered. So you see, Dr. Small, the reason Mr. Hone was on asylum property is very much my business. It could be an essential clue in the investigation of his murder should he, for example, be trespassing."

Strumm corroborated, "I'm afraid Mr. Holmes is correct, Dr. Small."

"Very well, then, Mr. Hone was in our employ."

"How can that be?" I said, taken completely by surprise at Small's response. But the expression on Holmes' face was one of expectation rather than amazement.

Small went on to explain, "Mr. Hone had a wife and family. He needed his job. The day after your friend so thoroughly denigrated his reputation, he returned, his hat in his hand, and begged me to allow him to continue to work."

Holmes interrupted, "Character, Dr. Small, is the tree; reputation is but its shadow. Only the tree has substance."

Small bristled, "He had six children to feed and said he didn't care what the work entailed." He looked from Strumm to me, ignoring Holmes, "Under the circumstances, what could I do?"

"Under the circumstances? I would say the circumstances were that Mr. Hone had taken advantage of his position as well as Miss Baker," said Holmes. "The circumstances were that he gave little thought to his family while he was abusing both his authority and your patient, not to mention your trust. Under those circumstances I would say sacking him was being exceedingly lenient."

"He was thoroughly contrite, Mr. Holmes."

"Was he, Doctor? I've run across many a contrite criminal in my line of work. Contrition often follows exposure, but is it remorse for the crime or the capture? It's the truly penitent man who asks for forgiveness before being caught."

"Nevertheless, I am the Director here, Mr. Holmes, and in my judgment Hone was sincere. I didn't wish to harm his family due to his petty failings."

The taxi came to a stop in front of the asylum's main office. "I thought he was found in the cellars of the north wing," Holmes said, looking out the window in suspicion.

"Unfortunately," Strumm said, "when the doctor found him, he had him immediately taken to the infirmary on the second floor."

"It seemed the proper thing to do at the time," came Small's rationalization.

"I see, I should have expected as much. Very well, we shall have an examination of Hone first and of the scene of the murder second." With that, Holmes opened the door and bounded out of the cab.

On the way into the building, I caught up with Holmes. "How on earth could Small have let Hone stay on after he misused the Baker woman so callously?"

Holmes replied under his breath, "Corvus oculum corvi non eruit". And though I was familiar with the phrase, in this context I didn't understand quite what he was getting at.

The second floor infirmary was immaculately painted all in white with lights enough to illuminate even the most remote corner. Hone was laid out on an examining table beneath a brilliant white sheet. His clothes were neatly folded and sitting on a table nearby. I could sense Holmes' irritation even before I heard his "Tsk, tsk".

The inspection of Hone took the better part of thirty minutes as Holmes examined, then re-examined the wounds on his throat and then, just when I thought he'd concluded, he examined once again the fatal flaw. He then gave a careful, but brief, examination of the clothing. I could tell there was something weighing on his mind by the way he lighted his pipe on the way to the cellar where the body was discovered. I was curious about what it was that concerned him, but judged it better to wait before asking him.

After examining the cellar, Strumm asked, "So, Mr. Holmes, what can you tell us about the murder of Mr. Hone?" I could see Small attempting to feign disinterest.

"Beyond the obvious that Mr. Hone's throat was punctured and then lacerated and that he was drained of blood, I'm afraid the movement of his remains away from the scene of the murder make it difficult to deduce further."

"And what of the murder scene itself? What can you tell us from it?"

"When I've seen it, I would be most happy to offer an opinion." Small's eyes narrowed for just a moment.

"What do you mean?" Strumm said.

"I mean that I've not yet seen where Hone was murdered. It certainly wasn't in this cellar."

"I don't understand?"

"Then perhaps you should ask Dr. Small."

Small stiffened. "This is ridiculous. Why on earth would I lie about where Hone was found?"

"Why, indeed," Holmes said, relighting his pipe.

"I beg your pardon, sir. I am a doctor, the director of this facility. I am not even obligated to report murders on these premises in keeping with the agreement between the State Board of Health and the City of New York."

"I'm afraid that's true, Holmes," Strumm said. "Due to the nature of many of the inmates, Director Strong has the authority to deal with these matters on his own, so long as the actions are within the confines and deal only with the residents and staff of his hospital."

"What a preposterous agreement," I said. "It's as if within the confines of his hospital, the state of New York has declared Dr. Small

God himself." As I said the words, I could feel my skin crawl in revulsion to the thought that anyone could be so entrusted.

"Tell us then, Doctor," Holmes said, "why did you report the murder?"

Small shuffled his feet a bit as he spoke, "Well, obviously, I felt it was my civic duty to do so, Mr. Holmes. We are not above the law here, despite Dr. Watson's opinion of our agreement with the state. Our arrangement precludes the public spectacle when one homicidal maniac murders another. This was something decidedly different. All of our patients are accounted for, and none were at large when Mr. Hone met his death."

"What about those escapees from the night the *Redeemer* ran aground?" I said, incredulous at Small's attitude.

"I wasn't counting them. I'm sure they've long since left the island."

"Ah, but how can you be so sure, Doctor. Perhaps it was one of them who Hone came upon and in order to silence him, they murdered him."

"What about the blood, Mr. Holmes? Or lack of it I should say."

"That would make it appear to be related to the Grand Central murder, Holmes," said Strumm.

"Yes, what a happy circumstance for Dr. Small to have the murderer appear to have come from without, rather than within."

"Just what are you suggesting, Holmes," came the quick reply from Small.

"Only making an observation, Doctor, only making an observation." The two men stared at each other for a mean second before Holmes remarked, "Well, I'm sorry we couldn't have been of more service to you, Commissioner. But I think Watson and I shall get back to our hotel, if you don't mind."

"Of course, Mr. Holmes. Gardener will drive you back to the ferry landing."

Holmes turned, "It's been a pleasure seeing you again, Commissioner, Doctor." Not waiting for a response, he turned and headed toward the carriage.

Strumm looked at me questioningly, "He appears not to be quite himself today, Doctor."

"Any change would be an improvement, I'd say," said Small.

"I think he was a bit put off that things had been moved around is all, Mylo. Can't make bricks without clay, you know," I said and then followed behind Holmes and climbed in beside him.

Once we'd gotten back onboard the ferry to Manhattan and we'd taken our seats on the upper deck with the sea breeze coming down the river I said, "What did you mean about not seeing the murder scene? Do you really believe Small is lying?"

Refilling and lighting his pipe, despite the stiff breeze, he said, "I don't think there can be any doubt about that, Watson."

"Do you think he also altered the wound?"

"No, but I'm happy to see you noted my apparent confusion concerning the wounds. There appeared to be a second attack at the same area. Perhaps Barlucci was interrupted..."

Barlucci again. "Then you believe Hone was murdered by Barlucci? To what purpose?" But I could see there was no alternative in Holmes' mind.

"A madman needs no purpose. My only question is why, if he didn't need to even report the murder, Small would stage a false murder scene and lie openly about where he'd found Hone." He sat puffing for a moment gazing out at the water and then said again, "Why..."

Chapter 11
Found and lost...

Holmes did not return with me to the Gilsey after we departed Ward's Island but rather made an excuse that he had a few leads to run down and would return later. He'd become increasingly closed mouth about his movements of late, which I found most distressing.

The morning was gloomy with thick, dark clouds and by the time I took dinner there was a steady downpour of rain, which convinced me to eat in the hotel restaurant. As overpriced as I felt it was, it was a satisfactorily enjoyable meal and certainly preferable to braving the downpour outside.

I spent most of the afternoon smoking in the lobby, observing the other guests, and then I retired to my room where I took up my copy of Dickinson. It was late in the day when Holmes arrived back at the hotel, soaking wet and in a high state of agitation. "Julia Tremaine is dead."

"What? Dead you say? You mean you found her?"

"Yes, in an unfinished section of the underground tunnel."

"How did she die?"

"I'm not sure. She was placed in a recessed shelf in the diggings. There were no signs of violence on her except for two small puncture marks."

"Placed you say? What do you mean, placed? And what of the

102

puncture marks?"

"I mean she was placed upon a shelf in the diggings, as though she were being presented for a funeral viewing. The puncture marks were partially scarred over, probably of little or no consequence relative to her death."

"It sounds as though someone wanted her to be found, I'd say."

"Yes, that was exactly my thought. She was dressed all in white linen and there were candles all around her body."

"Candles...hmm..then someone did want her found. Who do you think would kill her and leave her in such a manner and for what purpose?"

"Only one person, Barlucci. But as for his purpose that is unclear, perhaps it was meant as a warning. But he must have miscalculated. He must not have known the work was temporarily halted in that tunnel while the engineers were working out the support of the Commerce Bank building a half-mile to the north."

"What makes you think that?"

"The candles, they were burned completely down and had gone out long before I found the body. As they were made of pure bees wax, assuming they were new when lighted, and considering the average length of candles of this sort, it means the body was lying there a minimum of twelve hours, but I'd say it had been there a good deal longer, judging from the thin layer of dust that had settled on the body."

"What do you intend to do?"

"Grab your bumbershoot and galoshes, Watson, we're standing watch tonight."

"Standing watch? For what, may I ask?" I said as he sped past me, throwing off his wet jacket and entering the bathroom. He emerged seconds later in a fresh shirt and dry pants looking considerably more like himself than when he'd arrived. "I say again, for what exactly are we standing watch?"

"For Barlucci of course. Before I found Julia Tremaine, I believe I discovered one of his nests."

"There you go talking about nests again. What does this mean? You can't really believe Barlucci is a vampire."

The look on Holmes' face as I spoke both frightened me and tore at my heart. By all common sense he should have been joking but I could see from the set of his jaw and his piercing gaze he was dead serious. I sensed my worst fears about him were coming true. His obsession was beginning to make him become detached from reality. I decided I needed to see if I could walk him back a bit from the precipice. "Do you hear what you're saying, Holmes? You don't seriously believe in all this vampire mumbo-jumbo, do you?"

Holmes hesitated. I could see the wild look in his eye slowly become calmer, tamer. With a most pained looking smile he clapped me on the shoulder. "Of course not, but you must remember Barlucci claims to be a vampire. It would be in keeping with his delusion to observe the habits of one."

"And how have you come to be an expert on the habitual activities of such fictional characters?"

He crossed the room to retrieve his pipe, regaining the composure of the man I knew and respected more than any other. "Ah," he said, "I have you to thank for that, old boy. From the moment you told me you were going to chronicle the adventure of the body snatchers I began my research of the legends surrounding these creatures."

"Whatever for?" I asked, astonished. I felt a pang of guilt as he again confirmed I had been the catalyst to this mad adventure.

"For the eventuality that your probing into past events might stir up some new line of investigation into Barlucci's whereabouts."

"That damned affair. I wish I'd never written a word of it; I wish I'd left it sitting at the bottom of my trunk. Look at what it's done, it's driven you to I don't know what madness."

"Don't be ridiculous, Watson. If you hadn't written about the Body Snatcher affair nothing would have changed. Your chronicle of it is unrelated to the facts that brought us to America. No, but it is fortunate, I think, that I had so amply prepared myself for this investigation and that, dear Watson, is directly attributable to your 'little chronicle'." He paused to light his pipe, releasing a cloud of smoke before going on, "I was also fortunate enough to seek the advice and assistance in my research from a mutual acquaintance of ours."

"Oh? And who would that be?"

"Mr. Abraham Stoker."

"You mean Sir Henry's assistant? The one we met on our voyage to New York?"

"The very same. Unfortunately, he's since passed on, but ever since our first adventure in America I've maintained a friendship with Stoker and his wife, Florence. It is from Stoker that I learned about the vampire legends."

"But what does a theater manager know of vampires?"

"When we met, I was surprised to discover that Stoker had quite an interest in the macabre. He's become, since the time we met him, quite an accomplished writer. It's a wonder you've not come across his work."

"I'm afraid I've no interest in the horror genre. Just a lot of clap-trap and dungabilly."

"That dungabilly, as you call it, has at its roots the very essence of the evil and mystery of eastern European myth, and myth as you know flows from fear, fear of the unknown."

"Fear and ignorance, you should say. And from where did Mr. Stoker gain his unusual expertise?"

"Ah, that is a very interesting story. One that became the genesis of his most successful novel, *Dracula*."

"*Dracula*? I've heard of it, though I never made the

association of the author with Sir Henry's man. I remember it caused quite a sensation when it was first published. Never read it myself."

"But I have. I've read it and studied it."

"Studied it? Coals to Newcastle, Holmes, why? It's only a novel. Fiction, and of the basest kind. Whatever did you expect to learn from it?"

"Only what I need to defeat Barlucci."

"Well, now I'm afraid I am confused. Your logic in this appears to me to be, and I hope you'll pardon me for saying so, convoluted. You expect a work of fiction to provide you with the knowledge you need to defeat a madman. How, exactly, does that make any sense whatsoever?"

"To answer that you need to know what the source was for Mr. Stoker's novel. Do you recall my response when you asked what my fascination was with Sir Henry's assistant?"

"No, I'm afraid I don't. It has been twenty-five years, after all."

"And yet you mentioned it almost verbatim in your Body Snatcher tale."

"Ah, but I had my notes to guide me then."

"Of course. Well then, what I told you was that Mr. Stoker and I had a mutual acquaintance, but I never divulged who that acquaintance might be," he said, his eyes narrowing as he conjured the image of our conversation in his mind.

"What? Do you mean Stoker was acquainted with Barlucci?"

"Correct, and it was much more than a mere acquaintance. It was from Barlucci that Stoker gained the knowledge to paint such a malignantly realistic character as Count Dracula. The two met several years before Barlucci came to our attention, when Stoker was traveling through Southeastern Europe. Stoker explained to me that Barlucci was amused at his interest in Romanian folklore. When he learned Stoker was working on a novel, he offered to collaborate, identifying himself as an authority on eastern European culture and legend. When Stoker returned to England, they continued to correspond. That correspondence suddenly came to an end in the fall of 1888. Stoker was unaware why, but you and I know. That was when Barlucci arrived in England himself, although Stoker was at that time traveling with Sir Henry. He told me Barlucci's assistance was invaluable in separating the ridiculous from the bedrock of the legends."

"But this *Dracula* is just a novel you said, not some scholarly journal on the vampirical legend."

"That is true, and because it is a novel, Stoker explained to me that he made certain changes, embellishments as it were, in order to serve the story of the novel."

"Well, then, how can this novel, which embellishes the facts, be of use in defeating Barlucci."

"Ah, but during the writing of this novel, Stoker maintained a personal copy of the manuscript. This copy contained detailed notes on what was fantastic and what was, in the words of Barlucci to Stoker, bedrock. I asked his wife if I might borrow that manuscript."

"And she gave it to you?"

"Yes, she told me that when Abraham was stricken this last time, he told her to keep the manuscript safe until I should come for it. I think he knew I would find a use for it."

"Then Stoker was aware that Barlucci believed himself to be a vampire?"

"Yes, I told him that much on our first meeting."

"Remarkable."

"Indeed. It was on that voyage that I began to think about the possibilities an existence such as a vampire possesses would have. That immortality, true immortality, in the right hands could become a panacea of the world's troubles. Think of it Watson." I did think of it, and while I was thinking of it, I saw the wild thing in Holmes' eye begin to once again come alive. It dawned on me at that moment that it was immortality, or the chance of it, that Holmes was pursuing as much as Barlucci. This was why he could not let Barlucci go.

"But surely if a thing such as immortality existed, it would tend to corrupt the individual. We weren't meant to be immortal. We were meant to live our lives, toil and make our marks as best we can and then move on, making way for the next generation."

"Yes, yes, but don't you see what a great advantage it would be to humanity if there were an individual or individuals to carry forth in a field of endeavor, or even several fields, without interruption, without the need to have it stop and then pick it up again, having to rebuild as it were on the decaying ruins of a city of knowledge? Instead of the start-stop-start-again of scientific research, there could be a continuous string of building and discovering." Holmes began to pace around the room, seeming to be speaking to himself rather than to me.

"But at what cost?" I reminded him, "Barlucci is a murderer of epic proportion. Anyone who gained immortality in the way he claims would of necessity follow that line."

Pausing in his steps Holmes said, "Yes, yes, there is that but I would think that could be overcome."

I laughed, "Overcome? How, by volunteers lining up to be the feast of an immortal demon?" Once again I could see common sense regaining its hold upon him. "Besides, I should think it would be a most lonely existence unless there were a society of such creatures."

Holmes smiled, "I should think anyone who would gain immortality in such a fashion might wish to keep it a secret, don't you?" Tying up his necktie and grabbing his jacket, he said, "Come. Let me show you the nest. We can wrestle with the wisdom of immortality another time." And with that we hurried down and hired a hansom to take us to 42nd Street and Lexington Avenue.

We got out of the cab and descended into the as yet unfinished subway station. Holmes led the way into what appeared a depthless abyss. Although at ground level this section of the underground—

subway to the native New Yorkers—had a grand looking entrance with marble pilasters and a rich looking stone staircase covered with an archway of wrought iron, one did not have to travel far before the light became thinner and the tunnel rough and unfinished. As we descended I got the uncomfortable feeling of a fly entering beneath a web.

At the bottom of the stairs we could see to the north that this was the direction in which the main thrust of the excavation work was concentrated. The work to this point had consisted of excavating from above and covering over as the excavation was completed, but from 53rd Street on for approximately a mile the construction was being carried forth in true tunneling fashion. The 42nd Street Underground station was the last one prior to the beginning of the tunnel construction. To the south the track was laid and the tunnel was completely covered over, although the interior was still unfinished relative to the fancy brickwork and painting we'd witnessed in the completed lines. It was in this, the southerly direction, where Holmes led.

After we'd gone no more than a hundred yards Holmes handed me his match tin and held up the dark lantern while I lighted it. What little illumination there was from the subway entrance was fading fast, both with the distance between us and it and with the approaching night. In another hundred yards we would be completely at the mercy of the darkness were it not for Holmes' lantern. I followed closely behind as Holmes quickened his pace. The air, which had been thick and cloying with humidity when we'd entered the station, had suddenly grown strangely cool, most probably due to the increasing depth underground and perhaps the proximity to the East River.

Since we had exited the hansom Holmes had barely spoken. Now he turned and said, "Just ahead, we'll need to remove the grating." He motioned to a large metal lattice structure covering a ventilation duct. "Ever since the police found that Braden fellow at

Grand Central, I've been studying the ventilation system. This shaft connects to the one at Grand Central, and if you look from this angle," he descended to one knee, looking from the lower right-hand corner of the grate into the shaft up towards the upper left, "you can just catch a glimpse of what may be a shelf upon which there appears to be some clothing or rags. I believe this may be where Barlucci has been hiding during the day."

"Ah, yes, his nest didn't you say?"

"Exactly. Give me a hand here, will you?" He was busy prying off the grate with a coach wrench he'd produced from under his jacket. I took my handkerchief from my pocket and removed my tie. Wrapping them around my hands as makeshift gloves, I grabbed the lower edge of the grating pulling as Holmes pried. It was extremely heavy and as it came loose, it crashed to the ground.

"Well, if he's in there, I'm sure that woke him up. Thank you."

"My pleasure," said I, feeling a little annoyed.

"Quite all right, I don't think he was using this particular nest today. I'm hoping, however, he will return to it this evening, or next. In the meantime, I shall search for others during the day until I discover him. Now, take the lantern. I'll go first." He stepped up onto the ledge and entered. The duct was of such size that once he'd entered past the opening, he was nearly able to stand. But as he turned, the twin overlapping doors of a steel ventilation damper slammed shut.

"Holmes," I called. "Holmes, can you hear me."

After a brief silence he said, "Yes, Watson, I can hear you. And although I can't see much, this appears to be some sort of emergency damper meant to seal the shaft in the event gas is detected."

"Gas? I don't smell anything."

"Nor do I, but I suppose there is the chance the gas may be odorless. In that event, I wouldn't risk discussing this too much further. The damper has a self-latching mechanism and I think it would behoove each of us to vacate the area as best we can."

"But Holmes, I can't leave you trapped like this."

"Nonsense, Watson. You forget I've studied the ventilation system in some detail. By the time you reach the street, I'll have found my own way out, most probably at a street grating near the 42nd Street station."

"Are you certain?"

"Yes, now let's waste no more time arguing the matter. If there is a poisonous gas leak, the longer we tarry the greater our peril."

"Yes, yes, of course. I'll await you at the station grate." I felt like a villain, leaving my friend trapped in the duct, but there was nothing I could do. I was also quite aware that having studied the ducting, he would most probably find his way out prior to my own escape. I hurried back to the station, aided by the light of the dark lantern. In just a few minutes I'd emerged onto 42nd Street and made my way to the grating just above the station. The rain had stopped and the air was heavy and warm. After ten minutes and no Holmes, I began to become worried.

It must have been time for a shift change in the tunneling endeavor because just then a wagon loaded with workers drove by in the direction of the dig. I hailed it and engaged the foreman in coming to my aid. I explained that Holmes and I had been investigating the ducting when the damper, apparently triggered by a gas leak in the tunnel, had slammed closed trapping my friend inside. He told me that this was impossible since the dampers were not yet connected. A panic consumed me as I realized Holmes must have fallen into a trap.

The foreman and three of his crew followed me back into the tunnel, back to where Holmes had disappeared. Using the tools of their trade, the men worked on the damper, finally prying it open. I raised the lantern I'd only minutes before taken from Holmes. Climbing inside, I called, "Holmes." He was nowhere to be found. I was answered only by silence.

Chapter 12
Watson carries on…

It was late when I finally returned to the Gilsey. I'd telephoned Commissioner Strumm at his home from the Grand Central Terminal after leaving the scene to ask him to dispatch officers to aid me in my search for Holmes. The workmen who'd assisted me in opening the damper had returned to their wagon and to their tunneling operation too soon for my taste, but they had no sense of the danger I felt and reassured me that he'd probably wandered into an adjoining duct and would find his way to an exit soon enough.

Inside the shaft there was no sign of Holmes anywhere, nor was there any sign of the 'nest' that had been the impetus of his investigation. I was especially ill at ease with this, as well as the total absence of any sign of a disturbance. I suspected a trap had been laid and then sprung for my friend.

Strumm insisted on personally coming to my aid, much to my relief. But after several hours of searching and not a sign of Holmes, he too was of the opinion that Holmes had probably long since found his way out and very likely would be waiting for me back at our hotel.

Had Holmes found his escape as everyone seemed to believe, I knew he would waste no time in making his way back to the station to meet me and put me at my ease. But reluctantly, at Strumm's insistence, I finally agreed to return to the hotel. After all, there didn't appear to be much else I could do here. Strumm promised he'd keep men on the search until Holmes turned up.

My sleep was fitful and short. I arose very early, having slept not more than an hour or two all through the night. I made my toilet and decided to take an early breakfast. Just as I was about to leave our rooms, the telephone sounded. I hurried to answer it, hoping it would be some news of Holmes.

Sadly, I was disappointed. It was Abel Jenkins. He rang my room to tell me that Miss Lucie Strumm was in the hotel and would like very much to speak to me. As distraught as I was over Holmes' disappearance, I could hardly refuse. I told Jenkins to let her know I would be down presently.

I met Miss Strumm in the lobby. "Oh, Dr. Watson, thank you for seeing me so early. Has there been any news about Mr. Holmes? My father told us he's missing."

"No, I'm afraid not. But don't worry," I said putting on an air of counterfeit confidence, "he always manages to turn up sooner or later. Now, what is it I can do for you?"

"It's Phillip. I don't know what I'm going to do, Dr. Watson." She dabbed her red eyes with a handkerchief that was already damp with spent tears.

"Of course, dear. Why don't we go into the dining room? I'll ask the manager for a private table away from both the entrance and the window. We'll not be disturbed at this time of day I'm sure." As I said this I led the young Miss Strumm into the dining room and motioned for the waiter to bring us a carafe of coffee. I held her chair as she sat down and then I took my place beside her. "Now, tell me dear, what has you in such a state? What is going on with Phillip?"

"Oh, Doctor. He's…he's…" she said before dissolving into sobs.

"Nothing's happened to him, has it?" I asked, instantly expecting the worst. This had the effect of startling her out of her tears for a moment.

"No. I mean, I don't know. He's become so very distant and now his mother—" she burst into tears anew.

The waiter brought our coffee and I poured two cups as her sobs began to subside. "I see. Well, why don't you try telling me all that you do know? When did this distance begin?"

"Very well," she said, dabbing her nose before sipping her coffee. "Three days ago things were fine, more than fine, actually. Especially considering he'd only so recently learned about his mother. Phillip worshiped his grandparents, and his Uncle Charles. He knew if they kept the fact his mother was alive from him it must have been in his best interest to do so."

"Very sensible."

"Yes, that's what I told him. And then, just before we'd learned Mr. Holmes found his mother, dead, he came to see me. He looked absolutely terrible, like he hadn't slept in weeks. He began to speak to me of things that didn't make sense. He told me that his parents weren't crazy and that he should have been told the truth from the beginning."

"A startling turnabout. Most unusual, remarkable even. Did he say what had changed his mind?"

"I asked him, but he wouldn't say." Miss Strumm gripped my arm as she continued, "But that's not all, Doctor. He said he was convinced his uncle and grandparents had hidden the true facts from him because they were afraid he would follow his father's mad schemes of experimentation."

"Did he explain to you of what experiments he was speaking and is that how he termed them, as mad schemes?"

"No, but that's what they are, don't you see? Phillip's father was insane too. I've heard my parents say as much. I felt Phillip wanted to tell me about them, but each time he began, he would falter and change the subject. He seemed to be quite distraught and angry with his grandparents and with his Uncle Charles especially. No matter how I tried to talk some sense into him, he simply would not listen." As she said this, I could see her countenance clouding over and the tears, which had been gratefully absent, once again began to fall. "That's when he told me that I was wrong and that he would show me and his family just how wrong we all were. And then he left." She sat there silently sobbing into her handkerchief. I patted her hand in an effort to console her.

"There, there, Miss Lucie. I'm sure this is just a temporary rumple on your road to domestic bliss. I'll drop by and see if I can talk to him. After all, I'm not unfamiliar with the situation at the time of his father's death. Sometimes it takes a disinterested third party, someone with a bit of distance, to talk through the issues and make some sense of things."

"Oh, Dr. Watson, that's why I came to you. I knew if anyone could get through to Phillip you could. I would be so very grateful if you would, if you could talk to him. I'm sure he would listen to you."

"Consider it done, then. I'll pop on over to see him this afternoon."

We finished our coffee and talked of lighter topics. By the time she left, her mood was much improved, but she reminded me of my promise as I escorted her out to a cab.

After Lucie departed, I dined alone again in the hotel restaurant, though Holmes' continued absence had a deleterious effect on my appetite. Afterwards, with still no word from or about Holmes, I decided I had nothing better to do than fulfill my promise to Miss Lucie. I hailed a hansom and made my way to the house I'd once known as the home of Julia and Dr. Alan Tremaine and which now belonged wholly to young Phillip Tremaine. His uncle, Charles Cabot, who raised Phillip after his mother was committed to the asylum, still lived in the house but when Phillip turned twenty years old, in accordance with New York Law, the ownership reverted to him.

I knocked on the door and for a moment I was again back in 1888 expecting at any moment to be greeted by the lovely and vivacious Julia Tremaine. I instantly realized this could no longer be and the emotion of the moment made me knock once again in an effort to clear the thought from my mind. The door was answered by a plump middle-aged woman with chestnut hair tinged with gray tucked up under a white muslin cap. Her wide eyes reminded me of a doe as she looked at me and asked, "May I help you, sir?"

"Annie, it's Dr. Watson."

"Oh my yes...Dr. Watson, as I live and breathe. So good to see you again. Are you here to see young Phillip?"

"Yes, I've come to see the current Dr. Tremaine." I reached inside my waistcoat and produced a card with my name. I handed it to her. "Would you give him this?"

"Oh, Doctor, you don't need to give Master Phillip your card. Since you were here last, he's read most of your stories about Mr. Holmes. But I'm afraid Master Phillip isn't home at present. However, if you'll wait just a moment," she said, "I'm sure Master Charles would like to meet you. Please wait here for just a bit," she said, closing the door. A moment later she returned. "Master Charles would be honored if you would take coffee with him in the parlor."

"It would be my pleasure. Thank you, Annie," I said as she showed me into the very same parlor where Holmes and I first met Dr. Alan Tremaine and his wife all those years ago. As I entered, I saw a tall gaunt figure standing by the fireplace, which was dormant in the heat of the day. He was straightening a picture of his sister Julia on the mantle.

"Master Charles," said Annie, "this is Dr. Watson."

Charles Cabot turned on his heel and took a step toward me. To my trained eye, it was obvious he had a wooden leg, even though his gate was almost without even the hint of a limp. "Ah, Dr. Watson, please come in. I'm so happy to finally make your acquaintance."

"I'm happy to meet you as well. I only wish it could have been on a less somber occasion. I'm afraid you were out of town on my last visit to New York."

"Yes, well, I was engaged in a little business but I'm really not at liberty to discuss that just now." He raised his eyebrows in a particularly conspiratorial way and then completely changed the subject. "The news of my sister's death has been very hard on both Phillip and me."

"I'm sure it has. I'm terribly sorry I've missed him. It was he I came to see."

"Well, he's been spending more and more time away from our home, I'm sorry to say. But at least your visit affords me the opportunity of meeting you. I've read a good deal of your writings, Doctor. I admire a man who can tell a tale with such alacrity and with such imagination. I congratulate you."

"Thank you, but I'm afraid I was merely reporting the facts of the cases I chronicled as they became known to me."

"Come now, Doctor, surely you don't expect me to believe you didn't embellish your tales in order to increase not only their sales, but as way of advertising the skills of your associate, Mr. Sherlock Holmes. Ingenious bit of marketing, I say."

I wasn't sure if I should be insulted or not. I decided to delay judgment on that count for the moment. "I assure you sir, no such thought entered my mind. Mr. Holmes needs no advertisement. His consultation is sought by heads of government and industry without...how did you put it...'marketing'."

Annie arrived carrying a tray with coffee and small sweet cakes. "Ah, please, Doctor, join me for some coffee and a light repast." He motioned for me to sit. "I didn't mean to upset you. I actually meant it as a compliment. I've been all over the world and I must say I've met many a detective and none of them measures up to this Holmes fellow. Your descriptions remind me of Poe's Dupin. You must forgive me if I'm a bit skeptical."

I relaxed a bit as his manner became less confrontational and more conversational. "My associate might take issue with that comparison," I said with a chuckle. "I suppose had I not witnessed most of the accounts I chronicled first hand I might be a bit skeptical myself. But I assure you, Holmes is the genuine article." I decided to steer the conversation more towards the direction I'd come here to investigate and away from my friend's own investigative prowess. "You say you've been all over the world?"

"Yes, that's true, I have."

"I'd learned from your parents that during the time I wrote of in my last chronicle, the *Body Snatchers*, you were an officer in the British Army. I'd often wondered about that, but they were adamant. How did you, an American, come to be an officer in the British Army?"

Charles put his hand over his mouth as this time he chuckled at my question. "I'm afraid my parents didn't quite grasp the situation. I wasn't exactly in the British Army. I was an American military attaché on a diplomatic mission in Egypt under the auspices of the British government and as such, I was attached to the British Army during my tenure there, up until the time I was injured."

"Yes, I'd heard you had a bad accident."

"Accident? I'm afraid it was no accident, Doctor, but that story too is for another day. But come, I've dominated the conversation since you arrived. My apologies. You certainly didn't come here to discuss old injuries. Belatedly I must ask, to what do I owe your visit today?"

"Actually as I said before, I came to speak with young Phillip." When I mentioned Phillip's name, Charles face took on a grave look. "I promised Miss Lucie I'd look in on him."

"I'm afraid Phillip is out. In fact, he didn't come home at all last night. I believe he may be with his new friend, a fellow by the name of Alex."

"Alexander Hume?"

"Yes, do you know him?"

"I only met him once, at the Strumm's home."

"I'm afraid I don't much care for him, don't trust him."

"What makes you say that? He seemed like a perfectly charming and engaging young man. He certainly came to the aid of your nephew and his fiancée, Miss Strumm. I would think you'd be in his debt."

"Of course I'm grateful, although I wonder at the coincidence of his being at the right place and time to be of such assistance. Did you get a chance to find out much about him?"

"Well, I shared a cab with him and we had a delightful exchange."

"Did he tell you much about himself?"

"Hmm..let me see, he told me he's a musician, and…"

"Ha. And not much else, I'll wager. Though I would guess he persuaded you into telling him much about some small thing or other, didn't he? He's a shrewd young fellow, I'll give him that. I've never met one shrewder and I've met some very astute individuals in my travels."

I thought back to how young Hume had engaged me in conversation and how much I'd told him about the Abigail Drake case and how very interested he appeared to be. "Yes, I suppose I did do most of the talking, but then that's not unusual for me. Why do you distrust him so?"

"I dislike the influence he seems to have over Phillip." He paused to take a sip of coffee. "Phillip and I used to get on, he'd tell me everything that was going on in his life, his plans, his dreams, even his innermost thoughts. But now, I've hardly seen him since this Hume fellow has appeared. The two of them are nearly inseparable and when they are together they speak in hushed tones or stop talking altogether

119

when I enter the room. It's all so...so..."

"Conspiratorial?"

"Yes, that's it exactly, conspiratorial. I don't know what this Hume is getting Phillip mixed up in, but I can tell you it's no good whatever it is."

"I see. Miss Lucie is concerned as well. She asked me to speak to Phillip, to see if perhaps I could discover why he's been so distant with her as well."

"She and I have spoken about Phillip on the telephone. She asked me to speak to him as well. She's concerned because he's begun to speak of his father and his death and of how he's been lied to all these years—about his father, his mother, everything. But I told her he'd been as distant with me as he had with her and I didn't think I would be of much help."

"Perhaps as a disinterested third party I can get through to the lad. As I told Miss Lucie, it's sometimes easier to speak to a relative stranger than it is to those with whom one has a close relationship. I'll see what I can do, then."

"I would be very grateful, Doctor, and I'm sure Lucie would be as well." He put down his cup of coffee and looked at me with a serious face. "There is something more, Doctor."

"Yes? What is it?" I said noting the crease in his forehead deepen with concern.

"He's begun looking through his father's old papers and the notes of his mad experiments."

"What papers? I thought all of Dr. Tremaine's papers were burned in the fire that killed him and consumed Abigail Drake." I was very well aware what those papers must contain.

"Alan was apparently very meticulous in his documentation. Julia used to scold him for making two copies of practically everything, including household bill payments. These papers were found not long after he died, hidden away in a secret compartment built into the bookshelf in his study."

"Why on earth weren't they destroyed?"

"Julia wouldn't hear of it. She said Alan told her where they were and that she should ensure they were safe for when he needed them."

"I thought you said they were discovered after Alan died."

"That's correct. This was an early symptom of Julia's mental disorder."

"But why not get rid of them once Julia was…was…"

"Committed? I was going to, but as I read through them, something about their utter orderly madness prevented me from doing so. I thought that someday, if Phillip were to ask about his father and his illness… Well, I thought I could use it to show him that his father, for all his madness, was a genius. Some of the work he did in blood disorders is still being used today. But genius sometimes borders on madness and it only takes something or someone to give a slight push from one to the other."

I immediately thought of Holmes and his recent obsession with Barlucci and immortality. "Yes, you are quite right." Holmes, I thought, what had become of him?

"Oh, I know I should have burned them all. If I had, perhaps Julia would have come to her senses, but at the time…I just couldn't. I was so afraid to upset her."

"Yes, of course. You did what you thought best. No one can fault you for that. Are the papers here?" I asked, thinking it might be worthwhile to take a look at them.

"Why yes, Phillip has taken over the study as his own, of course, and he maintains them there. Would you like to see them?"

"Yes, if you think it would be all right."

"Well, I don't think Phillip would offer them, but if you care to take a look, you would see what we are dealing with." He arose from his chair and this seemed to be the only movement where the fact he was wearing a prosthesis was evident. "Please, come with me. I don't expect Phillip will be back anytime soon. In point of fact, I don't know when I can expect him."

I followed him into a large study with a set of three expansive windows spread across the wall behind an ornate walnut desk with a marble top. Each window had a wrought iron grill-work in a diamond patter that was continued in the fan windows above the center.

It was quite evident young Dr. Tremaine was engaged in reviewing his father's work. The papers were arranged in neat stacks on the desk and a nearby side table. I began my perusal by trying to ascertain the method of organization. It appeared experiments and results were all on the side table, and the desk was covered with the research that went into those experiments, along with notes and what appeared to be a journal. It was the journal that caught my attention. I read the first page,

'I open this journal on September 8, 1888, to record a very unusual dinner I attended at the home of Baron Antonio Barlucci. I had met the baron just over a week before at a reception he had thrown in my honor as I concluded a series of lectures on blood disorders throughout Europe that culminated with my final lecture at the Royal Scientific Society in London.

The dinner was absolutely sumptuous and afterward the baron told me the remarkable story of how he became a vampire.'

I stopped reading and looked at my host, "Have you read this?"

"Of course. Why do you think I kept it? I thought anyone reading that would realize Alan Tremaine was unstable."

"Does it continue on like this?"

"I'm afraid it does. He goes into great detail about how the baron proved to him he was a vampire and asked him to search for a cure."

"Would you mind if I took this journal with me? I'd like

122

Holmes to…" Once I spoke his name I realized that although I'd certainly not entirely forgotten Holmes had disappeared, somehow by not speaking of him I was able to delude myself that he was simply back at the hotel. But at the mention of his name, the horror of the night before and of his disappearance came home to me once again.

"You'd like Holmes to what? To read it?"

"Yes, I believe he would find it most enlightening." Somehow it seemed wrong to tell Charles about Holmes' disappearance. In point of true fact I didn't know if I could say it out loud without breaking down. I suddenly felt the need to return to my hotel and give Commissioner Strumm a call for the latest news.

"If it were up to me, Doctor, I would allow you free reign, but I fear that would be quite out of the question. All of the papers here now belong to Phillip and even though I am quite concerned about both his physical and mental well-being, I feel I would be betraying his trust were I to let you remove any of the documents. But should he care to stop by when Phillip is away, I would be most happy to allow Mr. Holmes access."

"In that case, if you don't mind, I think it's time I returned to my hotel and, er, find out what Holmes has been up to in my absence."

"Wait. Here." He scribbled something on a small slip of paper and handed it to me. "I've made some inquiries about Mr. Hume. Although information about him is scant, I would expect you may be able to find Phillip at this address. It's recently been leased by Hume."

I thanked Charles for his hospitality and left as quickly as I could without appearing to be in too much of a rush. I suddenly wished more than ever that Holmes were back safe and sound.

Chapter 13
Unexpected visitor...

As I entered the lobby of the Gilsey, I was at the low ebb of my emotion. I'd stopped by the 42nd Street station to see if there'd been any word on Holmes, but when I'd discovered there had been none I walked the short distance to the telephone pay station at the Grand Central Terminal. From there I again called Commissioner Strumm, this time to see if there'd been any news. He assured me the entire network of ventilation shafting, from its northernmost reaches at 46th Street south to 20th Street had been searched without result. They were still working the cross connections to other subway line ventilation systems as there was a complex system of cross and inter-connects, but the outlook was not hopeful. So, I was most dejected when I returned to the hotel.

As I crossed the lobby on my way to the lift, Abel Jenkins approached and said, "Doctor, I have your table ready for you. We have an excellent steak and kidney pie today I thought you might enjoy."

I tried to put on a pleasant face to Jenkins. He was aware, of course, that Holmes was missing and that I was gravely concerned for his safety. I supposed this was his way of trying to provide a bit of consolation, although at this particular juncture I was not in the least interested in food. I didn't wish to appear ungrateful to Abel, who after all was only trying to provide some comfort to me in my hour of need, so I turned to him and with a sad smile said, "I'm afraid I'm not very hungry for lunch today. Please forgive me if I turn down your kind gesture." I thought that would be the end of it, and turned back toward the lifts, but Jenkins quickened his pace to put himself between me and my destination.

"But it's a most exquisite kidney pie…" he said, and then after a pause, during which he inched backwards keeping himself between me and the lifts, he added, "…and you have a guest awaiting you."

Exasperated at this new invasion upon my dour mood I said, "I'm afraid I'm in no frame of mind to receive company. I'm sure you understand."

"But I'm afraid he was very insistent that I urge your attendance."

More than a little piqued, I said, "Oh, very well. I shall meet with this gentleman. What name did he give?"

"Well, uh, he…he didn't give me a name, Doctor."

I was now becoming incensed. Not only was Jenkins intruding on my solitary worry for my friend but now he was insisting on expanding that intrusion to one who did not have the decency to proffer his card for introduction. However, under the circumstances, I felt it would be less than charitable to poor Jenkins than to do other than accede to his entreaty. "Very, well," I said. "Lead on, then."

"Very good, Doctor." And with that he led me into the dining room, to my customary table where to my great surprise and greater joy sat Mr. Sherlock Holmes, puffing on his pipe as though he were deep in thought. He looked a bit tired and drawn, but otherwise in good health.

"Holmes," I ejaculated. "What are you doing here?"

"I'm about to have my lunch. I understand the Gilsey is serving a passable steak and kidney pie today. Do join me, won't you?" he said without the slightest indication that anything was amiss.

"This, sir, is beyond the pale," I said, feeling at once great relief in seeing his aquiline features again and abject annoyance that he could endeavor to act as though he owed no explanation of his recent whereabouts. "Where have you been? What happened to you after I left you in the vent ducting?"

A smile curled the corner of his mouth as he said, "I did exactly what I told you I would do. But I made a slight miscalculation as to how long it would take, owing, among other things, to the total darkness. By the time I arrived at the grating, you were nowhere to be found. I found the grating there to be too secure to move by myself, so I had little choice but to find another avenue of egress."

I took up my seat opposite Holmes and said, "Good heavens. And it's taken you all this time, nearly fifteen hours, to find your way out?"

"You must remember, Watson, it was pitch within the ducting and I could only gain my bearings at those places where the ducting opened onto the street or a lighted tunnel. It was a bit more difficult—"

"Oh dear," I said suddenly.

"What is it?"

"Strumm. I must call the commissioner. He's had men searching the ventilation shafts for you all night and all morning."

"No need. I called him from the desk when I arrived. Jenkins here told me what had transpired since we separated, and how brave a face you've put on, though he could well tell how distraught you were in spite of it." Having spent the tobacco in his bowl, he tapped the side of it on his boot, spilling the cinder onto the floor and stamping it out. "So, tell me what you've been up to, other than occupying the New York Police Department in a game of where's the detective," and again he smiled, a bit too roguishly for my taste.

By this time, the kidney pie had arrived and we each put a generous portion onto our plates. "I had a visit this morning from Miss

Lucie Strumm."

"Oh? Concerning her mother or her fiancée?"

"Her fiancée, but how did you…? Never mind, I suppose they would be the natural choices, since you'd spoken to the commissioner yourself. Anyway, she is very concerned about young Phillip Tremaine."

"I see…and what appears to be troubling Dr. Tremaine?"

"From what Miss Lucie says, he feels he's been lied to not only about his mother being shut away in an asylum, but also about his father's death and seems to believe that his mother wasn't mad but was put into an asylum because she was an embarrassment to the family."

"He seemed to be content with the explanations he'd been given when we met him at the Strumm's. What has happened to change that I wonder." With his meal nearly consumed, Holmes began to fill his pipe once again, a sure signal that this news was something to ponder.

"I believe it may be his new friend, this Alexander Hume."

"Oh? What makes you think so?"

"Oh it isn't only my own opinion. His Uncle Charles Cabot also believes as much. I've just come from speaking with him as well." I removed a slip of paper from my waistcoat pocket. "He gave me this address on Blackwell's Island, where he says I might be able to find Phillip."

Instead of taking the address, he struck a match and lighting his pipe said, "Indeed, You've been busy in my absence. Bravo, good for you. I half expected to find you fretting and moping about." Though his words were nonchalant, I could swear I noted a tinge of pain in his tone.

"I must admit I didn't sleep a wink all night, even though Commissioner Strumm assured me his men would find you by morning." This had the apparent desired effect of lifting his spirits.

"Never mind then," he said with the shadow of a smile on his lips. "Tell me about your visit with Miss Strumm and Charles Cabot."

"Well, as I said, Miss Strumm is quite distraught because young Phillip Tremaine is increasingly distant and suspicious of the motives pertaining to his mother's commitment to an asylum. She asked me to have a word with him so after lunch I went to his house to see if I could reason with him."

"And were you able to talk with him?"

"Why, no, when I arrived he was out. That is how I came to meet Charles Cabot."

"Ah, the older brother of Julia Tremaine and member of the US Army's version of a *cabinet noir*."

"You know he was a member of his country's SIS? I thought as much from what he said, or I should say what he didn't say." The SIS is the royal Secret Intelligence Service, the world's premier spy service.

"Not was, my dear boy, is. He's still active from what I've been able to learn."

"Even with his false leg?" I asked, astonished.

"What would make an agent less likely to be an agent than a wooden leg?"

"Yes, I suppose you are right," I said, considering in a new light all that had passed between Phillip Tremaine's uncle and myself.

"So tell me, what did Charles Cabot have to say about young Phillip's distancing himself from his fiancée?"

"Ah yes, well he told me that Phillip has been spending a good deal of his time with Alexander Hume."

"The young man who saved Phillip and Lucie from those ruffians?"

"The very same. Mr. Cabot is terribly concerned this Hume fellow is having an undue influence on young Tremaine. He believes Hume is encouraging in him a hostile attitude towards his family and all who had a hand in denigrating, as he puts it, his father's reputation. Tremaine has also been reading his father's notes from when he was in England."

"I thought all those papers were destroyed in the fire."

"Exactly what I asked Mr. Cabot. He told me that Tremaine's father was extraordinarily meticulous in his record keeping and had made a copy of all of his more important notes and research. Most likely he made copies of these during his voyage from England to America."

"And Phillip Tremaine now possesses these papers?"

"Yes, and Mr. Cabot showed me a copy of Alan Tremaine's journal of when he was working with Barlucci. I thought you would be particularly interested in that. He wouldn't let me borrow it, lest young Phillip Tremaine discover it was missing, but he assured me he would make it available for your inspection whenever you should occasion to visit."

"I must remember to stop by sometime and have a look," Holmes said, surprisingly with no particular sense of urgency.

"I must say I thought you'd be more enthusiastic regarding the journal at least."

Holmes said with a yawn, showing no interest at all, "At a document that was written more than twenty-five years ago? I hardly think it deserves more than a passing interest."

"You surprise me, Holmes."

"Come, Watson, we've more to worry ourselves about than the journal of a madman."

"Then you believe Dr. Alan Tremaine was mad?"

"I believe he was involved in madness and as a result, has left a legacy of madness in his wake."

"Well, then, where do we go from here?"

"I don't know what you are going to do, Watson, but I am going to finish what's left of my coffee, which by the way I find surprisingly excellent today, and then I shall most probably sleep away the majority of the next twelve hours."

Long after Holmes arose and went to our rooms, I sat at the table looking at the slip of paper still in my hand, perplexed by his attitude. I couldn't fathom what appeared to be a complete change in his manner.

The Holmes I knew would have found interest in anything relating to a case in which he was actively working and yet he seemed totally and pointedly disinterested in either the journal or the goings on at Blackwell's Island. The Holmes I knew would have eschewed nourishment for days while in the midst of such an investigation, but he scarfed up his meal like a man without a care in the world other than feeding a voracious appetite. And then there was the assertion he planned to sleep the day away. It was completely unlike Holmes to give in to creature comforts when pursuing a case. The Holmes I knew would go for days on end without sleep or nourishment. This was all quite irregular for Sherlock Holmes—quite irregular indeed. What could it mean?

Chapter 14
Watson investigates...

I removed the slip of paper Charles Cabot had given me and looked closely at the address. Apparently Mr. Hume valued his privacy. The address was a place called the Octagon, located on Blackwell's Island, which was a nearly uninhabited strip of land in the middle of the East River halfway between Manhattan and the borough of Queens. I was rather surprised as I remembered Blackwell's Island at one time was home to the penitentiary and asylum that now occupied Ward's Island. It was apparent New Yorkers believed there to be some safety in separating themselves from their insane and their criminals and their criminally insane with a stretch of water. But now, the only building in use on this particular island was the lighthouse on its northern tip.

I took a trolley from Manhattan across the Blackwell Bridge, which stretches from Manhattan to Long Island, passing directly over the island. Halfway across I debarked at the Blackwell station and took the lift down to the island below. Unfortunately to my surprise, due to the relative isolation and obscurity of the island there was no commercial transportation accommodation—no taxi, no conveyance for hire. I did, however, discover an abandoned bicycle, to which I availed myself.

I began pedaling north on the island, toward the lighthouse. I passed a boat landing where no doubt a ferry tied up. I made a mental note to use that conveyance should I visit the island again as my breathing was already beginning to become labored and my leg throbbed as I pedaled forth. I was pleased to see, not far from the ferry landing, the octagonal shape of a building ahead. I dismounted the bicycle and leaned it against a tree and walked the short distance to the Octagon, which was apparently the entrance to the abandoned insane asylum. I wondered at the selection of this ruin as a place of residence.

The building sat on a spate of land that was barren of vegetation for a short distance from the structure and then thick with weeds and coarse plants growing up all around it, giving the feeling that the structure was being expelled from the earth. A bit further away was a thick copse of trees such that the building was practically hidden from sight until you were nearly upon it. There was a conspicuous absence of noise such that my own labored breathing was that much more noticeable to me. There was no sound of movement, no songbirds or frogs, not even crickets. In fact the only sound I could detect other than those I made myself was that of the wind through the trees, a gentle whispering sound that could lull one to sleep easily I thought.

The stairway leading up to the broad portico entrance was covered with vines, as was much of the front of the structure, giving it a bearded appearance. I climbed the staircase and tried the door. It was locked. But upon examining the lock I discovered it was of a very elementary type and in less time than it took to re-secure my tie pin I was inside the front door.

Immediately upon entering the building I realized this was no residence—it was a laboratory. In my mind I was immediately taken back to the library at Mauldin Place, where Abigail Drake had financed the laboratory set up by Dr. Alan Tremaine and where they had both met their deaths. But what I saw before me far eclipsed that meager construction. There were tables along the walls, each covered with white linen and supplied with sparkling glass beakers, tubes, and funnels. There were chemicals of all sorts in glass jars, vials, and bottles. There were forceps, scales, graduated glass cylinders, pipettes, clamps, ring stands, burettes, volumetric and Erlenmeyer flasks as well as crucibles and mortars with pestles. It was clear that if this was where young Phillip Tremaine was spending his time, he was undoubtedly dabbling in his father's mad experiments.

On the far side of this large open room was a staircase spiraling up to a second floor loft space. Beneath the long arc of the stairs, I saw a desk scattered with books and papers. I crossed the room to examine them when the door opened behind me. "Dr. Watson? Is that you?" came the voice of young Phillip Tremaine. "What are you doing here? And how did you get in?" To my relief he sounded more curious than annoyed.

"I came looking for you, Phillip. Your uncle thought you might be here. The door was unlocked."

He looked at me somewhat with disbelief, but said nothing of it. Instead, he said, "Uncle Charles? How did he…" he hesitated and then laughed under his breath. "Never mind. I should know better by now than to think anything can long go unknown to Uncle Charles." His manner, though surprised and somewhat disturbed at my intrusion and his uncle's knowledge of where he'd been spending his time, didn't appear to me to be the least unfriendly. In fact, he crossed the room to shake my hand. "You'll have to excuse the mess. I've been too busy to clean up, I'm afraid." But I could see in his eyes there was something amiss.

"Well, I hope you'll excuse my barging in on you, Phillip, but I do so with the best of intentions."

"Lucie?"

"Yes, she's worried about you." I could see by his expression that something worried him as well.

"I know. This has all been so unfair to Lucie. She doesn't understand now, but in time she will, when I've..." His voice trailed off as he began straightening papers on the desk.

"When you've what, Phillip? What is it you're doing here? And how did you come to find this place?"

"Oh, I didn't find it. Alex did. He's been assisting me in my father's work. He's quite an extraordinary fellow. He was able to secure a lease and loaned me the money to outfit it with all this equipment."

"But what I don't understand, Phillip, is why you are continuing this...this work. A cure for a disease that is a figment of your late father's imagination—"

"You think my father was mad too, don't you?" There was sudden venom in his voice. "We'll prove you're wrong. My father will win back his reputation," he said without realizing how mad his words made him sound.

"Phillip, aren't you allowing your love for your father to cloud your judgment? You must realize that your Uncle Charles, Lucie, and yes, even I am only concerned for your well-being."

When I mentioned Lucie's name I could see the harsh look on his face soften for just an instant, but his voice took on an even more poisonous edge, "Yes, I know. My grandparents were only concerned for my well-being when they locked my mother away in an asylum and told me she was dead. And Uncle Charles was only concerned for my well-being when he told me my father was insane when he died. Everyone was more concerned with my well-being than they were in telling me the truth. Instead, they fed me with nothing but lies—all for my well-being."

"Phillip, I am afraid the truth is never as simple as we'd like and rarely pure. Your grandparents, God rest their souls, did the very best they could by you, I'm sure."

It was quite evident Phillip had conflicted feelings. The anger he'd shown just a moment before dissipated as he spoke of his grandparents, "Yes, yes…I don't blame them. And Uncle Charles, I'm sure, believed Mother was unbalanced and allowed his parents' will to…" He paused and turned aside. I could tell he was thinking of his mother alone in that asylum for all those years.

"Phillip, I know how difficult this is for you to only find out the truth so recently."

"No. It isn't the truth, only more lies." He said and began gathering together some of the loose papers on his desk. "My parents were not insane," he said in a voice so soft that I barely heard it. After a moment he'd composed himself and turned back toward me, an almost pleasant look on his face, "Thank you for coming to check on me, Doctor, but if you would be so kind as to excuse me, I have to get back to my experiments." As he walked me to the door, he said, "I believe you will find the ferry still at the landing. He generally takes a nap before returning to the city."

True to Phillip's word I found the ferry moored at the landing, the ferry captain asleep on the bridge and his deckhand, a disheveled and disreputable looking character, was examining the bicycle I'd discarded.

"This belong to you, Mister?" he said as I drew nearer.

"Why no, it isn't. I found it abandoned."

"Damned right it ain't yours. It's mine. I leaves it by the elevator for folks like you to ride, if you've a mind. But it ain't for free, you know. No sir, it ain't for free."

I had the distinct impression he was lying but if that was true, how did he know I'd found it by the lift? "I'm terribly sorry, how much do I owe you?" I said.

He looked me up and down as he took off his sweat-stained hat and scratched his head. "Two dollars," he said.

"Two dollars? I only rode the thing, I don't want to buy it," I said, my voice rising a bit at his cheek.

He cringed and hid his face in his hat, and then peeked above the brim. "Three cents, then," he said.

"That's more like it," I said and handed him three shiny copper pennies. "I say, will the ferry be returning to the city?"

The deckhand looked up at me with one squinty eye. Straightening his obviously arthritic back a bit as he pocketed his 'fare', he spat a brown spew of tobacco juice on the ground, splashing it up onto my shoe. "Always does," he said and cleared his throat with a phlegmatic noise that appeared to rack him with pain and ended in a coughing spasm.

"Yes, well, perhaps you could tell me the approximate time of its returning?"

Without looking up from his broom, he hooked one thumb over his shoulder and said, "When Cappy gits up, we go."

I looked up towards the wheelhouse and saw the ferry captain stirring. It appeared I'd arrived just in time.

It was late afternoon when the ferry pulled into the landing at East 79th Street. After paying the master, I debarked and hailed a cab to take to the home of Commissioner Strumm. I wanted to report to Miss Lucie about my meeting with her young man. As I was getting into the cab, the deckhand came sidling up to me and said, "Ain't you forgettin' something, Mister?" and held out his grubby hand, which was wrapped in a dirty handkerchief.

"What's that?" I asked.

"I usually gets paid for puttin' out the plank for passengers. Three cents a trip," he said, rubbing his grime encrusted fingers together.

"Oh very well," I said and counted out three more coppers from my purse. "A bit dear for my money."

"Oh well," he said tossing the coins in the air and snatching them with other hand, "'S my money, now, sir." And with that he walked back to the ferry whistling a tune I recognized as *Let Me Call*

You Sweetheart.

By the time I arrived at the Strumm home I'd come to the decision to soften my impression of young Phillip's emotional state to Lucie. I didn't want to worry the poor dear unduly. I knocked on the door sure that I could satisfactorily assuage her worst fears. My second knock was answered by Emily Strumm. "Good evening, Emily," I said. "Is Miss Lucie home?"

"Why, yes, Doctor, she is. Won't you come in? It's so nice to see you again."

"Thank you, I might have thought you'd be tired of seeing me by this time."

"Don't be silly, Doctor."

"At any rate, it's always a treat to see you, dear. Where's Mylo, still at work?"

"Yes, he's been working late ever since that 'ghost ship' arrived." she said as she ushered me into the parlor. I could tell something was troubling her and she must have seen the concern on my face, "You'll have to excuse me, Doctor, but I'm afraid I'm not feeling very cheery tonight."

"Oh, and what seems to be the trouble?"

"It's Ilsa, the girl I told you about, our housekeeper from Sweden?"

"Yes, I remember. The young thing with consumption. She hasn't gotten worse, has she?"

"I'm afraid so. She died last night, in her sleep. The undertaker took her away this morning. Lucie and I have been packing her things."

"I'm sorry to hear it. And with Julia's death so recent too. You've certainly had more than your share of sorrow of late."

"Yes, it's been a very difficult week for all of us."

"Pardon my curiosity, Emily, but is that the missing pendant you're wearing?"

"Yes," she said, touching it to her throat. "It is."

"At least that must bring you some cheer, then?"

"I wish that it did," she said with a bit of a frown. "Oh, I don't mean I'm not happy to have found it, but…well, we found it among Ilsa's things."

"Oh dear, you don't mean she stole it?"

"It appears so, Doctor. I never would have thought it of her."

"Thought what about who, Mother?" Miss Lucie walked into the room looking beautiful if somewhat sad.

"I was just telling Dr. Watson about finding my sister's pendant."

"Oh, that…it was quite a surprise. I mean, who would have thought Ilsa would do such a thing?" Miss Lucie said, a look of genuine surprise on her face.

Emily agreed, "That's just what I was telling the doctor. She seemed such an honest girl, humble and sweet."

"I suppose you can't be too careful these days," said Lucie.

"Well," said Emily, "Dr. Watson has come to talk to you, so I guess I'll just go see how supper is coming along."

After she'd left the room, Miss Lucie took my hand and guided me to the settee. "Have you seen Phillip?"

"Yes, yes, I've seen him. I took the train out to Blackwell's Island."

"Blackwell's Island? I don't understand."

"Young Phillip is working there. It seems your Mr. Hume has financed a laboratory for him."

"Alexander? I didn't think he had two nickels of his own to rub together, though I suppose he might trouble his parents for the money. And what is it that Phillip's working on—" Suddenly she gasped. "His father's work?"

"Yes, I'm afraid so."

"Couldn't you talk some sense into him?"

"Miss Lucie, I'm afraid he's not willing to listen when it comes to his father, nor his mother. But I must say, on any other topic he seemed perfectly reasonable. I wouldn't worry too terribly much. As soon as he gets this out of his system, I'm certain he'll be his old self again."

"Oh, Doctor, I hope you're right."

"It might help if perhaps you could persuade him not to associate quite so much with Mr. Hume. He apparently has had a deleterious effect on your fiancée."

"Alexander? I don't believe it. He's been nothing but kind and helpful to Phillip as well as to Mother and me. He came to see us just last night to let us know Phillip is all right."

"I'm afraid Phillip's uncle doesn't agree with you. He says Hume has been encouraging Phillip's investigations of his father's notes and records of experiments."

"I don't believe that. He's been as worried as I about Phillip. We speak of it often."

"You've been seeing Mr. Hume, then?"

"Well...he's come to dinner a few times and he visits us when he can. I even think he's been talking to Mother about Phillip when I'm not here, explaining that we've nothing to worry about."

"I see. Well, perhaps Mr. Cabot has gotten it a bit wrong. Parents and their surrogates often tend toward over-protectiveness of those they love most."

"Yes, I know very well about that."

I began to rise. "Well, I'd best be going."

"Won't you stay and have lunch with us? You haven't told me how Mr. Holmes is. It must have been awful being lost underground all that time. I would have been terrified."

"No, I'm afraid I couldn't impose. And as far as Mr. Holmes is concerned, he's very well. He doesn't terrify easily. Speaking of him, I want to be back at our hotel when he arises from his nap. I'm sure he'll want my assistance with his investigations and I've a thing or two to attend before I can return, so if you will excuse me, I'll be on my way."

"All right, then," she said as we walked to the door, "but I'm sure Mother will want to say good-bye before you go. Wait here and I'll get her."

I did as she requested and in just a few minutes Emily met me at the door. "Doctor, Lucie tells me you don't care for my cooking."

"What? Not a bit, I assure you. But as I told Miss Lucie, Mr. Holmes will be wanting my assistance I've no doubt."

"I'm happy to hear he is all right. I was so worried when Mylo told me he'd gotten trapped in the ventilation tunnels."

"Yes, I too am relieved."

My face must have betrayed my thoughts for she asked, "What is it, Doctor? Is something troubling you?"

"What? Oh, it's nothing," I said.

"Come, come, you aren't the only one that can read a worried expression. What are you thinking?"

I laughed. "I was just thinking about Mr. Cabot and his apparent distrust of Mr. Hume."

"Charles is uneasy about Alex? I find that hard to believe. Alex has been so very helpful here. He comes by nearly every evening to check on Lucie and me, you know."

"So I've heard. What does Mylo think about him?"

"What could he think? If it weren't for Alex, heaven knows what might have become of our Lucie."

"Yes, I suppose you're quite right. I'm sure Charles is most likely only being a bit over-protective where his young charge is concerned."

"I'm afraid Phillip isn't his charge any longer. He's a man of his own accounting now. Perhaps Charles is just finding it a bit hard to let go."

"Perhaps you're right. I suppose it's only natural after caring for a child all those years."

Emily laughed. "You may depend on it, Doctor. I too am concerned about young Phillip. But I don't believe Alex would allow any harm to befall him—or anyone."

"Spoken like a true mother," said I, to which we both laughed and I took my leave of the Strumm household.

I had yet another visit to make before returning to the hotel. Since it was only just past noon, I was certain it would be a few hours before Holmes would be stirring and I thought this would be a good time to meet Mrs. Ernie Jenkins. I hailed a passing hansom to take me to Police Headquarters.

I'd learned from Abel that Ernie's wife, Matilda, worked as secretary in the Records Division of the police department in the same building as the Commissioner's office. I intended to introduce myself as a friend of Ernie's and thereby make her acquaintance and perhaps get a glimpse of her personality. I knew from speaking with Commissioner Strumm the Records Division was in the rear of the headquarters building, in the basement, and upon entering I made my way down a long corridor past the briefing rooms and the downstairs lockup. The main hallway ended upon a smaller corridor that crossed it like "T" at the back of the building. At opposite ends of this corridor, there were two narrow stairways leading down to where the records were maintained, one was labeled 'UP' and the other 'DOWN'. I noticed a young woman near the top of the 'UP' stairs carrying a box of papers stacked so high I could only see her eyes and realized the segregation of traffic was a wise strategy.

I descended the proper stairway down into a cavernous room filled almost to capacity with desks, secretaries and filing cabinets. Dozens of men and women walked this way and that with their arms full of file folders and reams of paper, stacking, filing and transferring them from desk to desk. How anything came to be fashioned into any semblance of organization was certainly beyond me, but the good people of the records division appeared not to be perplexed at all.

I stopped at the first desk, where the occupant was affixing labels to some of the piles upon her desk. "Pardon me, Miss, but could you tell me if there is a young woman by the name of Matilda Jenkins who works here?"

At first I wasn't sure she heard me for her head bobbed this way and that without looking up at me as if she'd lost something and was trying to discover where it had gotten to. Just as I was about to repeat my request, she said, "There she goes just up the stairs, there, that's Matilda." And without ever looking directly at me this denizen of the department of records resumed her labeling without uttering another word.

I turned in time to see a slight young woman ascending the proper stairs and hurriedly made my way in that direction in hope of catching her before she disappeared. When I reached the top of the stairs, I saw her pulling on a hat, the kind that ties beneath a woman's chin, and hurry out the door, a cloth woman's handbag hanging limp to her side and her eyes darting down the hallway as if to be sure she was unobserved. I made up my mind to follow her without her knowing to see what I might discover about her daily routine.

Once out in the street, I quickly saw in which way she'd started and I surreptitiously followed, maintaining a discrete distance. She'd gone no more than a block and a half before she stopped, looked nervously up and down the street and then entered a shabby little establishment that specialized in the sale of tobacco and spirits. Her manner before entering appeared to me to be one of someone not wishing to be seen entering such a place and so I walked by, not stopping until I had passed the door of the shop. I waited at the corner, buying a penny-paper from the boy there and stood reading it, or appearing to read it, until she came out again.

When Mrs. Jenkins exited the store, the bag she had been

carrying was noticeably heavier as it weighed down on her considerably. I deduced she must have purchased a quantity of spirits, which made me very curious. I followed her back down the street and to the rear of the Headquarters building. She entered by way of a different door from whence she departed. This entrance was at the corner of the building and appeared to be a service entrance leading to stairway that allowed access either to the first floor or to the basement. I arrived in time to see her skirts ascending to the first floor and decided that I needed to follow no further. Instead, I retraced my steps with the intention of speaking with the proprietor of the *Cigars and Fine Spirits* establishment to find out what I might.

I entered the shop as though I were familiar with the area, walking up to the counter, "Pardon me, my good man, I'm interested in a box of hand-rolled *Las Morenas* cigars. A friend of mine, Ernie Jenkins, said I might find them in your shop."

The hulking man with the thick black mustache behind the counter looked at me suspiciously and said, "I don't know no Ernie Jenkins and I ain't got no lamurenas cigars no how."

"Oh dear," I said looking about, "I'm sure he said this was the shop. In fact, I just saw his wife, Matilda, leaving a few minutes before I came in. Surely she was buying Ernie his *Las Morenas*."

"Ain't been no Matilda buying no cigars for no Ernie in this store, Mister," he said in a most ungracious manner while he chewed the stub of a clay pipe between his yellow teeth.

"You're surely mistaken. I saw her leaving here not ten minutes ago. She appeared to be laden down with the weight of cigars in her bag."

"You the one's mistaken Mister. That weren't your friend's wife. That was Tillie. She comes in here twice a week buying bourbon for her husband."

"Twice a week, you say? For her husband? Bourbon?"

"That's what I said."

"I'm sorry, then, I must be mistaken. I'm terribly sorry to have bothered you," I said and turned to leave.

"You mean you ain't buying nothing?"

"I'm afraid not, sir, I only smoke *Las Morenas*," I said and left the store, wondering to myself how I was going to break the news to Ernie and Abel. It was only too obvious that Ernie's worst fears were true, his wife was having an affair—one fueled by alcohol. Poor Ernie. I would have to think about this for a time and decide how best to break the news.

I caught a cab in front of the shop and as it was getting on toward evening now, I was anxious to get back to the hotel, lest Holmes awaken and be gone without me. He'd told me precious little of his adventures in the ducting and I was sure there was more than he was letting on. Perhaps I could get his advice on this matter before broaching the topic with the Jenkins cousins.

Chapter 15
A fateful call...

It was not yet dark by the time I arrived back at the Gilsey. I managed to avoid speaking to Abel Jenkins by going straight to the lift without looking in his direction. I knew that sooner or later I would have to tell him and his brother Ernie about what I'd discovered regarding Ernie's wife, Matilda. But I felt I owed it to Ernie to discuss it with him first. At any rate, I didn't feel this was the right time and decided the best course would be to avoid speaking to Abel entirely.

I found Holmes still asleep, although it was quite apparent by the thick atmosphere and pungent aroma of his pipe that he'd at least stirred long enough for several bowls of shag. Strewn about the room was a collection of maps and literature on the underground system and its construction schedule. Lying open on the desk was Holmes' manuscript of Stoker's work, *Dracula*. I read a few pages, paying a keen interest to the notes written in the margins. But when I read a note ascribing the ways in which one may become a vampire, drinking the blood of another vampire being chief among them, I had to put the book down and wonder to myself how anyone of Holmes' intelligence could lend any credence to such drivel. I closed the book and with a troubled mind went to bed and fell asleep.

Early the following morning I was awakened by Holmes as he threw aside the curtains allowing the sun to shine directly onto my sleepy face. "Come Watson, the day is wasting away and I am famished. Let's see what delights the Gilsey chef has prepared for breakfast, shall we?"

I made my morning toilet and soon after found Holmes reading the daily paper in the overstuffed chair beside the window. "Ah, freshly shaved and ready for a new day, eh Watson? Come, let's go down and have our morning repast," he said pulling his pipe from his pocket and tamping into it a generous bowl of shag.

We got into the lift and on the way down I asked if he would like to visit the Tremaine home today and read for himself the journal Charles Cabot had promised to make available to us. When I received no response other than a shrug and a grunt, I suggested that perhaps instead he might like to take a trip out to Blackwell's Island. He lighted his pipe, obviously considering his words before answering, "As I told you before, I'm not certain anything of any use can be gleaned from a journal written over twenty years ago. And as far as young Tremaine's current endeavors, recreating his father's experiments, they appear to me to be a fool's errand, don't you think?"

"Well, I…" I said, astonished that neither of these things seemed to interest Holmes in the least. "Very well then, what do you think we should do?"

"I plan to continue my investigation of the tunnels."

"I would have thought you'd have had quite enough of those after your recent experience."

"On the contrary, it is due to my experience that I find them most fascinating." Not knowing quite how to respond to Holmes' inexplicable behavior, I stood silently as the lift made its way to the main level and the doors opened.

As we crossed the lobby on the way to the dining room, Abel Jenkins came around the end of the desk, waving his hand in the air. "Mr. Holmes…Mr. Holmes."

We stopped under the crystal chandelier and waited for Abel

to meet us, "Yes, Abel," said Holmes. "Have you another message for me?"

"No, Mr. Holmes, a telephone call. You can take it at one of the lobby booths, sir." Jenkins indicated one of four curtained booths that had been installed for the convenience and privacy of the guests to make and receive telephone calls, two on either side of the bank of lifts.

"Excellent. Perhaps one of my inquiries has borne fruit." Turning to me he said, "Why don't you go on ahead and secure our table. I shall be only a moment."

I proceeded into the dining room and since our usual table was occupied, I selected one on the opposite side of the entry, where I had a clear line of vision to the phone bank. I ordered two coffees and awaited Holmes. In just a few minutes, I saw his unmistakable tall, lean form come out of the booth and with a determined step come straight on to our table, a very satisfied smile on his face.

"I trust the call was important and expected?"

"On the contrary, it was quite unexpected, though crucial I'd say."

"Come, come, out with it. You look like the cat that got the cream with that smile on your face. Who was on the phone and what did they want with you?"

"The man on the phone called to warn me that Miss Lucie Strumm is in very grave danger."

"Good heavens. What does this mean? Who was he?"

"It was our old friend, Baron Antonio Barlucci."

I was shocked as much by Holmes' apparent cavalier attitude as by the news, as distressing as it was. "Holmes, this is no time to joke. Who was it? Did he actually say he was Barlucci?"

"He didn't give his name, but I tell you, Watson, it was Barlucci. I would recognize his voice anywhere. It was exactly as I remember it, except for the accent."

"What was different about the accent?"

"That's just it. He didn't have one, or at least not an Italian accent."

"Really, Holmes, if there was no accent how can you be sure it was Barlucci."

"Oh, there was an accent all right. But it wasn't Italian, exactly. It was more of a mix of East European with a slight Italian undertone. It was this that prompted me to listen more closely to the timbre and tonal quality of the voice itself."

"Then again I ask, how can you be sure it was Barlucci?"

"Perhaps you remember the monograph I wrote some years ago on the perception of sound. In it I posited there are six qualities of sound perception: volume, phase, direction, distance, pitch and timbre."

"Yes, yes, it was during the Gustafson murder case. You proved the sound of Gustafson's voice heard by the only witness to the crime had been generated in the basement and not in the locked room where Lord Balmert had been found shot."

"That's correct. Ventilation ducting played a crucial role in that case as well," he said with a smile. "Since that time, in my retirement, I have been doing sound experimentation with some sophisticated recording devices and have discovered that regardless how one tries to change the sound of their voice, there are certain qualities of timbre and pitch that remain, qualities the trained ear can detect through the disguised voice."

"Holmes, that's all very well, but it's been over twenty years since you were held prisoner by Barlucci."

"No, actually it's been less than 48 hours since I last spoke to Barlucci."

"What's that? What are you saying, Holmes?"

"Only that I had a most interesting chat with the baron while I was in the 'catacombs' of the underground system. I didn't tell you about it immediately because I didn't wish to distress you. I knew if I did tell you, you would look at me just as you are looking at me now."

I flushed involuntarily as I realized he was right. I was looking at him as if he were mad. I couldn't help myself. It was all just too fantastic.

"That's all right, Watson. If 'twere I in your shoes, I might think much the same of you. But I assure you upon my honor the conversation I am about to relate really occurred."

I was more than a little embarrassed that my great good friend felt the compunction to swear upon his honor—something I'd never heard him do before, so unnecessary it had always been. And yet, in this particular case his act of swearing an oath seemed just a bit justified in my mind. The fact that it did was not lost on me, for it showed the immense confidence I'd always had in Holmes' judgment had somehow eroded. I made, however, a valiant effort to conceal it from my friend. "Tut, tut, your honor is always understood with me," I said as I touched his arm. "Please, tell me all that occurred while you were…while you were absent."

"Very well. As you recall the ventilation damper slammed closed just after I'd entered the shaft. We, of course, thought this to be a reaction to the detection of gas in the tunnels. As it turned out, this was hardly the case. The sensor wasn't connected."

"Yes, I found that out. The foreman coming on duty told me as much."

"Good. My story, then, is somewhat corroborated thus far."

His need to say as much was poison to my heart as well as my ears. "Go on," I said, in an effort to get us past this uncomfortable pause.

"After our agreement to part and find our own ways out of danger, I immediately turned to make my way down the shaft to where I knew the first connection lie. I cursed my own stupidity in handing you both the lantern and my matchbox. The shaft was absolutely pitch.

I wanted desperately to investigate that shelf I'd spoken to you about."

"Yes, the nest."

"Exactly. But, without so much as a glimmer of light in the shaft, I pushed onward, to the connector leading toward the station where you were headed at that instant. But before I had gone thirty feet in that direction I was aware I was not alone. I felt a presence in the shaft, a familiar presence, a presence I'd not felt for a very long time."

"A presence, you say? You mean...?"

"Yes, Barlucci."

"What do you mean you felt his presence?"

"I knew he was there...I felt it, although it's difficult to explain exactly how I felt it. It was the same presence I felt when I was his guest in Darthmore Hall."

"I see," said I with an effort to keep the incredulity from my voice.

"I'd been in total darkness then as well, you remember."

"I do," I said simply.

"At first I made no effort to discover him. I neither spoke nor moved to touch him. Instead, I continued toward the connecting staff, believing the only inference he could make that I'd noticed his presence would have been from the slightly retarded progress I made and I was sure that would have been imperceptible from the caution one takes when one is moving about in total darkness. But that was apparently enough. He spoke to me, 'So, you know I'm here, even though you cannot see me. You always were a most remarkable man, Mr. Holmes.' His voice was exactly as I remembered it, though it didn't have the edge to it that it had on our last encounter.

" 'Baron,' I said. 'It's been a long time. Where have you been keeping yourself?'

" 'Surely you have deduced that, Mr. Holmes.'

" 'Let me see if I can reconstruct what has occurred since last we spoke,' I said as I tried to pinpoint from where in the darkness his voice emanated. 'You left me at Darthmore under the care of Garrett, with orders to murder me.'

" 'A precaution as regrettable as it was necessary at the time. But I told Garrett only to kill you should your friends approach before I'd had time to make good my escape, I assure you. I had no wish to end your life. That would have been, as I've said, regrettable?'

" 'Also regrettable was your final assault on Whitechapel, a Miss Kelly, if memory serves.'

" 'I'm afraid I didn't know her name, and yes, it was regrettable and unnecessary except for your meddling.' His tone was scolding but not shrill.

" 'Ah yes, you mentioned that at the time. Pray tell me again how it was laid on my head?'

" 'That is, in part, what I wish to discuss with you this evening, Mr. Holmes.'

" 'Then our meeting tonight was not merely a happy coincidence, I take it.'

" 'Obviously not.'

" 'You have me, once again, at your disposal, Baron. Please go on.'

" 'In due time, Mr. Holmes, in due time. At the moment I'm curious to hear your narrative of deduction on the events since that night.'

" 'Very well. As I said, you took your final victim in Whitechapel, leaving this calling card,' I said, taking a handkerchief from the inner pocket of my jacket. It was the very handkerchief he left draped over the slash in Mary Kelly's throat the night he butchered her. I brought it along on our trip for just such a moment as this.

" 'Ah, then you did find it. I was afraid the local constabulary would have discarded it before you arrived, if Garrett had indeed not deemed it necessary to dispose of you.' "

I interrupted, "You mean to say he could see the handkerchief? I thought you were in total darkness."

"Yes, apparently Barlucci has a keen sense of sight even in near total darkness, not unlike the bat, which many mistakenly believe are blind."

"I see, please go on. What did you say about his man Garrett and his apparent regret at aiding him?"

"When he mentioned his order to Garrett concerning 'disposing' of me as he termed it, I said, 'I'm afraid you overestimated Garrett's loyalty, that or else you underestimated his character. He hanged himself rather than do your last bidding.'

" 'You will find this difficult to believe, I'm sure, but I am very glad of it.'

" 'As am I, which I'm sure you'll find no difficulty believing. At any rate, you took your latest victim in a most savage fashion, and afterwards either met, seduced, or kidnapped Miss Abigail Drake and made for your ship, the *Animus Lacuna*.'

" 'Miss Drake and I were very much in love.'

" 'How touching, and you flew to her with Mary Kelly's blood still on your hands. Tell me, Baron, was the savagery you showed in the murder of Miss Kelly all for my benefit, or do you derive some sadistic pleasure from such a grotesque display?'

"It was at this moment that you and the workmen must have arrived at the vent damper for I felt a cloak thrown over me and my arms were strapped to my sides by what I thought at the time must have been steel bands. Barlucci whispered in my ear, 'If you value your life and that of your friend, you will be absolutely silent.' I could hear, then, the attempts you were making to open the damper, and then I was carried further into the shafting. I didn't know how far, but I could tell I was being carried along at a swift pace. The sounds of my imminent rescue faded swiftly until they were gone. When I was released, I was again in complete darkness, I guessed in some remote bypass of the ventilation system. Barlucci resumed, 'You ask if I derive pleasure from what to you is senseless savagery? I assure you I do not. What you believe to be a savage display, as you put it, was the result of a combination of deprivation and the resultant intoxication that is inevitable when that deprivation has ceased.'

" 'You'll forgive me if I find that a bit hard to believe, won't you?'

" 'Sadly, yes. Please, continue your narrative.'

" 'So, you escaped the official police by leaving on the morning tide before your handiwork had been discovered. Then, no word was heard of you for a fortnight. In the meantime, we'd dispatched Inspector Walter Andrews in hopes he might intercept you in New York, if indeed that was where you were going.'

" 'How did you determine my destination, if I might ask?'

" 'Garrett. He left a note, as best he could. Had we found it sooner, we might have apprehended you. As I said, a fortnight went by before we received word that your ship might have met with disaster. Here I had to rely on conjecture and never decided on whether this was a natural disaster or one in which you played a key role.'

" 'I assure you, it was a natural catastrophe. We were caught up in a storm which took us far north of our course and into that of an iceberg.'

" 'I see, then it follows that something occurred to prevent your departure with Miss Drake, leaving her to the elements.'

" 'I'm afraid she would not have lived either way. We had taken precautions, however, to enable her survival.'

" 'Curiosity compels me, Baron. How can you say on the one hand she would not have lived and on the other that 'precautions' were taken to ensure her survival?'

" 'It was necessary that Abigail become Undead, temporarily, in order to survive the elements.' "

Again I interrupted, "Undead? Then you're saying he still

insists he is a vampire?"

"Exactly what I asked him, 'Temporarily? Undead? Are you saying that Miss Drake became a vampire also?'

" 'Yes, it was necessary just until we could get to New York and Tremaine could cure us both.'

" 'But then things went awry and you were somehow separated from Miss Drake? How unfortunate for her.'

" 'True, but she did, after all, survive the ordeal.'

" 'Ah, but survival at what cost? If I were to suspend my disbelief for just a moment, then it would seem she became a beast of prey not unlike yourself, one that left in her wake the bodies of more than a few innocent and good men.' It was at this point I noted...I felt something in the baron's manner change. I thought that perhaps I'd hit upon some point that affected him in an unforeseen way.

" 'Abigail,' he said in almost a whisper. 'What did I do to you...?' He fell silent and for a moment I thought perhaps he'd gone. But then he spoke again, his voice taking on its former confidence, 'She wasn't prepared for her life as one of the Undead.'

" 'Exactly how does one prepare to become a vampire, Baron?' I asked.

" 'You scoff, Mr. Holmes, and why shouldn't you. You think of me as evil incarnate, is that not correct?'

" 'Evil is as evil does, Baron.'

"I heard a muffled laugh escape him. 'Were it only that simple. Tell me something, Mr. Holmes.'

" 'If I can.'

" 'Is a lion in the jungle evil? Even if he hunts and kills the gazelle?' I didn't answer; he went on, 'Or when a falcon snatches a partridge off the moors, is it evil? Or is it only acting as its breeding commands, as its nature demands?'

" 'You can hardly compare yourself to a hawk or a lion, Baron. You're a man, and men in order to live in a civil society must accept the responsibility of their actions. You repeat yourself. We've gone over this ground before.'

" 'Yes, I remember. You called me mad then. Do you still believe I am mad, Mr. Holmes?'

" 'That remains to be seen, Baron.'

" 'When you speak of civil society you are assuming that we are all equal within that society, but equality can only go so far, don't you agree? By that I mean surely a man of your intellect can hardly believe himself to be the equal of a common laborer or tradesman, even a very clever one.'

" 'I shall grant you that in intellect one man can certainly be superior to another, but that instance of superiority does not imbue the one with rights exceeding those of the other. As one of the founders of this very nation stated, all men are endowed by their creator with certain rights which are unalienable, life being chief among them. The man with a superior intellect therefore does not have the right of life and death over his intellectual inferior.'

" 'Spoken like a true egalitarian, Holmes. But these 'natural' rights of Jefferson cannot supplant natural law, or the laws of nature. If it should, then we humans would not have the right to deprive even the lowliest of creatures its own life, and yet we slaughter all manner of animal to feed ourselves with rarely a thought. We are only indulging our nature as omnivores, are we not?'

" 'What of it?'

" 'What of it indeed. Man is superior to the beasts, just as one beast is superior to another, such as the lion and the gazelle, the hawk and the hare. I submit to you, Mr. Holmes, that nature's imperative is adapt or perish. When one species is the prey of another, which is at fault?'

" 'Man's ability to rise above his nature is what marks him as superior to the animal kingdom.'

" 'And yet man is the only animal who wages war, Mr.

155

Holmes. I argue that the laws of man are suitable only to men. I ceased to be a man long ago and had to discover my own way from that time to this, to adapt in order to survive.'

" 'That is thin reasoning, Baron. Your claim that man's laws no longer apply to you is based on what? That you must kill in order to survive?'

" 'Do you believe I enjoy the taking of human life? I assure you I do not. I find it repugnant just as I find the drinking of human blood abhorrent and debasing in the extreme.'

" 'And yet you kill and murder and mutilate.' At this he grew silent once again. I waited. Finally, I asked, 'Have you nothing more to say, Baron?'

" 'I had hoped that you of all men might be able to understand. That you, a man of intellect, a man of science, when given the facts would have the capacity to see past your own prejudices and understand there are things beyond the reach of current scientific understanding. I had hoped you could appreciate the possibility of a disease that could make a rational man behave in ways that would seem to be irrational, but when informed by a greater knowledge would be revealed to be merely fulfilling his nature, as abhorrent as that nature might be to you as well as to me. Science, Mr. Holmes, is the movement from darkness into the light, the antidote to superstition and ignorance. I am not a deliberate murderer. I suffer from a disease that makes me appear to be a maniacal monster. I tried to explain to you once before that I am as much a victim as those whose lives I've taken.'

" 'I remember, but I doubt your victims would agree. It makes no more sense now than it did then. It assumes there is some credence to your claim of being a vampire.'

"He then said something that gave me pause, 'Mr. Holmes, do you have any experience with addiction? What I mean by that is, are you at all aware of the lengths to which an addicted person will go to satiate that need?'

"I of course knew very well the grip of addiction, as I know you can attest, although as a true friend you've made only the most circumspect mention in recording our little adventures. I replied, 'I'm somewhat familiar, yes.'

" 'I want you to recall, if you will, the worst case of drug addiction you can evoke and then double it, double it again, and again, and again, and yet again. This can only scratch the surface of my affliction.'

" 'Go on,' I said.

" 'You see, I've come to understand that vampirism, among its other manifestations, is an addiction, an addiction so strong that when the need reveals itself no human will can resist it. It is combined and intertwined with an equally strong will to survive such that even if the intellect is abhorred by the action to satisfy that addiction, the need wells up inside like another being taking over the body, making the need to ingest blood, human blood, the overriding and all-consuming motive, a compulsion so strong that the addict—the vampire—will do whatever it takes to sate his need. Abstinence only inflames the fever of the addiction, as you witnessed during our last encounter.'

" 'So Mary Kelly was…"

" '…was the manifestation of the beast within me and its rage at being held at bay for so long.'

" 'Held at bay?"

" 'Yes, Dr. Tremaine had devised a serum that was, day by day, allaying my symptoms.'

" 'Are you saying the serum worked?'

" 'Of course. Dr. Tremaine was quite brilliant…is quite brilliant. It was the first time in over six hundred years that I felt hopeful of being free again. And on that night when we first met, Mr. Holmes, you seized upon a case from my bookshelf, a case that contained the serum that had arrested the symptoms of my peculiar disorder.'

'Ah yes, vampirism.'

'That's correct, vampirism. I see you can speak of it now without the derision in your voice I heard on the night of our last encounter, though you still do not truly believe. Can you imagine my furor when you destroyed the vials he'd left to sustain me until I could meet him in New York?' This time it was I who was silent. 'Ah, that's right, you are not yet convinced of the existence of vampirism.'

"I could see that this back-and-forth banter was leading somewhere, though I wasn't quite certain of his aim. 'Come now, Baron, you didn't trap me here to have yet another debate on fictitious diseases. What is your purpose?'

" 'My purpose? My purpose, Mr. Holmes is to demonstrate that you have nothing to fear from me. My purpose is to convince you that once I am cured of my affliction, which can only be a matter of time, I will no longer have a need of human blood. My ultimate purpose of course is as it has ever been, to rid myself of the yoke of oppression under which I've labored these past six centuries.'

" 'A pretty speech, Baron, but a leopard doesn't change its spots. Even a leopard who claims to be a vampire.'

"I could hear him release a long sigh, and then I was again trapped, this time without the cloak. From behind he grasped me in such a fashion that I was unable to move my arms. I'd never felt strength such as his before. I realized those weren't steel bands I felt before, but only his arms. He again whispered in my ear, 'You are the only man alive I have reason to fear, Sherlock Holmes. Were I the beast you believe me to be, I would dispose of you with no more thought than flicking off a fly.'

"I struggled to get free but it was no use. His embrace was like a steel vice. 'Is that your intent? To rid yourself of me once and for all?'

" 'Not at all, Mr. Holmes.' And as suddenly as he had seized me, he released me. I turned to grasp him but he had moved out of my reach without making a sound. 'You cannot win, Mr. Holmes. I have ten times your physical prowess, which includes the ability to see in total darkness. Now, how can I convince you of my condition?' I quite thought for a moment he was offering to drink my blood.

" 'If you will permit me,' I offered, 'I have done some little research in the area of vampirism.'

" 'Mr. Holmes, you never cease to amaze, but I'm afraid there is more misinformation concerning my condition than there is information. What texts did you consult?'

" 'The *De Graecorum hodie quirundam opinationibus* to name one,' I said.

" 'Allatius the Greek, I'm impressed. But I'm afraid that work is rife with inaccuracies.'

" 'Yes, so I've been told.'

" 'Told? Told by whom? Whoever it is appears to be better informed than most.'

" 'He should be, he was informed by you personally. I've consulted with Abraham Stoker.'

" 'Ah,' he said with evident appreciation, 'the writer. Very good, Mr. Holmes, very good indeed. So, with what you've learned from Mr. Stoker, what do you propose?'

" 'I don't suppose you'd have a stake close at hand, would you?'

" 'Mr. Holmes, you are a caution. Even under these conditions you jest. No, I don't believe we're quite ready for that at the moment.'

" 'Pity. In that case, perhaps you'd allow me to take your pulse.'

" 'You have been doing your homework. You shall find a pulse a difficult quarry. Yes, excellent.'

"I could hear the sound of him rolling up his sleeve. He came

159

forward and gripped my right forearm, more gently than before, but I could feel the steely hardness of his fingers. He guided my hand to his naked wrist. It was chillingly cold to the touch. I searched in vain. First one wrist, then the other, and then his throat. All the while he chuckled. As I probed I thought about the throats of the women in Whitechapel he'd slashed and wondered if he ever gave them any consideration. He must have sensed my thoughts for he answered my unspoken question.

" 'Were it possible for me to exist without taking a human life, I swear to you, Mr. Holmes, I would have done so, or were it possible for me to end my own misery and thus foreswear this abhorrent curse I would do that as well.'

"I took advantage of his distracted attention and seized from the inner pocket of my jacket a set of handcuffs and applied them to both his wrists before he realized what was happening.

"I could hear the clang of steel echoing in the dark ventilation shaft as he spread his hands to the full length of the chain separating the manacles. 'You disappoint me, Mr. Holmes,' he said, and he handed me back the empty and twisted manacles. 'Did you really think you could capture me with this children's toy? Perhaps now you will believe.'

"As you can imagine, I was dumbfounded. I tested the steel of the manacles and could not get them to budge. 'You make a very convincing argument, Baron. And what is it you wish me to do with my newfound knowledge of your condition.'

" 'Simply to allow me to be, Mr. Holmes. I've set into motion a series of events that will at long last result in my cure. I ask only that you do nothing to interfere.' And then he simply disappeared."

I sat stunned for some seconds. "What do you suppose he meant by that?" I asked at last. "Do you suppose he has somehow discovered young Dr. Tremaine has taken up his father's mad experiments?"

"I suspect that somehow he may have influenced young

160

Phillip, and he is now engaged in creating a cure for the baron, either wittingly or unwittingly. And I'm convinced that was Barlucci on the phone just now."

"But if it was Barlucci, why would he warn you about danger to Miss Lucie."

"I don't know. We must be on our guard. Barlucci has the cunning of a predatory animal. He may be trying to lead us off the scent. Perhaps we've gotten too close and he hopes this will divert us. And yet, we cannot take his warning too lightly, lest the danger to Miss Lucie be real."

"What shall we do?"

"First, we shall eat. Then we shall visit Miss Lucie and ask her if she has noticed anything unusual lately."

\#

When we arrived at the Strumm home, Lucie and her mother were preparing for the upcoming funeral services for Julia Tremaine. Since the death of Mrs. Charles Cabot, Sr., there were no women to handle the delicate arrangements for a funeral and so Emily and Lucie took it upon themselves to step in and help Phillip and his Uncle Charles in their time of sorrow. The funeral was scheduled for the following day in the late afternoon and the Strumms were hosting a gathering for the family thereafter. It wasn't expected to be a large affair under the circumstances, but Emily and Lucie wanted everything to be just so, as women are wont to do.

We discretely asked Lucie if we could speak to her in the garden, as we didn't want to cause her mother any undue concern. She made some pretense of showing Holmes a new species of rose she and her mother had been nurturing.

Once in the garden, Holmes turned to Lucie and very gently said, "Watson and I would like to know if you've noticed anything unusual of late."

"I don't understand, Mr. Holmes. What do you mean,

unusual? Of course there's this business with Phillip, I would call that unusual."

"No, what I mean is, have you noticed anyone, a stranger perhaps, asking you questions, or following you, anything along those lines?"

Lucie started and took a step backwards, "Following me? Oh dear, why do you ask? Is there…"

Holmes took her arm to steady her as she appeared near swooning. "Please, Miss Lucie, it may be nothing at all, but I received a communication this morning that you may be in some danger." He led her to a garden bench where they both sat down.

"What kind of danger, Mr. Holmes? From Phillip?"

Her reaction stunned me and I could tell by the expression on Holmes' nearly expressionless face that he too was somewhat surprised by her question.

"No, I don't believe the danger is from Phillip. What made you think of him?"

"Well, he's been so queer lately, and distant, and he's mixed up in his father's mad experiments. And from what Alex said last night…" The words escaped her lips before she could harness them.

"And what has Mr. Hume told you?"

I could see a sudden cooling in her temperament, as if Holmes had tread on some forbidden turf. "Only that Phillip is consumed by his work," she said with an air of caution.

"Is that all Mr. Hume said?"

Suddenly she turned and looked Holmes straight in the eye. "No. He said he thought that perhaps Phillip had been working too hard, taking this nonsense about his father's work too seriously."

"How did he mean that? I had thought he encouraged Phillip, that he in fact had supplied him with the means to carry on these experiments."

Her mood softened a bit. "Yes, that's true, but it was only to get it out of Phillip's system. Alex thought if he pretended to help that soon Phillip would see for himself how mad it all was."

I'd been standing quietly by until now, but could not help but interject, "He certainly went to a great deal of expense in that regard."

"What does money matter to Alex? He's quite wealthy, you know."

"I'm afraid I didn't know. I thought he was a musician. I can't imagine the pay is all that substantial. The last time we spoke you yourself said you didn't think Alex had two sixpence to rub together."

"Come now, Watson. I think Miss Lucie means that Mr. Hume comes from money, isn't that right?"

"Why yes, I suppose it's his parents who are the wealthy ones. I must say when Phillip and I first met him, he didn't appear to us to be more than an itinerant musician."

"I see," said Holmes. "And when did you discover he was more than a musician."

"Well, I don't know. I suppose it was when he brought Phillip and me to his parents' home for a late supper. They're vacationing in Europe for the summer."

"And when was this?"

"A few days before you arrived in New York, I believe. Yes, it was the Friday before Papa said you were to arrive. I remember because Ilsa had just taken ill, poor thing."

"Where, exactly, does Mr. Hume live?"

"I don't know."

"But you had supper at his home. Surely you must remember where it is."

"I'm afraid I don't. You see, Alex said that as a consequence of his parents' wealth, he needed to keep the exact whereabouts of where they lived a secret. So, when he came for Phillip and me in a coach, he drew the curtains and made us promise not to peek."

"Didn't you find that a bit odd?"

"Never mind that," I said, "didn't your curiosity get the better of you? I don't think I could have resisted peeking myself."

Miss Lucie laughed. "You are quite right, Doctor, I was terribly curious and lifted the curtain once we were on our way."

"And what did you see?" said Holmes.

"Why nothing. Alex had shuttered the windows on the outside as well as having curtains inside. I was quite frustrated by the time we arrived."

"Most interesting. I assume you were returned home in like manner?"

"Yes, that's right."

"I see. Well, I'm sure we've taken up enough of your time, Miss Lucie," said Holmes standing. "Come, Watson. I think it's time I visited young Dr. Tremaine's laboratory."

Chapter 16
Surprising encouragement...

After we said our good-byes to Emily Strumm, Holmes and I took a cab to the 79th Street ferry landing. "Unusual fellow this Hume, wouldn't you say, Watson?" said Holmes as we cantered by the underground digs near 53rd Street.

"Quite unusual," I agreed and then thought about it and added, "in what way?"

"Well, at first he appears to be nothing more than a poor musician who happens by at just the right moment to come to the aid of our two young lovers, Phillip and Miss Lucie, and in the span of just a couple of weeks, he has all the appearances of being Phillip's benefactor in the pursuit of following his father's experiments."

"That is quite a remarkable turnaround."

"Yes, I wonder if he also has designs on Miss Lucie and means to supplant Phillip in her eyes. Encouraging Phillip to take up his father's work might be a wedge he could use to come between them."

"Do you really think so? I don't see that at all, Holmes. Miss Lucie was most concerned about Phillip when she came to see me, to the point of tears."

"Yes, but I didn't see any sign of tears today, did you?"

"No, I can't say that I did. But what does that prove?"

"Prove? It proves nothing, but it does add a thread for us to ponder." A far-away look came to his eyes, as if he'd just remembered something unpleasant. "Or perhaps he has some other plans in mind."

He withdrew his pipe from his pocket and by the time he lighted it, I could see by the brooding look he'd taken on that the rest of our trip would be passed in silence.

When we arrived at the landing, Holmes bounded out of the hansom to speak to the ferry captain while I paid the driver. When I caught up with him, he was making ready to draw in the gangway and instructed me to release the lines from the bollards.

"I say, where's the captain's man today? He should be tending the lines and the boarding plank."

"I believe the captain said he is otherwise occupied today. In fact, he said he hasn't seen his helper since the day you last made the crossing from Blackwell's."

"What an impertinent lout. I expected as much from a man of his demeanor."

The cool breeze off the water made the brief crossing pleasant on the warm August afternoon. I sat on the passenger bench while Holmes went forward to the bow.

"Thanks, Cappy," called Holmes to the ferry captain as we arrived at the landing on Blackwell. It was a short walk to the Octagon, made even shorter by following Holmes' long stride.

Holmes approached the door and knocked loudly. No answer. "Phillip?" he called. Still no reply.

"Perhaps we should come back another time?" I said.

"Nonsense. Lack of a host didn't stop you, did it?"

"Well, no…but, how did you…" but he was already working the lock with his pick. In less time than it takes to write these words we were inside the front door. Instantly Holmes was on scent, looking here, looking there. One minute he was stretching up, glass in hand, inspecting the walls, the next he was crawling along the floor examining every stain and piece of lint. Several times he stopped to scrape up a bit of dust or powder, which he deposited into separate papers and put into his pocket.

When he'd concluded his investigation of the physical clues, if that's what they were, I directed his attention to the stacks of papers on the desk beneath the stairs. "These are what young Phillip was working on when I visited him."

Holmes shuffled through the papers, slowing to read in places, scanning in others and said, "Hm, it appears he's made rather rapid progress in his experiments."

"What makes you say that?"

"He makes mention of several 'epiphanies' that he attributes to his late father speaking to him from beyond the grave."

"Beyond the grave?"

"Yes, look here," he said as he pointed to one of the pages. "It reads: 'I could never have made this leap of experimental deduction had it not been for the guidance of my late father in how to properly combine the chemicals. Who would believe the order in which they were combined would be of such paramount importance.'"

"Good heavens. He's talking as though he actually spoke to his father."

"That's one interpretation, of course, but I think it more likely that he found something in the notes of his father that eluded to the methodology with which he has met with apparent success."

At just that moment there was a sudden draft that shuffled the papers on the desk. "What was that?"

"Sh…don't make a sound," Holmes said as he turned and stepped noiselessly toward the source of the draft, which was a trap door in the floor that slammed shut before Holmes could take more than two steps in its direction. Finding the handle and latch, Holmes attempted to open it. It held fast. "Watson, give me a hand."

We combined our strength but were still unable to lift the door. "Perhaps it's locked from beneath."

Holmes looked around the room. Near the door there was a fire axe behind glass. Holmes broke the glass and with the axe began working on the door. In less than two minutes, he'd hacked his way through the plank with the handle and threw the axe to the side. "Bear a hand, Watson."

Together we lifted what remained of the door. Beneath was a stairway leading down into a dark room. It was sparsely furnished and might have been abandoned from the time when the asylum housed by the Octagon closed nearly twenty years ago except that in one corner the thick dust that covered the majority of surfaces was conspicuously absent. It looked as if someone, or something, had been using that spot as a place of repose.

Holmes walked about the small room testing the walls all around. "Halloa, what's this?" he said. "Watson, take hold of this torch-sconce...there, that's it." He got down on his knees. "When I tell you, pull on the sconce with all your might." He readied himself and then said, "Now."

After a second or two's hesitation the section of the wall where Holmes had been prying swung aside revealing a crawlway, dark and foreboding. "This way," said Holmes and he began to crawl down the shaft with me reluctantly following behind.

The passage was dark and we didn't have the aid of the lantern this time. After shuffling along on our hands and knees for some few minutes, Holmes came to a stop so sudden I nearly ran into him. "What is it? What's wrong?" I said. I looked up at him and noticed there was a dim beam of light shining on Holmes as he rose to his feet.

"I'm afraid we've come to the end of the line." I could see the narrow passage suddenly shot up about eight feet in height where Holmes stood. Just on the other side was a grating of steel bars. Holmes was testing the strength of those bars without success.

Failing in our quest of the phantom who'd been hiding below the laboratory, Holmes and I returned the way we'd come. As we ascended the narrow stairs leading up to the lab, we saw Phillip Tremaine tidying up the papers that had blown from the desk as we pursued the phantom.

When he saw us emerge, there was a look of shock on his face as he said, "Here, what's this? What are you doing down there?"

"Chasing phantoms, I'm afraid," Holmes said.

"Phantoms? Who or what did you expect to find down there?"

"We were rather hoping you could tell us, Dr. Tremaine."

I said, "Yes, Phillip, it appears there was someone staying down below your laboratory. Do you have any idea who it may have been?"

There was a telltale hesitation before he said, "Who…I…I don't know." His gaze dropped to the still open trap door. "I didn't even know there was a room down there."

"I see," Holmes said. "No matter. Perhaps it was some vagrant looking for a warm, dry place to sleep."

"Yes, that must be it. Whoever it was, you and Dr. Watson must have scared them off. Did you get a look at them?"

Holmes peered at young Phillip as he answered, "No, I'm afraid he was too quick for us. He scurried down a shaft like a rat escaping two terriers on his tail."

"Well," Phillip said turning back toward his desk, "I'm fairly certain we've seen the last of whoever it was, now that you and Dr. Watson have exposed their trespassing with your own."

"Yes, I'm sure we have. Very sure indeed." Silence hung in the air like so much dirty linen until Holmes continued, "Well, I'm sure you must have work to do. Watson told me you've been engaged out here and I wanted to come and give you my personal condolences for your loss before the funeral."

"Thank you, Mr. Holmes. In that case, I apologize about the trespassing remark, but you didn't need to come all the way out here for that. Although in a way, I'm glad you did. It gives me the chance to thank you for finding my mother and bringing her out of that place."

"Of course, you're welcome. I only wish she'd been alive when I found her."

"Yes."

Another even more awkward silence followed, again broken by Holmes, "So, Watson here also tells me you are continuing with your father's experiments."

"Yes, that's right," he said with a look of expectation on his face.

"I'm sure he'd be proud to know you are pursuing his work."

A surprised and pleased expression replaced the apprehension of a moment before. "I'm sure he would. And thanks. Thanks for understanding," he said, extending his hand to Holmes, who grasped it, giving it a firm shake.

"Well, as I said, you must have work to do and I believe the Gilsey has a meat pie on the menu today."

I shook young Phillip's hand as we departed. "I promise, next time I come here and no one is home, I shan't enter without your permission."

"That's all right, Doctor. You and Mr. Holmes are welcome, although you might let me know you're coming so I can arrange to meet you."

"Fair enough," I said. As Holmes and I walked back to the landing, I said to him, "I say, Holmes, you appeared to be more supportive of this experiment nonsense than I expected."

"Let's just say I didn't think Phillip needed to have yet someone else tell him how foolish his efforts are. I thought he could do with a bit of benign benevolence. Besides, I learned a good deal just now. Some of those threads I've been collecting are beginning to weave themselves together. I need to smoke on it."

"Huh," I huffed. "I was there with you the whole time. I didn't learn anything. What was it you saw that I didn't?"

"You should know the answer to that, Watson."

"Yes, yes…" I said with a sigh, "…it's not what you saw that I didn't, but rather what you observed that I did not. Isn't that it?"

"Precisely, my friend, precisely."

Chapter 17
Julia Tremaine is laid to rest…

The following evening was the funeral ceremony for Julia Tremaine. I arrived at approximately 6:45 p.m. for the service that was to begin at 7:00 p.m. sharp. The St. James church was of the Roman Catholic persuasion and was situated at 32 James Street, just a few blocks east of Commissioner Strumm's offices in lower Manhattan. The building was Revivalist Greek in design, with a recessed portico behind two large Doric columns of alabaster. Above and behind the pediment was a bell tower topped with a domed cupola adorned with a Roman cross at the apex.

I arrived alone, as Holmes had some errand to run and promised to meet me at the church. The evening was warm and muggy and the full array of candles adorning the altar made the atmosphere quite close. As I approached the front of the church, the immediate family had just taken their seats in the first pew and the rest of the small cadre of guests was passing by the open coffin to view the deceased. I took my place in the queue and when I reached the casket I was absolutely stupefied by how very fresh and lifelike Julia appeared. I paused, admiring the work of a skilled undertaker. Despite her long incarceration in the asylum, she appeared not to have aged at all since our first meeting in the winter of '88.

As I stood there, remembering how sweet and lovely she'd been, I felt a familiar hand on my arm and Holmes whispered into my ear in a low voice only I could hear, "She looks to be only sleeping, eh?"

"Yes...yes, they've certainly taken care in the preparation of her remains I must say."

"Not at all. I took the liberty of speaking to the funeral director. After some assurances I wasn't from the state authorities, he confessed that they didn't use any embalming fluids at all."

"Not embalmed? For heaven's sake, why not?"

"Apparently on the request of Phillip Tremaine. He told the director that he didn't want the body embalmed on religious grounds. And the director, due to the unusual state of preservation of Mrs. Tremaine's body, obliged despite funereal ordinances to the contrary, no doubt pocketing the funds normally used for such services. He told me they only had to clean the body, dress her and fashion her hair. What you see are the unadorned remains of Julia Tremaine."

"Astonishing. Absolutely incredible."

"Indeed. Now, I think we should take our seats. We don't wish to appear obtrusive."

We sat a respectable distance apart from the family and close friends, not wishing to impose upon them in their hour of grief. As the priest executed the quaint funeral rights, I looked about the nearly empty church at the assemblage. In the first pew, of course, was young Phillip Tremaine and his uncle, Charles Cabot. Seated beside Phillip was Lucie Strumm and her parents, Mylo and Emily. I observed Phillip, with his head down and Lucie comforting him with her gloved hand upon his shoulder. Two rows behind where Holmes and I were seated was Alexander Hume. His gaze seemed fixed neither on the casket nor on the minister but rather on the pew in which the family was seated.

I wondered silently if a similar scene to this was played out shortly after Phillip Tremaine's birth when it was said that his mother had died. Did they go so far as to stage a false funeral? The assembly would have included her parents at that time, Mr. and Mrs. Charles Cabot, Sr. Also present would have been Charles, Jr., of course, as well as Mylo and Emily.

My thoughts were interrupted as the coffin was sprinkled with Holy Water and the procession out to the hearse began. It was not until then that I noticed a dark figure in the rear of the church, just opposite to where Hume was seated. He was kneeling in one of the little alcoves where one can light a candle for a personal intention. I supposed him at first to be one of the Hibernian order whose calling it was to watch over the church and building ensuring no trouble befell it from the Catholic-haters in lower Manhattan of which there were more than a few. When the service ended and the coffin was carried down the center aisle of the church, he rose and departed through the side door.

It was as the coffin passed by the area of devotion that the first disturbance of this somber affair occurred. As the funeral was a somewhat hurriedly put together proceeding, the pallbearers were all drawn from the members of the same Hibernian Society. It is believed, due to that, one of them may have been a bit under the influence of alcohol and managed to drive the corner of the coffin into the side of a pew in such a manner as to cause the lid to spring open.

This was, of course, bad enough but what happened next was of such a horrific consequence as to cast a veil of gloom over the entire ceremony. The pallbearers all claimed, to a man, the eyes of the corpse sprang open when the lid flew up and caused them such a state of fright that they dropped the coffin onto the granite floor with a resounding crash.

Anyone who has any experience with corpses of course knows it isn't unusual for muscles and tendons as they dry out to twitch creating unexpected and sometimes horrifying movements in the dead limbs. This particular case was made that much more horrifying by the pallbearers faltering in their duties and dropping the casket.

The commotion took some time to clear and calm down, with Phillip Tremaine and his uncle upset as much with those carrying Julia Tremaine's remains as with the whole horrid scene. Emily Strumm was, as befitted a woman, in tears at the spectacle while Lucie tried to comfort Phillip.

The ensuing confusion was so great that I failed to notice Holmes had exited the church through the same egress as the mysterious dark figure. He caught up with me outside the church where we shared a carriage I'd hired for the evening.

"Where did you get off to?" I said as we settled back into the carriage.

"I wanted to see who that fellow lighting the candles was. Did you see him?"

"Yes, I wondered who he was myself, but thought perhaps he was one of those Hibernian chaps."

"No, I don't believe he was."

"He didn't appear interested in the ceremony, perhaps he was just a parishioner making a votive offering."

"It wasn't what he was doing that drew my interest."

"What was it then?"

"The coffin, and the corpse of Julia Tremaine."

"I don't understand."

"There is a legend that says if the victim of a vampire passes by that vampire, the coffin and the eyes of the corpse will open in accusation of its master before succumbing to him."

I could scarcely believe my ears. He was speaking as if he suspected this poor pilgrim who was innocently praying of being a vampire. But his own words created a paradox that I was quick to point out, "But Julia wasn't the victim of a vampire, at least it wasn't the bite of a vampire that caused her death."

He looked at me and said, "If that is true, what was the cause of death?" This stopped me cold. I had the occasion to examine Julia when she was first taken to the mortuary and I could not detect a cause of death. In fact, other than a lack of pulse and respiration, I could scarcely believe she was deceased. Her color and skin and limbs were all much more like a sleeping woman than a dead one. I had no answer, so instead I asked a question, "Do you suppose she might have been poisoned? Perhaps injected into the closed wounds on her throat?"

"Perhaps, but I don't believe she was poisoned."

"Where did the gentleman go?"

"I'm afraid I don't know. By the time I got outside the church, he'd vanished."

At last we were at the cemetery where Holmes and I had discovered the desecrated tomb of Dr. Alan Tremaine. It was in this tomb poor Julia was to lie. Holmes and I were surprised to see none other than the superintendent, Mr. Lionel Manfried, tending the gate of the cemetery. He led the funeral party to the place of entombment.

As we stood alongside the open entry to the tomb, a most disagreeable odor was obviously emanating from below ground. Holmes and I, of course, recognized the odor to be that of a decaying corpse, though none was present within the tomb, according to Mr. Manfried. He was most apologetic explaining to the family that the tomb had been opened all afternoon but the odor persisted. He said that he had never had this sort of issue in all the years he'd been associated with the cemetery.

As one might imagine, the ceremony at the graveside was considerably shortened due to the obnoxious fumes. The Strumms invited everyone to their home for refreshments after. Holmes and I remained behind a bit to speak with Manfried, but I accepted the Strumms' invitation for the both of us explaining we'd be along just a few minutes behind the rest.

When everyone was gone, Holmes walked over to where Manfried had the wagon apparatus poised above Julia's tomb ready to lower the stone in place. "I was a bit surprised to see you tending the gate today, Mr. Manfried. I thought you'd have a new man by now."

"We've had two, Mr…uh, Mr…?"

"Holmes. Sherlock Holmes, and this is Dr. Watson."

"Oh, yes, of course. You'll excuse me for forgetting your name, sir, I've been quite scattered of late." He began lowering the stone in place.

"Quite all right, think nothing of it. You were saying, you've had two men since we saw you last?"

"Yes, that's right. Both quit within a day or so of having signed on. There, that should do it," he said as the stone came to rest, sealing the tomb.

"Did they happen to mention why they quit?"

"Well, I really shouldn't be discussing this, professional ethics you know," he said, while retrieving the lift bits from the stone. "But it's all so foolish I don't see the harm. They claim the cemetery is haunted."

"Haunted?" said I. "Ridiculous."

"That's exactly what I told them", he said, wiping the soil from his hands. "Superstitious balderdash. I tell you the cemetery business is no different than any other business except for the people who you have to deal with day by day. It's the living that are the most troublesome if you ask me. Haunted. I never—"

Holmes interrupted, "Did they give you any explanation as to upon what they based their claim?"

"Dark shadows moving on the grounds, voices. May as well be ghoulies and ghosties and long legged beasties as far as I'm concerned. It's all nonsense after all."

"I see. Thank you, Mr. Manfried, and I hope you find a reliable man to tend the gate soon," Holmes said and then turned to me, "Come along, Watson, we mustn't keep the Strumms waiting."

In the taxi on the way to the Strumms' home Holmes appeared to be quite agitated. "What is it, Holmes. What's troubling you?"

"Don't you find the haunting of the cemetery to be quite telling?"

"In what way?"

"Well, let's look at the facts. This is the same cemetery where Dr. Alan Tremaine was laid to rest, the same cemetery with which Julia Tremaine was obsessed and that obsession landed her in the insane asylum."

"All true, yes, but what has all that to do with the haunting, and how is the haunting telling?"

"Let us surmise for a moment that Barlucci was onboard the *Redeemer* when she was wrecked on Ward's Island. Let us further surmise that, as a diversion, he was the cause of the inmates of the prison and asylum escaping, including Julia Tremaine."

"Do you mean to say you believe it was purposeful that she was an escapee? If we take your theory that Barlucci was onboard for fact, how could he have known Julia was in the asylum?"

"Perhaps he didn't. Perhaps it was merely a fortunate happenstance.

But how else do you explain the carnage we saw at the site of the Tremaine tomb? Perhaps Barlucci is using the tomb as one of his nests. Don't you see how well it ties in to the haunting?"

I couldn't believe what I was hearing. "But Holmes, this is all conjecture, not something you normally engage in. I'm surprised. Haven't you always said that to theorize without all the data leads to twisting the facts to fit the theory?"

"Not at all. Don't you see? I'm afraid it's becoming quite clear. But you are right. I must have more data...more data...more data." He sat there, withdrawing into himself, steepling his fingers in front of his eyes, his lips moving and I could see he was reviewing the 'data' in his mind. I sat and watched him, wondering if my friend was on the verge of a nervous breakdown. I prayed he was not.

Chapter 18
Watson's most unkindest cut…

Holmes and I arrived just as the guests were gathering in the dining room to sit down to supper. "Please excuse our tardiness," I said.

"Not at all, Doctor. You and Mr. Holmes are just in time, I'm so glad you could make it," said Mrs. Strumm with her usual graciousness.

Seeing an unfamiliar face, Holmes stepped forward. "I beg your pardon, I saw you at the funeral but I don't believe I've made your acquaintance," he said to Hume.

I stepped forward to make the introductions. "Oh, that's right, you haven't met Mr. Hume, have you, Holmes. Alexander Hume, let me introduce you to Mr. Sherlock Holmes, the world's foremost, and only, consulting detective."

"Mr. Holmes, I'm honored, though you hardly need introduction. You are exactly as I pictured you. I've read all of your many and varied exploits as recorded ably by Dr. Watson, as well as a few accounts written by others. I feel almost as if we are old friends. It's a great pleasure to make you acquaintance," Hume said, extending his hand and giving a short bow.

With an air of cool effrontery Holmes took Hume's hand and shaking it firmly said, "Hardly an American greeting."

"Beg your pardon?" Hume said, a quizzical look on his face.

"The bow," Holmes explained as we all sat down at the table. "I say it's hardly an American greeting. Something I would expect from someone with a European background."

Hume looked around the room with a somewhat uncomfortable smile on his face, "I dare say your powers of observation are quite as exceptional as has been written of you, Mr. Holmes. It's true, I have spent a good deal of time in Europe, first studying violin and then playing in orchestras in Vienna and Budapest."

"Oh? And under whom did you study? I've travelled to Vienna myself. Perhaps we have mutual acquaintances." Holmes' nearly confrontational manner took me totally by surprise. He was acting as though he were a barrister for the prosecution and poor Hume was in the dock, but Hume handled it with great aplomb.

"Er, well, let's see, there was Maestro Mahler, with the Hofoper in Vienna; Giuseppe Verdi in Milan; others of whom you would probably not have heard."

"You must have been very young to have known Verdi," Holmes said with a glint in his eye. "He died a dozen years ago."

"Yes, I was but a boy. He was a great man and I didn't study under him so much as study his compositions, though I knew him."

"Very interesting indeed. Then if all that is true, you spent a good deal of time in Europe."

"Yes, a great deal of time," Hume said returning Holmes' cold stare with one of equal suspicion.

"Thank goodness he didn't remain in Europe," said Mrs. Strumm, "or who would have rescued our Lucie and Phillip?"

This interjection broke the spell of Holmes' prosecutorial interrogation of Hume and the rest of the supper passed with more light and pleasant conversation all round.

When supper was over, Holmes pulled me aside as we were

on our way from the dining room to the drawing room for an after dinner cigar. "Watson, that man, Hume, do you know who he is?"

"Yes, of course. He's the young gentleman who rescued Miss Lucie and Phillip. I told you all about him, surely you remember," said I, matter of factly.

"No. It's him."

"What? It's who?"

"Don't you see? It's Barlucci, it's Baron Barlucci in disguise." I felt my knees buckle beneath me when he said this and for a moment I thought I might collapse on the floor. "He's altered his looks, his manner of dress, even his voice, but it's him. I would bet all that I hold dearest in the world it's him." Holmes breathed the words and had on his face that same mad expression I'd noted before when he'd fixed Barlucci in his mind, an expression that said he wouldn't let it go regardless the argument put before him. But I felt it my duty as his friend and confidante to try.

"Holmes, you know it can't be. Hume is much too young. Why, he looks barely older than Barlucci was when we chased him around London twenty-five years ago. How do you explain his not aging a wink in all that time? Besides, you remember what Mandible Pierce told Emily and Miss Drake." I decided that reason interspersed with a bit of ridicule might work the trick, might just shock him back to his senses. "Are you saying he was frozen and when he thawed out, he was still the fresh young man we knew and hunted back then?"

His reply shocked me, "Precisely, Watson. A vampire does not age like you and I. He can take on the appearance of practically any age he chooses or, if deprived of fresh, rich blood he may assume the trappings of old age—gray and thinning hair, wrinkled skin—but when he's nourished himself once again, he resumes his former vigor."

I could not believe what I was hearing. "A vampire? Now you are saying that young Hume is a vampire?" Holmes had never spoken so unguardedly about vampires before. This was a new and most distressing turn of events.

"Not a vampire, Watson. THE vampire, Hume is Barlucci, a wicked and vile creature from the blackest reaches of hell come to wreak his vengeance on mankind for his own distorted reasons."

Holmes was absolutely raving. Would that I could have torn my ears from my head rather than bear witness to the utter mental destruction of that genius of intellect I had come to admire, and yes, to love over the course of our many years association. I was heart-sick at his words for I knew it signaled a turn for the worse, from obsession to outright madness. I felt as though I might collapse on the spot. As much as it struck at my heart like a hot dagger, I knew what I must do and must do quickly before his madness drove him to only God knows what ends.

Rather than collapse, I looked Holmes squarely in the eyes and said, "Are you certain?" With this turn of events I felt it best not to confront him with the obvious folly of his assertion. I remembered well when he nearly exploded in temper when I questioned his theories after we explored the desecrated tomb of Tremaine. I thought perhaps I should just play along and in that vein I might find a way to make him come around to seeing his own error. I didn't want to embarrass our hosts, but most especially I didn't wish to embarrass poor Holmes.

"I'm absolutely certain. Take away the long hair, the beard, and that affected accent of his and you'd be certain too. He obviously believes his disguise to be impenetrable. Did you notice the way he purposefully sought me out? His cockiness will be his undoing."

"But if it is Barlucci, does it necessarily follow that he is a vampire?"

"Nothing else fits the facts. He survived twenty-five years in a frozen prison only to return now as a young man. And let's not forget the trail of bloodless corpses he's left in his wake."

It was thus clear. My friend and colleague Sherlock Holmes

had taken that last step toward the abyss of insanity. I suppose I'd known this was coming but I refused to allow myself to believe it. Even now my hand trembles as I write these words. But I was faced with an even more daunting question than Holmes' sanity. What to do about it?

I knew it was no use trying to persuade Holmes on my own to submit himself to the care of a physician. I would need assistance. I would need to enlist Commissioner Strumm to aid me. "Well then, I think the thing to do is to inform Commissioner Strumm," I said, suddenly feeling more like a conspiratorial traitor than a colleague, or a friend.

"But the Commissioner doesn't believe Barlucci is alive."

"Then we shall have to convince him. I'll get him aside and explain the matter while you engage Hume, or Barlucci rather, in conversation. We shall then confront him and demand he submit to a test, else be arrested."

"Yes, then when you've examined him and can find neither pulse nor heartbeat Strumm will have to be convinced. Then we will have our vampire." Holmes reached into his pocket. "Here," he said. He withdrew two vials of water and two cloves of garlic. "Holy water and garlic, give one each of these to Strumm and keep the other yourself. With these we can surround and entrap him."

I came very near to weeping as I took Holmes' pathetic offering of the talismans from his hand and placed them in my jacket pocket.

"Now, go, I'll engage our friend, Barlucci."

Holmes crossed the room and began a conversation with Hume about violin construction and I signaled to Commissioner Strumm that I wished to speak to him in the relative privacy of the other side of the room. When he came over I said to him, "I'm afraid this whole Barlucci affair has driven Holmes over the edge."

"What do you mean, Doctor?"

"Holmes believes Hume is Barlucci."

Strumm laughed. "I thought for a moment you were serious." And then, seeing the character of my face he said, "You are serious. What...? How...? Whatever has given him the idea that Hume could be Barlucci? It's ridiculous. Absolutely mad."

"I agree. It is ridiculous, but not to Holmes. And that's not the worst of it. Not only does he believe Hume is Barlucci in disguise, he's also convinced Barlucci is a vampire." I grasped his forearm tightly. "You must help me."

The look on my face must have persuaded Strumm of my seriousness, "But how? What can we do?"

"My thought was to demonstrate the fallacy of Holmes' fantasy to him. The hope is that even in a muddled state, that magnificent mind of his would not fail to grasp what his own eyes observe." What I didn't say was that our only alternative would be to commit Holmes to an institution in order to prevent his harming himself or anyone else, least of all Hume, who we would also need the cooperation of, if we were to have any hope of convincing Holmes of his deductive delusion. "We'll need Hume to cooperate, of course."

"I'm sure he will be only too happy. He seems quite taken with Holmes, at least as you have portrayed him in your chronicles."

I didn't bother to tell Strumm it was partially due to Hume's apparent infatuation that Holmes thought Hume to be Barlucci. He was utterly convinced Hume, or Barlucci, was indulging in a bit of hubristic fun at his expense. "Good, I'll pull Holmes aside and tell him that you aren't convinced but are willing to allow a test. I'll say you insist we move to another venue, one away from your family, that they not be put into any danger should Holmes be right."

"Excellent, and I will deal with young Hume, impress upon him the urgency that he cooperate no matter how mad the whole thing might seem, that you and I are only concerned with Holmes' well-being and that he might play a key role in assisting us."

At my first opportunity I caught Holmes' eye and motioned for him to join me. He excused himself from Hume's company and as he walked over to me, Strumm began talking to Hume in a low voice. "I spoke with Strumm. I told him you believe Hume to be Barlucci."

"Yes, what did he say? I'll wager he was quite surprised."

"He thought I was joking."

"I should have known," he said, raising his brow. "Strumm's a fool."

"Holmes you must admit for you to accuse Hume of being Barlucci stretches the corridors of credulity just a bit. And then to add to that the business about him being a vampire…"

Holmes didn't appear to be listening. "Then he won't assist us?"

"No, I'm not saying that."

"Well, come, come, what are you saying then?"

"It took some doing, but I did get him to relent a bit. He's agreed to assist us in getting Hume to stand for a test if we conduct it someplace other than his home."

"He probably only agreed because he thinks I'm wrong and wants to gloat when he's proven right."

"I thought that too, at first, but then it dawned on me that if that's the case, why would he insist we not conduct the test here? That shows he must at least allow for the possibility that you are correct."

"Yes, yes…you're right. Even though he doesn't wish to admit it, he knows deep down that I'm right." Holmes gripped my arm firmly, "Watson, we are very close to the end of our journey, and the end of Baron Barlucci." I thought bitterly that he was right, but not in the way he expected. "Did you give Strumm the garlic?"

"What? Er…ahem…yes, yes, of course," I lied.

"Good," he said. "Now then, Hume is a musician, we'll use my Stradivarius to lure him back to our hotel room. We'll do the examination there. He won't be able to resist a chance to play it."

"Excellent. That will do the trick."

Minutes later we were on our way to the Gilsey. "How did you come to own such a wonderful instrument for such a small sum?" asked Hume as our brougham ambled down Fifth Avenue.

"It was by a stroke of the most fantastic luck," Holmes said in a relaxed tone. "I happened to be walking in central London, on one of our early adventures. Watson wasn't with me but was, rather, nursing a devilish cold as I recall. I happened by a small pawn shop run by a merchant named Rothstein. He was testing a violin he'd purchased from the widow of an Italian immigrant. I heard the notes struck by the pawn broker and even in his untutored hand I recognized the mellow sound of a fine instrument."

"Ah, yes, the sound is most unmistakable to one with a luthier's ear. Were you in the market for a violin, then?"

"Actually, I was not. My own violin, a domestic copy of an Amati, was quite adequate for my needs. But when I heard the sound, on a whim I walked into the shop as though I were looking for a steamer trunk and casually asked the shop owner what he would take for the violin."

"And he asked only fifty-five shillings?"

"On the contrary, he asked for five pounds. I countered with two. He quickly dropped his price to three pounds, five shillings. I offered two pounds ten to which he countered three. We finally settled at fifty-five shillings."

"I can see you are as shrewd a bargainer as you are a detective. But if you knew it was a Stradivarius, why quibble over such a petty sum?"

"It was obvious to me that this old peddler of odd merchandise didn't know the worth of what he was holding. If I'd appeared too eager to meet his price, he might reconsider, have it appraised. Then where would I be? I'd be without my Stradivarius. Besides, he was an impertinent fellow and I enjoyed the amusement of haggling with him.

This particular shopkeeper, I knew, had a reputation for being a singularly hard bargainer. Ah, here we are at our hotel. You can see for yourself if I made a wise bargain."

As we entered the hotel, I could see that Strumm had arranged to have three rather burley plainclothes detectives waiting in the lobby. This may not have been obvious to Hume, who would have no experience in this sort of thing, but I knew it would not be lost on Holmes. I was relieved when he said to me in a low voice only I could hear, "I see Commissioner Strumm has taken the proper precautions, though I believe with the accoutrements I've supplied you we shall have no difficulties. I think it safe to have them wait in the lobby."

"I agree," I said reluctantly. It was apparent that Strumm had already made that arrangement for as we got into the lift, they did not follow, at least not immediately.

We four rode the lift up to our third floor room with barely a word spoken. Each of us apparently had a different expectation of what would occur when we arrived.

As we entered, Hume said, "Now, Mr. Holmes, where is that violin you told me about?"

"It's right here," he said, reaching into the closet and pulling out a battered violin case. "The epitome of violin-making," he said producing the beloved instrument.

"Ah, it's wonderful. More than 180 years old and," Hume plucked a string, "a tone more beautiful now than the day it was made."

"You should know," Holmes said.

"Thank you, Mr. Holmes. You pay me a great compliment."

"I meant that you should know it sounds better today than it did 180 years ago."

Hume had a strange look on his face. "I don't understand."

Strumm, who had been standing silently by the door said, "I think what Mr. Holmes means is that he believes you're a bit older

187

than you appear."

"I'm afraid I still don't understand."

Holmes looked at Hume with an accusing eye. "It's quite simple, Mr. Hume, or should I call you by your title, Baron Barlucci."

"Who? Barlucci? Who is this Baron Barlucci?" Hume said, then a look of recognition passed over his face. He turned to me and said, "Isn't Barlucci the man you said perished in a shipwreck over twenty years ago?"

Holmes didn't wait for me to answer, "Come, Baron, enough of these games. I know who and what you are, and we've come here tonight to unmask you."

"Oh, really, Mr. Holmes. And how do you propose to do that?" Hume said, overplaying his part a bit, I thought.

"By exposing you for the vampire you are."

"A vampire? Are you mad?"

"When you first told me you were a vampire, I could have sworn you were mad, but in the ensuing years, I've come to realize that however improbable vampirism is, to say it is impossible only serves to prove my own predisposition."

"You are mad," Hume said.

"You can easily prove it, if you dare. If, as you say, you are not Baron Barlucci, you should have nothing to fear in submitting to a few simple tests, tests that if you fail will prove you to be a vampire and by extension, the vampire Barlucci." Holmes now turned in my direction. "Doctor, will you please retrieve your stethoscope from the bureau drawer and check Mr. Hume for a heartbeat?"

It was such a bizarre request. The entire scenario was most disorienting, like a fantastic dream from which I was wont to awaken. I reluctantly went to the bureau, removed my scope and approached Hume. "Would you mind removing your jacket?"

"This is ridiculous."

Strumm said, "Please, Alexander, allow Watson to listen to

your heart and we can have done with this."

"Quite so, Commissioner," said Holmes, who had withdrawn the clove of garlic from his jacket pocket.

"Very well," Hume said and removed his jacket and then opened his shirt. "I'm at your disposal, Doctor," he said, opening his arms while giving Holmes a long cold stare. For just a moment, looking at the malice in those eyes, I almost believed he could be Barlucci, despite my misgivings.

I fitted the tubes to my ears and then placed the diaphragm against Hume's bared chest. I knew, of course what I would find. The steady, strong heartbeat of a young man. I listened carefully. I glanced up at Holmes' eager face and shook my head. "I'm afraid he displays a normal, if somewhat slower heartbeat than I'd expected. Certainly within the normal standards for a young man."

Holmes' face, suddenly ancient, fell. "Impossible," he said.

I removed the tubes from my ears and held out the instrument. "See for yourself," offering it to Holmes.

Holmes took the scope and listened. He roughly removed them from his ears and with a voice that was rising in crescendo said, "What form of trickery is this, Barlucci?" and raised his hand as if to strike Hume.

Strumm caught his arm. "Holmes, what are you doing?"

A wild look had come across Holmes' face. "It's a trick. My God! Don't you see? Can't you see? It's a trick. Of course it is, a cursed trick. Don't let him fool you. This is Barlucci." He was shouting now. I rushed to assist Strumm in restraining him, feeling a bit like Brutus to Holmes' Caesar. But at this moment I had no time for recriminations. That would come later.

Strumm gave a call and the three burly detectives we'd seen when we entered the lobby came into the room. The shock of what was happening was most acute. I watched in agonized silence while the detectives placed handcuffs on Holmes and carried him out of the room. All the while Holmes continued to rant about vampires and Barlucci. His eyes pleaded for us to believe him, to listen. They fell upon me and all I could do was look away.

"Where will they take him?" I asked Strumm once they left the room.

Strumm answered, "The asylum on Ward's Island."

"I must go to him."

"No, Doctor. Not tonight. They'll sedate him and take good care of him. You can go visit him tomorrow."

I knew he was right. There was nothing I could do tonight. This was the most sorrowful day of my life, watching Holmes, the man I'd come to think of as closer than a brother, being hauled away in chains blathering like a madman.

Hume, who'd fallen silent while Holmes raged, said to me, "I'm very sorry, Doctor. He was a great man."

"Is," said I.

"What?"

"Is." I repeated resolutely. "Holmes is a great man."

Chapter 19
A Small retribution…

Abominable. That is the only word to describe it.

I visited Holmes at the New York Asylum the following day and what I saw there was abominable. Holmes had been secluded in a small, dark room in the south wing. It was no more than eight feet by eight feet. The walls and floor were padded and Holmes—dear God, Holmes was huddled in one corner of the room in a dressing gown and strait-jacket. Over his mouth was a gag of some sort to prevent him from calling out. My heart was rended in two when I saw him through the small viewing grate in the door.

"Must he be confined so?" I asked the Director. I couldn't bear seeing Holmes like this and made up my mind to get him out at once.

"He put up quite a fight when they brought him in," he said. Although his manner was professional, I detected what I thought was a bit of glee in his eye. No doubt after being humiliated by Holmes on two separate occasions, the director took grave pleasure in my friend's mortification.

"I wouldn't wonder. Any sane man would," I said trying not to show my ire. "I've come to see to his release, in my custody, of course."

"I'm afraid that isn't possible. His commitment papers were signed by Commissioner Strumm and only Commissioner Strumm can sign for his release."

"That's preposterous. I am this man's doctor as well as his friend. I demand he be released to my custody at once. I accept full responsibility."

The director smiled, "I'm afraid your medical degree holds no authority in the state of New York, Dr. Watson. I'm unable to release Mr. Holmes to your custody. There's nothing I can do. Now, if you'll excuse me, I have a hospital to run." The director turned his back and began walking away.

"Now see here," I said but it was no use. He either didn't hear or, more likely, ignored my protestation. I was left standing in the passage outside of Holmes' room. I'd never felt more helpless and ashamed in my life. I felt entirely responsible for Holmes' current predicament and I made up my mind to go directly to Strumm's office and demand he have him released immediately.

When I arrived at Commissioner Strumm's office, I was in such a tizzy that I didn't wait for his secretary to announce my presence, but instead barged right into his office. I was surprised to find the commissioner with a recently emptied glass in his hand and a bottle of Four Roses Bourbon, three-quarters empty, on his desk.

"What's the meaning of this, Doctor?" he said in some alarm as he put down the glass refilling it and quickly downing the contents. He looked a wreck. This time he didn't offer me a drink, but kept a niggardly grasp on the bottle and glass. His expression, one of self-loathing, was not unusual for a man in his state of alcohol addiction and my heart immediately felt for his dear wife and daughter.

"I'm here about Holmes. You've got to get him out of that place. It's beastly what they're doing to him there."

He turned his back toward me and strode over to the window, "I'm sorry, Doctor. Holmes is a danger, to himself as much as anyone. You should know that."

"I know no such thing. If I had known how he'd be treated in that place, I never would have gone along."

Strumm turned around and looked me in the eye, sweaty strands of hair falling across his brow. "Go along?" He laughed derisively. "Doctor, you didn't just go along. Hell, you led the damned parade," he said, emptying his glass once again.

The truth of his words were a buggy whip to my ears. "Yes," I admitted, ashamed for my part in Holmes' humiliation. "I was afraid."

"You were afraid his rantings would lead him to hurt someone, or himself, isn't that right?"

"Yes, I suppose, but now I see I was wrong." Unwilling to give up the fight, I said, "Holmes doesn't belong in that place. See to his release and I'll take him back to London. We'll be on the first ship out of New York, I promise you."

Strumm wiped the sweat from his brow and neck with a handkerchief, "I can't, Doc. I can't take that chance now." As he put the handkerchief back in his pocket I noticed a smudge of bright red. His drinking had apparently gotten so bad that it must have occasioned a nose bleed now and again.

"What do you mean you can't? You're the only one who can, Mylo," I said, beseeching him with my eyes. "I beg of you, allow me to take him home where I can look after him."

"I'm afraid that's impossible, Doc. He's exactly where he needs to be for now," he said, looking down at the remaining contents of the bottle in front of him. "Now, if you'll excuse me."

"Does Emily know you're drinking again?" He looked up at me with defiant eyes. I turned to the door and said without looking back at him, "I'll find a way to get him out. I'll get a court order. I'll..." and as I closed the door behind me, I thought I heard him say to himself something to the effect of, 'I pray you do, Doc...I pray you do.'

After spending much of the day negotiating the various courts and magistrates of the state of New York, at least those located in the city, I came at last to the court of one William O'Brien, Chief Justice of the New York State Supreme Civil Court, the court of last resort in a case such as this. Unfortunately, Commissioner Strumm had apparently called ahead of me as his secretary was expecting my visit. "I'm very sorry, Dr. Watson, Justice O'Brien is not available to see you."

"But this is an urgent matter. A man's life may be at stake."

The young woman lowered her voice, glancing at the closed door to Justice O'Brien's office, "I'm afraid he's been forewarned, sir."

"Forewarned? What do you mean forewarned?"

In a bare whisper she said, "Forewarned of your visit." She glance toward the Justice's close door before continuing, "I'm sorry, Doctor, I can't say any more. I really shouldn't have said that, it's just that I don't think it's quite fair to have you wait for nothing. He really won't see you."

"But why?"

She looked down at the typewriter in front of her and said, "I'm sorry, I've said too much already. I could lose my job. No, I can't say anything more."

I could see it was no use and felt quite certain that whatever Commissioner Strumm had told Justice O'Brien could not have been the whole truth. But whatever it was it appeared to be enough to convince the judge to do as he asked. I was angered and surprised that the commissioner would interfere in this way. I decided that I would have to speak with Emily Strumm and try to enlist her aid in getting my friend released.

The long shadows of the late afternoon cast their gloomy spell as I arrived at the Strumm household. My hope of having Holmes released was waning much like the day. As I approached the front of the house, Emily Strumm opened the door. "Oh, Doctor, I was just on my way out."

"I apologize for this interruption, Emily, but I'm afraid I must speak to you. It's most urgent."

"Of course, Doctor, please come in," she said as she backed into the foyer. I closed the door behind me. "Would you like some coffee or tea? I can make some, it'll only take a minute. What is it? You look so serious."

"Yes, well, some tea would be—"

I was interrupted mid-sentence by a furious knocking on the door. "Oh, my," said Emily, "who can that be?"

We both turned to face the door as she opened it and when she did my heart leapt in my chest as I saw Holmes standing there. "Quickly, Miss Emily," said Holmes, "where is your daughter? Where is Lucie?"

"Holmes," was all I could manage to say.

"Lucie? Why, she left just a few minutes ago. Her father called her and asked her to meet him downtown. Why?"

"Holmes, how did you…" he ignored my interruption for the moment.

"Thank God," said Holmes. "At least, then, she'll be safe. May we come in?" It wasn't until Holmes said this that we realized he was not alone. Standing back away from the door was another figure, a woman huddled in a hat and shawl, despite the warmth of the August evening, making it quite impossible to see her face.

"Why, of course, yes, please come in. My husband told me you'd taken ill and had to be rushed to the hospital. I'm so glad to see you looking so well. I was just about to make Dr. Watson some tea. You're most welcome to join us, both of you."

"I'm afraid your husband both under and over stated my illness."

"Well, I'm glad at least you are all right now. Please, make yourselves comfortable," Emily said and then offered to take the wrap of the young woman.

Holmes turned to me, "Watson, you're wondering how I managed to escape the New York Asylum. I can tell you it wasn't as easy as I'd first believed it would be."

The sudden intake of air from Emily's gasp alerted me that something was amiss. I turned to look and saw Julia Tremaine standing there, as beautiful and youthful as I remembered her twenty-five years before. I was able to reach out and steady Emily as she began to swoon. "My God," I ejaculated. "What does this mean?"

"It quite means that you will now have to believe me, Watson, for I bring you irrefutable proof of the existence of vampirism."

"This is some trick," I said, not wishing to believe my own eyes.

"No, Doctor, I'm afraid it isn't," Julia said, a tear forming in her eye. "I…I am a vampire, but—"

"It can't be," said Emily. "It can't be…" Turning to Holmes with a frightened stare she said, "Why would you bring her here? You know she's…she's…"

"Evil? No, I'm afraid that isn't quite true, Mrs. Strumm. Julia isn't evil. Please rest assured, you have nothing to fear from Mrs. Tremaine."

"How can you say that, Mr. Holmes? You know what she is, what she's capable of."

"Mr. Holmes is right. You don't have to be afraid of me."

I said, "I wish we could believe you, Mrs. Tremaine, but how can we be sure?"

"I've promised Mrs. Tremaine a cure and safe passage to that cure."

"How can you promise such a thing, Holmes?"

"I'm afraid I've violated my own rule, Watson." He fixed me in his gaze, a wisp of a smile on his lips. "I've started this story in the middle. Perhaps I should begin at the beginning. But first, Mrs.

Strumm, I believe you had offered some tea?"

"Yes, yes of course, I..." Emily said, still looking stunned. "Please, make yourselves comfortable. I'll only be a moment."

"That's all right, Emily, I'll give you a hand," I said and we went together into the kitchen while Holmes and Mrs. Tremaine moved into the front parlor.

"Doctor, do you think it's possible?"

"That there is a cure? I've known Holmes for a very long time, Emily. I'm sure he wouldn't have promised unless he was certain he could deliver." Emily had a far-away look in her eyes as she put some snack cakes on a tray while we waited for the water to boil. "What is it, dear?"

I was just thinking about...about Abigail," she said and I gave her a fatherly hug.

When we returned to the parlor with refreshments, Holmes was standing near the empty fireplace smoking a cigarette. Mrs. Tremaine was seated on a small settee directly opposite a matching chair. Emily placed the tray on the table between them.

"I say, Holmes, if you wouldn't mind, please catch me up, it would appear I'm a bit in arrears so far as this matter is concerned."

"I owe you my deepest apology, Watson. But it was absolutely essential to our plans that you be left temporarily in the dark, so to speak."

"Our plans?"

"Yes, that's right, mine and the Baron's."

"The Baron? You're in league with that devil?"

"No, he's no more a devil than you or I, or..." he said, indicating Mrs. Tremaine. "Do you remember what I told you about my experience in the ventilation shaft?"

"Yes, of course I remember," I said, turning away, embarrassed that at the time I was quite convinced he'd gone round the bend.

Noticing my discomfort, Holmes said, "There, there, Watson. You thought and did exactly what you were supposed to think and do. I gave you what must have seemed an outlandish story without so much as a whit of proof. I'm surprised you didn't have me committed on the spot."

His generosity made me all the more ashamed.

"I didn't tell you the whole story. In fact, I stopped just short of the critical juncture. Once Barlucci had shown me he was more than my physical equal and that he intended no harm, we had a very long discussion, one we needn't go into just now. It suffices to say that during the course of it I came to realize he was quite a remarkable man who'd been placed in an impossible predicament."

"But how can you trust what he says is true?"

Holmes smiled and said, "He gave me his word."

"His word?"

"Yes, he gave me his word, along with a wooden stake and a mallet. And then he allowed me to wrap him in chains. He told me that if, once I'd heard all he had to say, I still believed him to be evil I should drive the stake through his heart."

"Good God, Holmes. Why didn't you do him in?"

"I considered it, but under the circumstances I thought it would do no harm to hear him out first."

"Dear God," said Emily, placing her delicate hand over her mouth.

"He then warned me, should I determine to do it, to destroy him, I should not hesitate in the least or he would instinctively do whatever he could to stop me, even if it meant killing me."

"Chilling. And so you believed him?"

"Once I had heard all he had to say, I could hardly disbelieve him. In fact, I offered my assistance."

"Do you mean to tell me the two of you have been conspiring all this time? How then can you be certain there is a cure that will work?"

"You astound me, Watson. You should be able to attest to the efficacy of the cure. After all, you yourself examined the patient."

"I examined..." I thought for a moment. "Hume...you mean Alexander Hume is Barlucci, just as you said?"

"Yes, and he's been cured of vampirism, thanks to Dr. Phillip Tremaine carrying on the work of his father, Alan." Turning to Julia, he continued, "And now young Phillip will have the pleasure of also curing his mother." Julia sobbed quietly as Emily went to comfort her.

"But how does all of this...how did Julia..." I tried to form the words but was concerned at deepening Mrs. Tremaine's discomfort.

"Perhaps I should take Julia into the drawing room while you gentlemen..." began Emily, but Julia touched her arm to stop her.

"No, it's best you both hear all of this, especially under the circumstances."

"What circumstances?" I said.

Holmes began, "I'm sure you're both wondering how Julia came under this curse."

"Mr. Holmes, I think it would be better if I told them." Julia dabbed her eyes and her nose before continuing. She turned to Emily, "Some of this may be difficult for you to hear, Emily, but I think it's important you all have a complete understanding of what we're dealing with."

"What we're dealing with?" said I, "I don't understand, I thought there was a cure."

"Yes, I'll get to that...let me explain." Julia took Emily's hand as she continued, "Twenty-five years ago, before the fire in which Alan and your sister died, Abigail came to me in the night."

"Came to you? But you came to her, I mean me," said Emily recalling the afternoon so long ago when she first met Julia Tremaine.

"Yes, I came to speak to Abigail, though I knew her as Emily.

I later realized that it was really you to whom I spoke that afternoon and that the two of you were engaging in a charade in order to protect her. But in the evening on that same day, Abigail paid me a visit. She left this as a calling card." As Julia spoke, she turned her head to the side and pulled open the collar of her dress.

Emily gasped as the wound on Julia's throat was revealed. Two round reddened marks were on her throat. "Abigail...did she...?"

"Yes, the marks on my throat were left by your sister, by Abigail. And from that point on until she died, I was her willing vassal, a slave to her every whim. Once she died, I began to recover. I gained back my strength. I was able to carry and deliver Phillip with very little ill effect. Even this wound on my throat began to heal, leaving only a scar."

"What was it that occasioned you to be committed to that hideous asylum?" I asked.

"I had been too ill to attend my husband's funeral and for many months after I could not bring myself to visit his gravesite. But once Phillip was born and I was feeling more like my old self, I felt compelled to go and say good-bye to my husband—to Alan, my love. But while I was standing there beside his tomb, saying a silent prayer and speaking to him in my mind, perhaps even murmuring a farewell, I felt a sudden headache, as if my mind were being pulled from me by some invisible hand wrapped around my consciousness and I became terribly nauseated. I put it down to having been up and around too soon after Phillip's birth, for it was a difficult delivery."

Julia arose from her seat and walked over to the window, gazing out to the street. "After that day at the cemetery I was never the same. Each day I felt a stronger and stronger compulsion to return to Alan's tomb and I did so, repeatedly. It was while I was standing there on my second visit that I felt as though I could actually hear Alan's voice though I couldn't understand what he was saying. From that point on I became obsessed with being at the cemetery. Day and night

I would venture back, back to his side. It was about this time that I noticed the wound on my throat had stopped healing, had in fact reversed itself and was now oozing once again."

"You poor dear," said Emily. "What could have caused this change?"

Julia turned back and looked at Emily. "It was Alan. He caused the change."

"But he was dead, Julia," I said to her.

"Not dead, Doctor. Alan was Undead."

"What? We found him in the house, the night of the fire. He was poisoned. The hypodermic we discovered in this throat…it was full of strychnine."

"Yes, it's true. Alan was poisoned that night, poisoned by the serum he himself had tainted with strychnine."

"Why would he do such a thing?" asked Emily quietly, as if she suspected the answer.

"He did it to destroy Abigail. He'd been working on a cure for her and for Barlucci. But the morning before I came to visit you I told him that if he continued, I would leave him, ruin him. However, after I became slave to Abigail's will, I pleaded with Alan to forgive my foolish jealousy and continue working on the cure. He did so, happily thinking I understood the importance of what he was doing." Julia crossed the room, standing near Holmes, by the fireplace. "Then, just before he was to administer the interim serum to relieve her 'symptoms'—"

Holmes interrupted, "You mean to stop her need for human blood."

"Yes, it was a first step to a cure," she explained and then went on, "just before he was to administer it, he discovered the marks on my throat and he knew. He knew that I'd become her victim, a pawn in her cruel game. How enraged he must have been. He knew she had taken me even though she knew I was pregnant with Phillip. She knew even before Alan. So, he plotted to murder her, knowing I would never be free while she lived."

Holmes took over the narrative, "And that's when he 'doctored' the serum. He knew she was too clever for him to use straight poison, so he disguised the lethal dose in the serum that was to cure her. What he couldn't know was that Abigail had no intention of being cured, at least not yet, not without Barlucci."

"I don't understand, Holmes. Why would she postpone a cure for this horrid existence?"

"Yes, it would seem horrid to you and me, and indeed Mrs. Tremaine feels the same, isn't that so?" he gently took Julia's hand. She nodded, once again dabbing her eyes. "But to Abigail Drake it must have been a feeling of immense power. And she knew a cure would allow the aging process of which we are all victim to begin again. She knew from the account given her by Mandible Pierce that Barlucci had been buried under a mountain of ice and snow. But she also knew that time was on Barlucci's side. Eventually he would be uncovered, either by some salvage operation such as the *Redeemer* or even through a natural climate change, which might take eons. Perhaps she even contemplated hiring some sort of search expedition. But regardless how he returned, she was convinced that in time he would return. The only question left to answer was, return to what? If she allowed Tremaine to cure her, she might be an old woman when Barlucci came back to her."

"I see. She wished to remain just as he remembered her. And so, what, she switched the serum?"

"Yes, the serum Tremaine injected into Abigail that night was merely her own blood. Since the real serum was a compound composed primarily of her blood to begin with, it was a simple task for her to create a fake syringe, secreting the actual syringe full of serum—and poison—most likely in her dress pocket. When Abigail realized Tremaine had attempted to murder her, she turned on him. At some point in the struggle, she injected the poisoned serum into Tremaine, causing his death."

"That must have been after I arrived. Abigail turned on me too. She was mad, accusing me of horrid things," said Emily through tears as she remembered that terrible night. "But how does all of that lead to Julia becoming a…"

"A vampire?" said Julia. "Remember, the syringe that killed Alan didn't just contain poison. It was a mixture of the serum and the poison, and the serum was composed primarily of Abigail's blood. The same act that ended Alan's life cursed him to become a vampire."

"One of the ways in which a vampire is 'created' is to ingest the blood of a vampire," Holmes explained. "Although the traditional way is to drink the blood, which is, in fact, how both Julia and Abigail became vampires, it appears an injection works equally well. When Barlucci knew the *Animus Lacuna* was doomed, in order to ensure Abigail's survival of what would surely have been, and in fact was, her death, Barlucci had her drink his blood. In a like manner, when Dr. Tremaine was injected with the serum containing poison mixed with blood it was as if he had drunk of Abigail Drake's blood. Most likely even Abigail didn't realize the outcome would be to create yet another vampire."

"Alan Tremaine, a vampire? But why haven't we heard of this before?" I said. "If this is true and Alan Tremaine became a vampire all those years ago why have we not heard anything about his victims?"

"Unlike Abigail, who awakened on the mortician's table, Alan was unable to escape his tomb," said Julia quietly, looking down to the floor.

I said, "But Holmes, I thought you intimated a vampire to have extraordinary strength, surely Tremaine would have…"

"Yes, it's true. A vampire possesses the physical strength of ten men."

"Then why could he not escape his tomb?"

"When a vampire first awakens, he is not yet truly a vampire, not until he takes his first blood prize. Only then does his strength and other abilities manifest themselves to their full capacity. That is why Alan Tremaine could not escape his own tomb and that is why he continually sought Julia's assistance."

"And that is why poor Julia was committed to an Asylum?"

"Precisely. Because she had been a victim of a vampire, and in particular the same vampire line of which Alan was now a part, she had a peculiar sensitivity to his mental probing. Once he'd made contact with her when she visited his tomb, she could not escape."

Emily rose and went to Julia, putting her arm around her. "And you spent all those years with Alan in your mind, asking for your help?"

Julia broke down into tears. "Yes, I…I tried to tell him I couldn't help him…"

Holmes said, "Fate would give Julia her chance to help Alan when the ghost ship, which carried Barlucci, ran aground on Ward's Island. Barlucci, in an effort to hide his own tracks, affected an inmate escape at both the prison and the asylum. It was only by the most fortuitous coincidence that Julia was one of the escapees."

"Fortuitous for Tremaine, at least. Poor Julia." I said in sympathy to Julia's plight.

"And eventually for Julia as well, as she is now free of the asylum and will soon be free of vampirism," said Holmes.

"Yes, and when her husband is cured as well, perhaps there will be a happy ending to this whole ordeal." After I said this, Julia's sobs began anew. "What's wrong, dear?"

"I'm afraid it may not be so for Alan Tremaine. You see, he's spent the last twenty-five years trapped in his own tomb, unable to escape and unable to fulfill his destiny. It's taken its toll. Alan Tremaine is quite mad. Irrevocably so, I would say, and as such he's quite dangerous, which is why we came directly here after securing my escape."

"I thought perhaps you were tracking me down," I said.

"I feel extremely fortunate you were here, but we were actually coming to warn Lucie and the Strumms about Alan Tremaine."

"Warn us? Why?"

Julia looked up, her tears now dry, "Mrs. Strumm, Alan is mad and his madness has made him believe Abigail is still alive. He means to destroy her once and for all."

"But that's ridiculous. How…"

"He's seen Lucie's picture, he believes she is Abigail and that she is using Phillip. He plans to kill her."

"No, he can't. We must stop him."

"I'm afraid he can, Mrs. Strumm," Holmes said. "But if she is with your husband, she may be safe for now. Do you know where she was to meet the commissioner?"

"Why, at his office."

"Then we must go there at once. Tremaine isn't mad enough, I don't believe, to attack her at Police Headquarters."

It was then that I remembered why the wound on Julia Tremaine's throat seemed so familiar. I'd seen it before, and recently. "They may not remain at Headquarters," I said.

"What makes you say that?"

"I should have remembered. The wound on Julia's throat. It reminds me of something I've seen before."

"Of course, on Dr. Rudalac…"

"No, I've seen it recently. On the throat of Mylo Strumm."

Holmes turned and fairly shouted, "What?"

"Well, I…didn't see the wound exactly, but I was with Mylo earlier today, he was sweating profusely and when he wiped his brow and then his neck, his handkerchief came away, stained crimson."

Emily gasped and then said, "Then Mylo has—"

Holmes finished Emily's thought, "…has become Tremaine's victim and accomplice. Quickly, we've not a minute to lose."

"But where will he take her," I asked Holmes as we headed out the door and hailed a passing Growler.

As we all climbed into the cab Holmes shouted at the driver, "79th Street ferry terminal. An extra dollar for your best speed." Once inside the cab he answered my question, "He'll take her to Blackwell's Island."

"Why there?"

"Several reasons present themselves," Holmes said as he sat scribbling a note on a dollar bill. "It's secluded, it's where young Phillip has his laboratory, so Lucie won't be suspicious, and it's the one place where Tremaine can take care of three problems at once."

"Three problems?"

"Yes, first he can rid himself of Abigail Drake, or whom he believes is Abigail. Then, since he will no longer need Commissioner Strumm, he can dispose of him as well."

"But what about Phillip?" I said, not believing Tremaine would harm his own son.

"Tremaine, in his madness, must of course believe Phillip is working with Abigail and thus is trying to kill him, so he plans to reverse the tables and do away with Phillip and Abigail together. But here we are. Come, the game's afoot."

Holmes commandeered the vacant ferry, offering the ferry master two dollars for the special trip. Holmes explained, "With any luck, we'll arrive ahead of them. Miss Lucie would have had to travel all the way to lower Manhattan. From there, it makes more sense to take the bridge to Blackwell's. That means they will have to take the lift down to the island. That can be a time consuming endeavor as Watson can attest. Then they will need to travel to the opposite end of island, the end adjacent to the 79th Street ferry terminal, a journey of nearly two miles."

"I hope for Lucie's sake you are right."

"So do I, Watson, so do I," Holmes said with uncharacteristic humility.

As the ferry made landfall, Holmes leapt ashore and sprinted toward the Octagon. I followed closely behind. Julia and Emily brought up the rear. As we neared the building, we could see the door was open. There was a dog cart left near the entrance. Holmes signaled me to be silent as he stopped short of going inside. I could see from his position he was listening and deduced we had arrived after Mylo and Lucie. I said a silent prayer we were not too late.

Chapter 20
Showdown at the Octagon…

As I caught up to Holmes I could hear voices coming from inside. Holmes asked in a hushed tone, "Watson, do you have your pistol?"

"No, I'm afraid not."

"No matter. Keep Mrs. Strumm and Mrs. Tremaine here while I try to disarm the situation. Before I could answer, Holmes burst through the door of the Octagon. After cautioning the two women to be silent, I listened carefully to what transpired inside.

Strumm said, "Holmes, what are you doing here? I thought you were—"

"Indisposed? Yes, Commissioner, thanks to you Director Small took special care to keep me under wraps, so to speak." He paused, and then addressed Alan Tremaine, "Ah, Dr. Tremaine, it's been quite some time since we've seen each other. I understand you've had a rather grave time of it. But here, what's happened to young Phillip?"

"Very clever, Holmes, but this doesn't concern you. This is a family affair. Phillip is merely unconscious, Miss Drake is attending him."

Lucie was cradling Phillip's head. At Tremaine's words she looked up at Holmes, "Why does he keep calling me Miss Drake?"

Fear and confusion were in her eyes.

"It's all right, Lucie. Dr. Tremaine is just a bit confused," Holmes told her and then turned to Tremaine, "Leave your son and the girl out of this. They are innocents in all this."

Tremaine laughed, a sickening, tremulous laugh, the laugh of a mad man. "Innocent? My God, Holmes, I took you for a more intelligent man than that. Abigail Drake is the reason for all of this, it is she who created me."

"No, Tremaine, you're wrong. Barlucci is the wellspring from which all of this has come, not Abigail."

Tremaine paused and then addressed Mylo with a tone as cold as his stare, "Strumm, take Mr. Holmes outside and shoot him. I'll tend to these two myself."

"Yes," said the cowed voice of Commissioner Strumm, "and then you'll...you'll..."

"...give you your relief, Strumm? Yes, but wait outside, I don't wish to be interrupted while I take care of these two."

Julia, Emily, and I concealed ourselves as we waited for Holmes and Strumm to come outside.

"Why are you doing this?" cried Lucie. "He's your son, and I've never even met you before. We both thought you...you were dead."

"Dead? Dead?" Tremaine's voice became louder.

Just then Holmes walked outside the door, his hands in the air. When they reached a point out of sight from the door, I pounced. Strumm struggled back but managed to maintain his grip on the gun. I could see the festering wound on his throat. Holmes turned, grabbing at the gun and it went off. Strumm staggered, then fell, his life blood pouring from his chest.

"Mylo," Emily said as she knelt beside him.

Strumm looked up at her. "Emily, I...I couldn't help..." he said between fits of coughing, a sickening pinkish foam forming in the corner of his mouth signaling the bullet had pierced his lung.

"Shh…I know, Mylo…I know…" she said as she cradled his head on her lap.

Strumm made a feeble attempt to rise. "Emily, I…I'm sorry…" he said and then fell back and breathed no more. Emily sat rocking him, tears edging down her cheeks.

I looked around and discovered that Julia was no longer standing beside us. Then I heard her voice inside the door, "Alan, you're making a terrible mistake. Your son has created a serum that can cure you, cure us, so we can be together again."

"Julia, don't be a fool. You're being tricked by her. You don't know her and what she's capable of…she's a devil."

I could see Julia through the doorway, but Tremaine was out of my sightline to the left. I started in after her but Holmes grabbed me by the arm, "Wait. Perhaps she can reason with her husband or maneuver him into a position of weakness."

Julia moved further into the room, shielding the two young innocents from the malevolence that was once her husband. As she did, Tremaine came into our view, his back to the door. He picked up what appeared to be a broken walking stick. "I tried once before to kill you with this," he said, brandishing the stick, "but I was weak." He slowly walked around his wife and spoke to Lucie, who kneeled crying beside an unconscious Phillip Tremaine. "This time I am much stronger," he said as he took the corner of the oak desk in one hand and hurled it across the room. Lucie jumped.

"Do you think you can impress me with your theatrical show of strength, Tremaine?" Emily had pushed past Holmes and me and moved to the right of Tremaine, as Julia approached his left.

Tremaine's mouth was agape as he looked from Lucie to Emily. "What…what sort of trickery is this?"

"That's right. You've been out of touch awhile, haven't you, Tremaine. Leave these two alone. You're fight is with me. She is not

Abigail Drake, Tremaine. I am."

Tremaine seemed thoroughly confused and Holmes and I took advantage of the moment to move into the room beside Emily. Holmes, with Strumm's pistol leveled at Tremaine, said, "Listen to reason, Tremaine. What your wife has told you is true. You can be cured, Phillip can cure you using the research you performed."

Tremaine seemed to falter and then said to Holmes, "Why should I believe you."

"Because I've seen it work."

"On who?" Tremaine said with a laugh. "All of the vampires are in this room."

"Not all of them," said a foreign voice just outside the door.

Tremaine's head snapped in the direction of the entrance. "Baron?" he said, his voice trembling for the first time.

In stepped Hume, and yet it wasn't Hume, it was Barlucci both in voice and manner. "That's right, Tremaine, Baron Antonio Barlucci." He turned to Holmes, "I came as quickly as I could when I got your message."

"And you are cured, Baron?"

Lucie looked up, "Alex, I don't understand. Why does he keep calling you Baron?"

"Let me explain, Miss Lucie," Holmes said without taking his eyes off of Tremaine. "Alexander Hume is a fiction. He never existed. The baron assumed that identity in order to continue to seek out the cure for his affliction incognito." Holmes began to slowly move to his left, pistol pointed at Tremaine, until Tremaine was fixed like a compass rose between the cardinal headings of Holmes, Barlucci, Julia Tremaine, and Emily Strumm. The double shock of seeing Emily and the baron together had temporarily frozen him. "It was the baron who originally commissioned Dr. Alan Tremaine to invent a cure for his vampirism. It was also the baron who, through a well-intentioned if misguided blunder, created a monster of the once innocent Abigail

Drake."

The mention of her name seemed to snap Tremaine from his trance. With a hideous hiss escaping his open mouth he raised the jagged stick above his head. Holmes fired three shots. Tremaine laughed. "You should know you can't kill me with bullets, Holmes," he said and came at Emily meaning to drive the stake through her heart. But Julia, who'd been watching her husband intently, was quicker. She leapt between her husband and Emily, the stake piercing her heart instead of Emily's. "Julia," he cried as he cradled her limp body to the floor, a contented smile forming upon her lips as she died in his arms.

Before we could react, Tremaine grabbed Emily around the waist. She screamed and scratched his face leaving deep crimson furrows in his flesh and yet no blood flowed down his cheeks. Tremaine cursed, striking Emily. She slumped unconscious from his savage blow and he ran for the door, casting Barlucci aside like a limp doll when he tried to stop him. Holmes, Barlucci and I ran after him, but he was already in the dog cart, heading to the bridge to escape with Emily in tow.

"Baron, did you bring a rig?"

"Yes, just here," Barlucci said and ran to the side of the building retrieving a carriage.

We climbed in and Holmes drove the horse for all it was worth. By the time we arrived at the bridge, we could see the first lift was already a quarter of the way up to the trolley terminal. We had no choice but to follow in the second. As luck would have it, this second lift was just slightly faster than the first, and we began to gain ground on Tremaine.

We arrived at the top just as the nearly empty trolley was pulling out. We managed to get aboard and could see instantly that Tremaine was not there. "He's taken her to the top level," said Holmes, and he and Barlucci jumped off the trolley car and began climbing up to the top level where the railway traversed the bridge. I remained in the trolley. Not being as agile as Holmes I thought it best not to burden them with worry over my falling to my death. I could hear the approach of the train above even as the trolley pulled out and headed toward the 59th Street station.

At the station, I hurried up the stairs to the train level just as the train arrived. If Tremaine were to get off, I would be awaiting him. Holmes and Barlucci alighted from the train with a look of dejection. "He's not on the train. I'm afraid we've lost them."

Just at that moment we heard a woman's scream and shouts of "Whattaya think you're doing..." We rushed towards the commotion in time to see a hackney speeding away, its driver seated on the ground nursing a bump on his head.

"What's happened?" I said.

"That sonabitch stole my cab," the man cried.

"Was he alone?" Holmes asked.

"No, he had a woman with him, he—" but Holmes was already on the move, hailing another taxi.

"Driver, follow that cab and don't lose it. It'll mean a fiver for you if you can catch it."

The driver didn't answer except to say, "Heeyah!" to his horse and off we went.

"Where do you think he's headed," Barlucci asked Holmes.

"I'm not sure. He surely knows that his digs at the asylum have been found. I would expect sooner or later he would head back to the subway tunnels."

"But what do you think he's going to do with Emily?" I said, knowing full well the answer.

"Tremaine is confused as well as mad, driven so by a combination of twenty-five years of solitude in that tomb and his inability to slake his thirst for blood all that time."

"Yes," said Barlucci, "to have the beast in himself denied for that long a span would drive any man to insanity. Had I not six centuries of experience, I too would have been driven mad while I awaited to be discovered. Luckily, I was frozen but even this didn't prevent my carnage aboard the *Redeemer*."

I was finding it difficult to feel sympathy for a man such as Barlucci, knowing the butchery he was responsible for, and I was surprised by that shown him by Holmes, who reached out and patted his arm saying, "That's all behind you now, Baron."

"Not until we rescue Emily," said Barlucci.

"He's stopping up ahead, sir," shouted down the driver. "Want me to pull alongside?"

Holmes jumped up to look, "No," he said, "we'll get out here," handing the cabby a crisp five-dollar bill.

We were in the shadows and it was plain to see from his unhurried movements that Tremaine believed he had lost us. We watched as he entered a large building on East 53rd Street. I was thinking it was an odd building without windows and with only one large door when I noticed a buzzing sound. "What's that?" I whispered as we approached the door.

"Electricity," came Holmes one word reply.

"Electricity, I've never heard..." I stopped as we reached the door. The buzzing sound was much louder now and accompanied by the whirring of machinery. Carefully we entered; I could feel a tingling sensation running through my body, even my teeth. Barlucci went to the left once we were inside while Holmes and I moved to the right, all of us looking for a sign of Tremaine, or Emily. The inside of the building was enormous and there was row upon row of large machines humming menacingly. I later discovered their purpose was to convert the high voltage alternating current coming from the massive power stations to direct current for running the subway and elevated trains.

The sound of metal creaking above drew our attention in time to see Tremaine drawing down a suspended ladder with a chain.

"Tremaine!" Holmes called. "Let Emily go, we can help you."

Tremaine laughed as he flung the limp body of Emily Strumm over his shoulder, "No one can help Abigail now, Holmes. You'd best tend to helping yourself." Tremaine picked up a wrench and hurled it down at us. Holmes ducked his head just in time and the wrench fell down into the generator, causing a small explosion of sparks, erupting in fire. Tremaine laughed and continued climbing to the next cat walk.

"Is this how you want your life to end, Tremaine? You have achieved a stunning scientific breakthrough, found a cure for a disease that serious men speak of only in whispers—vampirism. You would be famous, heralded as a genius. Let us help you, cure you, if not for your own sake, then for your son's sake, for Julia's."

When Holmes mentioned Julia's name, Tremaine faltered. "Julia's dead," he shouted. "She's dead and Abigail killed her."

"No, Tremaine. You killed her."

He continued his climb and suddenly I realized what he meant to do. Below the catwalk where Tremaine was headed was a row of high voltage contacts leading from the transformers to the converters. "Holmes, he means to throw Emily on those contacts, to burn her alive." But it was too late, Tremaine was standing on the catwalk, lifting Emily above his head.

Then, suddenly and without warning, Barlucci, who'd assumed a position unseen above Tremaine, leapt down onto the catwalk. Tremaine dropped Emily onto the rail as he and Barlucci became locked in a death grip. With a last effort, Barlucci forced the two of them over the rail into the nest of electrical contacts below.

I turned away, but was unable to avoid the sounds of popping and hissing as their bodies short circuited the equipment below and were burnt beyond recognition. When I opened my eyes, Holmes was up on the catwalk, looking down over the rail, cradling Emily, who appeared to be regaining consciousness in his arms.

Chapter 21
Endings and new beginnings...

The ensuing fire engulfed nearly a quarter of the building before the fire department arrived, interrupting power to a large section of the city's electrical rail system and creating havoc for late-night travelers as well as for the police. When the detectives arrived, Holmes explained what had occurred weaving a tale that captured all of the pertinent facts without alluding to vampirism. Commissioner Strumm's death was explained as an heroic act of bravery in attempting to rescue his wife, his daughter and her fiancé as well as Julia Tremaine, from a crazed madman who died in the fire after killing Strumm. Holmes explained Mrs. Tremaine's earlier death had been faked in the hope of foiling her assassin. Curiously, no mention at all was made of Alexander Hume, or Baron Barlucci.

The next few days were a bitter time for Phillip Tremaine and his uncle, Charles Cabot, as well as for Emily and Lucie Strumm while they buried their loved ones and helped each other cope with all that had occurred. Emily in particular seemed rather melancholy when Holmes and I called on her the day after Mylo was laid to rest.

"I hope we haven't come at a bad time," Holmes said as Emily invited us inside.

"Not at all, I was just gathering together some of Mylo's things for the church charity. Lucie isn't at home and I wanted to do this while she was out, but I'm glad you stopped by. I didn't get a chance to thank you."

"No need, we were only too happy to be of assistance," I said.

"Yes, of course I wanted to thank you for saving me and Lucie, but I meant what Mr. Holmes did for Mylo, for telling the authorities he acted heroically," a tear graced her cheek as she spoke and she quickly wiped it away.

I offered, "Mylo acted as courageously as he was able. His will was not his own."

"I know. It hadn't been for some time, well before all of this, I'm afraid. You knew about his drinking," she looked down at her hands, holding back tears. "I'd told him I was going to leave him, just as soon as Lucie and Phillip married. I just couldn't go on watching him destroy himself—destroy us." We sat silently for a moment while she dried her tears and then she looked up and said, "Mylo had his faults, but deep down he was a good man. A kind man."

"Yes, and a brave one in spite of all this," said Holmes taking Emily's hand. "He knew he was incapable of resisting Tremaine, so in our struggle, he turned the gun on himself."

"You mean…"

"Yes, he sacrificed himself for us, Emily…for you. To paraphrase the poet, in death all debts are paid."

I took the opportunity of an awkward silence to direct the conversation in a more congenial direction, "So, when do Lucie and young Phillip plan to be married?"

Emily's face brightened as she wiped her eyes, "They wish to do so as soon as it can be properly arranged. Of course, in view of all that's happened, they want a very small, intimate wedding, just family and a few close friends." She looked at Holmes and me expectantly, "Will you and Mr. Holmes be traveling back to London soon? We were hoping you might stay for the wedding."

Holmes smiled and said, "We should be delighted to stay until the wedding, Mrs. Strumm. I think we'd both like to end our visit to America on a happy note, eh Watson?"

"Of course, yes…of course."

"Good," said Emily. "And Doctor, Lucie would like you to give her away, since her father…"

Later Holmes would chide me for puffing up as I smiled and said, "I would be most honored, Emily, most honored indeed."

On our way back to the hotel I suppose I was unusually quiet, for about halfway Holmes said, "I wouldn't worry about it too much, old boy. I think you've probably gotten things a bit muddled anyway."

"Muddled? How…" I said and then realized Holmes was speaking as though he could read my thoughts. "Confound it Holmes, there is absolutely no way you can know what it is I am thinking of at this moment."

"Oh no? Hmmm…I'd say you had a bit of unpleasant business that you have been avoiding for some time and have realized that you will soon have to face the music and have done with it."

I sat stunned for a moment. "How could you possibly…?"

"Come, come, Watson. You know my methods better than anyone. Must I recount for you how I arrived at this deduction?"

"Yes, I'm afraid you must since I've not said a word and there is nothing here in this coach that could inform your deduction. Pray tell me how you've concluded it or be branded a witch now and for all time," I said in my most theatric manner, relieved at having some distraction to my own thoughts.

Holmes laughed in that wholly enjoyable fashion of his and said, "Very well, then. I noted it even before we entered the cab."

"Noticed what?"

"I noticed that after puffing up like a cooing pigeon at being asked to give away the hand of Miss Lucie Strumm you became sullen and quiet. That cued me to watch you intently."

"Can't a fellow even contemplate his duties without being accused of trying to shirk some other responsibility?"

"That's just it. You weren't thinking about giving away Miss Lucie."

"And how could you possibly know that?"

"Elementary. You were obviously very pleased at being given that singular honor. That is evident by the way you were preening and puffing out your chest. I was afraid you'd pop a button from your vest."

"Poppycock. Get on with it."

"As I said, had you been thinking of that, you would have been smiling in that insufferable way you do whenever you are pleased with yourself. But in this instance, almost as soon as we turned to get into the cab, your entire countenance changed, which I knew was the signal that you had a new and unrelated thought come into that grizzled old head of yours, and as I said, it caused me to watch you more closely."

"What of it. So you watched me more closely. That doesn't tell me how you think you know what my thoughts were."

"I was coming to that. Once we got into the cab your mood appeared to darken even more. As I continued to observe, you fell into some fairly familiar habits."

"What sort of habits?"

"Oh, let's see, there was the twisting of your mustache. This signaled a pensive mood but little else. Then there was the fumbling with your watch chain between your thumb and forefinger indicating that time was on your mind, that some deadline perhaps was looming. And when you weren't twisting your mustache or your watch chain, you were grasping your walking stick with one hand and rubbing the brass hound's head handle with the other. The only occasions upon which I can remember you doing this in such a robust manner were when you had some perceived unpleasant news to give, most often to me, or to your wife."

I laughed and said, "And what did I do before I carried a stick?"

"You would rub the face of your closed pocket watch, thus killing two birds with one stone. So tell me, Watson, how far from the mark have I fallen?"

A bit sheepishly I admitted, "Not far at all, I'm afraid...not far at all."

"Let's have it then, man, what is troubling you so."

"Well, I suppose I may as well tell you. It's Ernie's wife."

"Ernie Jenkins' wife?"

"Yes. I'm afraid she's taken to drink and is dallying with another man from her place of employment."

"Another employee at Police headquarters? A detective perhaps?" he said, with just the hint of a smile forming at the corners of his mouth.

"Yes, it very well could be I'm sorry to say."

"And how did you reach this conclusion? Pure deduction?"

"Not at all. I saw her." I said, a bit defensively.

"That must have been a bit embarrassing," Holmes said with that confounded look of superiority on his face.

"No, I didn't actually see them..." I paused and took a breath, I was beginning to feel more than a slight bit ill-used. "Oh, dash it all, Holmes, I saw Mrs. Jenkins purchase two bottles of liquor from a spirits and tobacco establishment within a block of the headquarters building. I followed her back and she entered very suspiciously into a rear entrance."

"And the man with whom she is dallying? Was he awaiting her?"

"Well, no, he wasn't."

"Beware of false knowledge, Watson. It deceives more often than ignorance. I submit there was no dalliance."

"But I asked the storekeeper about Mrs. Jenkins and he said she's a regular customer, that she comes in at least once per week and buys two bottles of liquor that she told him she was taking to her husband," I said with some satisfaction.

"And what should she have said? That she was buying whiskey for the Commissioner and that she'd been sworn to secrecy?"

"What?"

"Poor Watson. As I've told you so many times that I am beginning to lose count, you see but do not observe."

"I think I did a very good job of observing in this instance. You weren't there, how would you know?"

"But I was in the Commissioner's office."

"What are you getting at, Holmes?"

"Alcohol has the tendency to make even the most careful man sloppy." When I made no response he went on, "On our first day in New York, when we accompanied Strumm to his office, I noticed he left a bank draft on his desk, made out but not yet signed. It was made out to Matilda Jenkins for a total of four dollars"

"That's the exact amount Ernie was upset that she'd spent."

"Yes, no doubt Strumm had forgotten to pay her on at least one occasion."

"But why would Mrs. Jenkins buy the Commissioner's whiskey for him on the sly like that and not tell her husband?"

"Any number of reasons could be proffered. The most obvious being he made it a condition of her continued employment, with the possibility of a promotion, perhaps."

"That's it. Abel said she'd been a typist and had been promoted to secretary not too long ago. But why not buy his own whiskey?"

"The answer there is obvious. He didn't want his wife to know and didn't wish to risk being seen going in and out of an establishment that offers liquor for sale."

"But Emily did know, didn't she?"

"One thing I've learned over the years, Watson, is that wives always know, whether they wish to admit it or not."

I laughed, remembering my own experiences and said, "You're certainly right there." I felt greatly relieved and was able to report to Ernie and Abel a satisfactory conclusion to my investigation and when Ernie confronted Matilda with what I'd uncovered, she broke down in tears and promised never to hide anything from him again.

Preparing for the nuptials of Phillip and Lucie kept me busy up until the very day of the wedding and prevented my reviewing with Holmes how he made his escape and why he'd conspired to have himself committed in the first place. I didn't even get an explanation for why he'd left Barlucci's name entirely out of the report he made to the police until we were well on our way back home.

Holmes and I stayed only a few days past the wedding and then boarded a liner back to England. We were seen off by Emily, Phillip and Lucie Tremaine, and Charles Cabot. As we supped on our first night out, I said to Holmes, "Tell me, why is it you made no mention to the police of Barlucci, or Hume as he called himself?"

"I was trying to avoid the tangled web of introducing a being they could little comprehend or less believe. Had I mentioned Barlucci, or Hume as you say, it might have led to questions better left unasked, don't you agree?"

"I'm not sure I do. What happens when they extricate two burned skeletons from the wreckage of that substation?"

"I shouldn't worry about that, Watson," he said with a glimmer in his eye. "The fire was hot enough, I believe, to consume bone as well as flesh."

"Well, I suppose you're right there. After all, we haven't heard anything to contradict the story you told the police. But explain to me how you came to be aware that Tremaine had become a vampire."

"I suspected as much when we first opened his tomb and we found it was empty."

"You certainly didn't intimate anything of the sort to me at the time. It was all Barlucci from the way you described it."

Holmes smiled as he cut his steak, "And what would you have thought if I'd told you then I believed there were two vampires loose in New York, eh? It wasn't until I discovered ash from his cigar at Phillip's laboratory that I had actual proof beyond Barlucci's word."

I grunted. "Yes…yes, of course…"

Holding the bite of steak suspended on his fork, he said with a laugh, "You'd have had me trussed up in a straight-jacket a lot sooner, I'll wager."

"Please now, Holmes, I've already explained I feel just awful about that. Had I known…" my voice trailed off as well as my appetite.

"There, there, Watson, I know you didn't intend that. It appears Dr. Small, on top of having been a bad administrator, was a vindictive and vengeful man. Of course, it probably didn't help that I'd stumbled upon a lucrative business in prostitution he was running from that asylum. It turns out he was a man of small character as well as name and stature."

"Prostitution? Good heavens, no."

"Yes, that was why he had Hone's body removed from where it was really found."

"Where was that?"

"In the south wing. It seems Dr. Small set up a comfortable little brothel in the central quadrangle of the south wing. He found Hone there."

"I don't understand what caused him to report it at all."

"I believe I do. As you'll recall, Hone had a family. Small knew his death could not be hidden. Besides, I'm sure Small suspected the motive to be either revenge or a warning from one of the downtown gangs who run the more conventional brothels in Manhattan."

"But how did you discover Small was running a brothel?"

"That was one of the reasons I'd arranged to be committed. Barlucci had heard of it from Julia. Many of the victims in that vile scheme were women who could not vocalize what was happening to them, such as Miss Lorelei Baker."

"Dreadful."

"Yes, well I'm afraid Small won't be tried for his offenses."

"And why not? Surely his arrangement with the state of New York doesn't shield him from criminal prosecution. He should be hanged for what he's done and allowed."

"Fortunately, or unfortunately for Small, the state of New York has been spared the expense of his trial by Dr. Tremaine."

"You mean…"

"That's right, Small was Dr. Tremaine's last victim. He found him alone just before going to Blackwell's Island to await Strumm."

"Well, I can't say I'm sorry."

"Nor can I."

And thus were tied up all of the loose ends for this, the longest span of an adventure in the inimitable history of Mr. Sherlock Holmes. At last we could put to rest all thought of Baron Barlucci and what we came to think of as the Whitechapel Vampire saga. Of course it suffices to say that this also closes the casebook on Jack the Ripper, although we doubt very much anyone not intimately associated with all the facts would make the same conclusion. Despite all the fantastic things I've recorded in these pages, we haven't one shred of evidence to prove the existence of any sort of supernatural creatures. After all, vampires are only legend.

Epilogue

I thought I had closed the book on this extraordinary tale after penning the final chapter—that is until some months later when I visited Holmes in his comfortable country estate in Sussex. We were sitting by the fire enjoying a few glasses of mead, that wonderful fermentative by-product of Holmes' apiarist hobby, when I said to him, "You know, Holmes, you had me quite baffled by your behavior ever since I received your letter suggesting Barlucci might still be on the loose, or on the loose again, I should say."

"I shouldn't wonder at your bafflement. There were moments when I had a doubt or two, myself. But once we'd arrived and I'd gotten a look at the *Redeemer's* log I knew I was right."

"No doubts then from that time forward?"

"Well, not about that."

"What then?"

"I'm not sure I should say. I know your feelings about Barlucci and fear you might think me a bit too lenient in that regard."

"I did think you appeared to be in some sympathy with him. Too much so for my tastes."

"Well, we had quite a long chat within the confines of the ventilation shaft that night. I believe I learned as much about myself as I did about Barlucci."

"I have noticed you appear to be at peace at last. No more

recriminations about things left undone? No more silly notions about immortality?"

Holmes looked at me with a kindness he rarely showed and said, "Watson, I have my immortality."

"How's that?" I asked, feeling quite perplexed.

He reached out and placed his hand gently upon my arm. "You have given it to me, old friend. Through your writings, your little chronicles regardless their flights of romantic fancy from time to time, have truly made me immortal." He lighted his pipe and sank back into his chair. "Oh, I'm not vane enough to believe they'll stand the test of time. I'm sure as quickly as one age passes another subsumes it and my little contributions will wither in comparison to the next generation." He blew a long thick billow of smoke into the air, perhaps in an effort to hide the tear I'd seen forming in his eye. "But you have assured me that anyone who has an interest will be able to read about our exploits. You have given me, and by extension yourself, a measure of immortality. And for me, that is enough."

I was touched beyond speech. I didn't know quite what to say in response, so thrilled that my literary efforts appeared to be important to him, whom I admired so greatly. I was relieved that at about that time there came a knock at the door.

It was a postman with a package.

After thanking the postman and sending him on his way, Holmes brought the parcel back to his chair by the fire. "I wonder what this could be," he said as he carefully untied the string.

"From where was it posted?"

"New Zeeland, three weeks ago."

"Hopefully not another pair of ears," I joked, evoking from him a soft chuckle.

"No, this cardboard box is much less macabre," and as he said this he withdrew from the package a small piece of jewelry that I recognized immediately as the signet worn by Emily Strumm. He held it up to the window letting the last rays of sunlight coming through catch and play upon the bloodstone.

"I wonder what possessed Emily to send you her keepsake."

"Here's a note," Holmes said unfolding a small bit of foolscap. "It says, *'We won't be needing this any longer. Thank you for believing.'*"

"We? What do you suppose she means by we? And what in blazes is she doing in New Zeeland."

"I suppose they wish to make a new start," Holmes said rising and crossing the room. He'd retrieved a key from his waistcoat pocket and was unlocking one of the cabinet doors above his desk. I joined him there as he placed the signet inside.

"What do you mean, they wish? Who wishes?"

He handed me the note, "Here, see the signature? You must make your own conclusion."

The note was signed *'A.B.'* "Who the devil is…" The answer to my own question struck me like a lightning bolt, suddenly and with a great force. "You don't mean to say…but he's dead. We saw him die."

"Did we?"

I thought back to the night in the substation when Barlucci leapt from above and carried Tremaine over the rail, down to their deaths. At least, I'd thought they'd both died. I was in too much shock at that time to make a verification myself, but I saw Holmes looking down over the rail to where I assumed the two bodies were consumed by the electrical fire that erupted. Then I remembered seeing something else. I remembered seeing a wisp of a smile on Holmes' face as he peered down, one of satisfaction. At the time, I felt it was satisfaction of a just conclusion to our adventure, but now…

"You knew," I said, stunned by just how much my friend sometimes deceived me. "But why?"

"To be quite honest, Watson, I was torn by this more than by

227

anything else associated with this entire episode. Not just in keeping it from you, although that did bear heavily upon me, but also in allowing things to play out as they did."

"You mean by allowing Barlucci to escape."

"My dear Watson, he had already escaped."

"What do you mean?"

"He had escaped from over six centuries of imprisonment. I could see it in his eyes when he'd first taken the final serum."

"You were there?" I asked amazed.

"Of course. Who do you think injected him?"

"Well, I assumed it to be Phillip."

"Dear me, not at all. Phillip was completely unaware that Hume was Barlucci until that night in the Octagon, and I dare say he probably believed Hume was merely playing the part of Barlucci much as Emily played the part of Abigail. By the way, I almost forgot," he said digging into his pocket. "Here you go," and as he said it, he dropped six copper pennies into the palm of my hand. "I was also busy during this time making sure no harm came to you as well.

My head was now reeling. Holmes took my arm to steady me. "Then you were aiding Hume, er Barlucci, the entire time? He must have been very convincing."

"As I said, I was torn. I thought him to be sincere in his desire to be rid of his curse, and toyed with the idea of having him arrested after he was cured, as he would be much easier dealt with if he were merely mortal."

"Yes, indubitably."

"I had to weigh his past transgressions against what he was going through. In particular, the girl, Ilsa, bore heavily on my mind."

"Ilsa? The Strumm's house servant? What did she—" the meaning dawned upon me and caught up my breath.

"Yes, she too was a victim of Barlucci. Even before we had arrived in New York, he used her to retrieve the signet from Emily."

"Why on earth did he want that?"

"It belonged to him. He used it as a sort of identification device for accessing his vast fortune. That's why Abigail had it. He'd given it to her in the event they became separated, knowing a young woman alone, even if she were a vampire, would be in more need of money than he. That is how she could afford Mauldin Place and the equipment for Alan Tremaine's laboratory."

"I'd quite forgotten he was a financier. So, he still had a great amount of money. That would explain why Lucie at first believed him to be itinerant, he hadn't yet accessed his fortune. Poor Ilsa, used and discarded."

"Yes, as I said that was a difficult thing to overlook. But, if he truly was the victim of a condition such as he described, an addiction to blood coupled with a superhuman survival instinct, he could hardly be held accountable. Taking all of this into account there were only two sensible choices available, destroy him or cure him. After some deliberation, I chose the latter and having done so, it seemed to me to be dishonorable to seek his destruction in the gallows. After all, it was the vampire who committed those heinous crimes, and Barlucci was no longer a vampire. That part of him was destroyed."

"I see. And so when you saw that he survived his encounter with Tremaine, you—"

"I did what I thought was best. He'd willingly risked his own life to save Emily, knowing he had very little chance against Tremaine. I thought it only fair to allow him to make good his escape." Having steadied me, he continued now to put the bauble into his cabinet. "This, I would guess, is Barlucci's way of thanking me."

"But the signet had passed to Emily."

"Hence the 'we' in the note. The signet was given by Barlucci to Abigail Drake as a seal of recognition by which she could access his fortune. When Abigail died, Emily kept it to remember the sister she loved. Now, I suspect Emily and the baron have secured enough from his remaining holdings to travel to New Zeeland and start a new life together, most likely as Mr. and Mrs. Hume. Thus, they no longer have a need for Barlucci's signet."

Having said this, he placed the charm into his cabinet. "What's that?" I asked. There was a glass cylinder in the back of the cabinet in a stand alongside a thick leather-bound journal.

He reached inside and pulled out a glass vial with a cork in it, nearly filled to the top with a crimson liquid. "This? It's just a souvenir I took from Phillip Tremaine's lab. I'm afraid in my retirement I've become somewhat of a collector." As he replaced the vial back into the cabinet, I noticed a small label plate affixed to it with two initials inscribed upon it, '*A.B.*'

Also from MX Publishing

MX Publishing is the world's largest specialist Sherlock Holmes publisher, with over a hundred titles and fifty authors creating the latest in Sherlock Holmes fiction and non-fiction.

From traditional short stories and novels to travel guides and quiz books, MX Publishing cater for all Holmes fans.

The collection includes leading titles such as *Benedict Cumberbatch In Transition* and *The Norwood Author* which won the 2011 Howlett Award (Sherlock Holmes Book of the Year).

MX Publishing also has one of the largest communities of Holmes fans on Facebook with regular contributions from dozens of authors.

www.mxpublishing.com

Also From MX Publishing

London, 1920: Boston-bred Enoch Hale, working as a reporter for the Central News Syndicate, arrives on the scene shortly after a music hall escape artist is found hanging from the ceiling in his dressing room. What at first appears to be a suicide turns out to be murder.

www.mxpublishing.com

Also from MX Publishing

"Phil Growick's, 'The Secret Journal of Dr Watson', is an adventure which takes place in the latter part of Holmes and Watson's lives. They are entrusted by HM Government (although not officially) and the King no less to undertake a rescue mission to save the Romanovs, Russia's Royal family from a grisly end at the hand of the Bolsheviks. There is a wealth of detail in the story but not so much as would detract us from the enjoyment of the story. Espionage, counter-espionage, the ace of spies himself, double-agents, double-crossers...all these flit across the pages in a realistic and exciting way. All the characters are extremely well-drawn and Mr Growick, most importantly, does not falter with a very good ear for Holmesian dialogue indeed. Highly recommended. A five-star effort."

The Baker Street Society